Having Faith

(Callaghan Brothers, Book 7)

Abbie Zanders

To Kristine,
Always have faith.
♡ Abbie Zanders

Having Faith

(Callaghan Brothers, Book 7)

First edition. April, 2015.

Written by Abbie Zanders.

ISBN: 1515304604
ISBN-13: 978-1515304609

Acknowledgements

Special thanks to:

… to my wonderful beta readers Deb B., Anjee Z, Shelly S., Carol T., Tonya B., Carla S., Perryne D., Shayne R., and Susan J. (and a few of you who prefer to remain unnamed – you know who you are)

… to Aubrey Rose Cover Designs, for crafting an *amazing* book cover

… and to all of *you* for selecting this book – you didn't have to, but you did. Thanks ☺

Before You Begin

WARNING: Due to strong language and graphic scenes of a sexual nature, this book is intended for mature (21+) readers only.

If these things offend you, then this book is not for you.

If, however, you like your alphas a little rough around the edges and some serious heat in your romance, then by all means, read on…

Chapter 1

"I take it your date didn't go so well last night," Maggie Callaghan said with genuine empathy. She piled yet another scoop of vanilla ice cream onto Kieran's slice of apple pie and flicked a glance at him with those swirling green eyes.

"It went well enough," he answered with a lazy shrug. And it had. It had gone like every other date he'd had in the last six months. Nice. Normal.

The problem was, there was very little that was normal about Kieran or any of the men in his family. They were a strong bunch steeped in strength, loyalty, and honor. Highly skilled in weaponry and combat, they comprised their own special off-the-books ops team, and were often called to undertake the missions no one else wanted. Everyone in the small, sleepy town of Pine Ridge, Pennsylvania knew the rumors, of course; but only a privileged few knew the truth.

Maggie raised her eyebrows expectantly, so he continued. "I took her to see that new movie everyone's been talking about, then a late dinner. It was nice."

Maggie snorted softly. "Nice, huh? Callaghan

boys have about as much use of "nice" as I do a rat infestation in my cold cellar."

"Yeah." Kieran gave her a crooked, boyish grin. Maggie understood. She always got it.

As normal as they tried to appear to the rest of the world, they needed more to retain their mercurial interest past a few hours, days at the most. They needed women who embodied the spirit of their hearts – their *croies*. Anything less held only temporary satisfaction.

Unfortunately, Kieran hadn't found his yet.

All six of his older brothers had found their *croies*, or soul mates; he alone remained single and unattached. At six-foot-five, with two hundred and seventy five pounds of rippling muscle, blue-black hair and icy blue eyes – and the owner/operator of the hugely successful *BodyWorks* Fitness Center - he was quite the eligible bachelor. It seemed that every single woman – and even some not so single – wanted their chance to snag the last remaining Callaghan, to find themselves in the inner circle of the wealthy, powerful clan. While flattering, it was also disappointing.

So far, none had been successful in capturing his heart and soul, and Kieran was feeling restless. After seeing the kind of bond his brothers had with their wives, he couldn't help but hope he would be as fortunate. He wanted a woman who loved him because she couldn't help herself, not because of his business, his family name, or social status.

"You have to have faith, Kieran," she told him with an enigmatic smile that sent a shiver of foreboding through him. "Your time will come."

"Something you're not telling me, Mags?" he asked suspiciously, the fork suspended midway between the plate and his mouth. Besides being the one they all went to when they needed a place to unload, Maggie Callaghan was also known for her frequent flashes of prophetic insight. Though she routinely denied having any such ability, every one of them had witnessed the strange phenomenon – her emerald green eyes would gloss over and begin to swirl like there was a tempest within. Kind of like they were doing right now. Before he could call her on it, though, the swirling clouds stilled and her eyes were back to normal.

"Well," she said, her infectious grin growing to epic proportions as she set down the pot and sat down at the table with him. She leaned forward conspiratorially and whispered loudly, "I'm pregnant."

"Jesus! That's great, Mags!" Kieran said excitedly, reaching over to wrap a bear hug around her much smaller frame. "Mick didn't say a word."

Maggie's face flushed a pretty rose color. The moment he eased up on his steel-like embrace she rose and scooted back over to the stove. Kieran's eyes narrowed, immediately suspicious. "You didn't tell him, did you?" he accused softly.

"I made some fresh strawberry cream pie," she

responded, ignoring his question. "Even with the Goddess buying most everything I still have more than I know what to do with. I'll get you a slice."

The Celtic Goddess was a high-end restaurant run by their sister-in-law, renowned chef Lexi Kattapoulos Callaghan. Several years earlier they had contracted with Maggie's farm to produce the bulk of organic produce used in their one-of-a-kind menu offerings. Thus far the acquisition had been a highly successful and lucrative arrangement for all involved.

"Maggie."

"And I whipped up some fresh cream, too," she added, pretending she hadn't heard him. "Nothing beats fresh-whipped."

"Maggie."

"Or I've got some blueberry crumble still warm. We got a huge crop of the early ones this year…"

"*Maggie*." Every one of them – his six older brothers and their wives - knew that Maggie baked like a fiend when she was nervous or excited. He glanced over at the huge tubs of freshly made cookies and the tray of homemade cinnamon rolls she'd just extracted from the oven. Maggie wasn't just anxious. She was in full-on panic mode.

"You sound just like Michael when you say it like that," she told him. If he didn't know her better he would swear she was pouting.

"Why haven't you told him?" His older

brother Michael worshipped the ground his wife walked on, and loved their son Ryan as much as any father could. Kieran couldn't imagine him being anything less than ecstatic over the news.

She shrugged. A few more tendrils of dark cherry-cola colored hair escaped the clip with which she'd attempted to contain them, cascading around her face, coming to rest on the shoulder straps of the worn and faded full frontal apron that had once been her great-grandmother's. He'd been so absorbed in his own worries he hadn't paid her appearance much attention. Now that he looked closer, he could see that her skin was a bit paler than usual, and there were dark shadows beneath her eyes.

"He's going to figure something's up, Mags," Kieran said, looking pointedly around at all the treats.

"Yes," she agreed, drawing the word out slowly as she fixed him with big green eyes. "About that…you need to take all this back to the Pub with you. Or better yet, take it over to Lacie's. Her brother Brian loves this stuff, and heaven knows he could use the extra calories more than I can."

Kieran's brows knit together, at least as much as they could on his smooth, boyish face. At twenty-eight, he could have passed for much younger. "You want me to lie to my brother?"

"No, of course not," she said irritably. "I'm just asking you to not say anything just yet." He didn't miss the flash of hurt in her eyes, and felt a pang of remorse for suggesting such a thing.

She paused, and he could practically see the wheels turning. "Think of it like a 'need to know' type thing, and Michael just doesn't need to know yet."

Kieran's frown increased, prompting Maggie to add, "It's just, well, you know how he worries over the slightest things…"

It was true. Michael did worry. Like all of the Callaghan men, he was especially protective of his wife – the one who had captured not only his heart but also his mind and soul. And, given Maggie's nearly pathological fear of traditional medicine, Michael's concerns were often valid ones. In her stubborn avoidance of all such things, she often did not seek treatment of what she considered minor injuries, much to the chagrin of her husband and sometimes to the detriment of her health.

They understood why she felt the way she did. Poor medical care had cost Maggie not only her parents but also resulted in her spending a good part of her childhood in the hospital. It was her grandmother, skilled with homeopathic remedies, who had taken her in and given her a normal childhood. Her husband, a doctor himself, was slowly working on building her trust.

"Does he have anything he should be worried about, Mags?" he asked. Michael was his brother by blood, but Maggie was a cherished sister as well.

And Kieran had a very strong sense of family. Her health and well-being was every bit as important to him as his brothers'.

She bit her lip, her hesitation just a little too pronounced to stem the unease he felt building in his gut. He had been feeling it all day. Up till that point he'd assumed it had something to do with the funk he'd been in lately, but maybe it was more than that. His brothers all shared a sixth sense, instinctively knowing when one of them was in trouble. Their wives were such a part of them, fitting so seamlessly into their family, that it made sense such feelings would eventually extend to them as well.

"Everything is fine. I'm sure of it," she said. But she didn't actually believe that, and Maggie was quite possibly one of the worst liars on the planet. If he hadn't already figured that out, the unshed tears building in her eyes and her trembling bottom lip would have clued him in.

"Ah, Maggie." Kieran went over to where she stood at the counter, wrapping his arms around her. She virtually disappeared in his embrace.

"I'm sorry," she sniffed into his shirt, hugging him as if he was a cherished, albeit supersized, teddy bear. "I shouldn't have said anything. I didn't mean to put you in the middle. I just needed to tell someone…"

"Tell someone what?" Michael's deep voice reverberated through the kitchen, shooting his brother a questioning look.

Startled, Maggie backed away from Kieran, dropping the dish she'd had in her hand.

Kieran exchanged a brief glance with Michael as Maggie swore softly and bent to pick up the pieces. He kept his expression carefully neutral, but Michael's eyes narrowed. The very fact that his face gave away nothing probably told his brother everything he needed to know.

"Maggie," Michael said gently, kneeling beside her to take the broken ceramic from her hands. "What's going on?"

"Nothing," she mumbled unconvincingly.

Michael stood and turned to his youngest brother. "Kieran? Have you done something to upset my wife?"

Kieran shifted uncomfortably under his older brother's steady gaze, unwilling to lie but not wanting to rat Maggie out. As it turned out, he didn't have to do either. Michael's question brought some of the fire back into Maggie's eyes. She was fiercely protective of her family, and that included Kieran.

"Of course he didn't," she snapped, placing herself in front of Kieran. "You know, for such a smart man you can be such a donkey's backside."

One of Michael's dark brows formed a perfect arch over his luminous blue eyes. "A donkey's backside?" Kieran turned away in an attempt to stem the bark of laughter currently trying to escape.

"Aye," she said, and it was a sign that she was gearing up for something. Whenever Maggie got that slight hint of Irish brogue in her voice, everyone knew enough to brace for battle.

Kieran took full advantage of the opportunity and started backing away. A riled Maggie was every bit as dangerous as a highly-trained operative. Maybe more so, because there was usually some logic or rules of engagement for operatives.

"You cannot see what is plain in front of your face, Michael Callaghan."

Michael regarded her with a practiced calm Kieran envied. He tossed the remains of the plate in the trash can and leaned against the counter, crossing his arms over his chest. "Is that so?"

Maggie crossed her arms, too. It was hard to determine which one was more stubborn. "Aye."

"You wouldn't by any chance be referring to the fact that you are thirteen weeks pregnant, would you, Maggie?"

Maggie's mouth dropped open. Michael smirked.

"You knew?" Astonishment turned to anger in the span of a few heartbeats. Kieran didn't miss her quick glance at the cast iron skillet in the drying rack. Apparently neither did Michael, because he moved it smoothly out of her reach.

Michael sighed heavily. "I am a doctor, Maggie. And your husband."

"You *knew*? And you didn't say anything?"

"Neither did you," he pointed out logically. Maggie scowled. Kieran wondered at the dynamics of the pair. Maggie was Michael's passion; he was her rock, always. And he never let her get away with anything.

"By the way, you have a two o'clock with the OB." Michael checked his watch. "That gives you about ten minutes to get ready."

Her peeved expression turned quickly to one of fear. Her eyes widened and her arms uncrossed. "But I can't," she stammered. "What about Ryan?"

"Kieran's taking him back to the Pub. Taryn's waiting on him."

Maggie shot Kieran a look of ultimate betrayal. "Is that why you're here?" she said in disbelief. "All that shite about being the only one who hasn't found his *croie* yet, that was just to distract me?"

He shrugged. It was true enough that he was starting to feel restless, that he was ready to meet the right woman who would be the other half of his heart. He hadn't been lying about that. Sure, he had *BodyWorks*, the fitness center he owned and operated. That kept him busy. As did his martial arts classes and the occasional art work he did for his cousin Stacey's novel covers.

But he was growing more than a little weary of the single life. He'd give it all up in a second to have a woman look at him the way Maggie looked at his brother. To have a little guy of his own to bounce on his shoulders and toss baseballs with and take fishing.

"Judas," she mumbled, adding something in Irish that made his cheeks redden and actually made him feel bad.

"Now go on then," Michael said sternly, tapping her backside and giving her a gentle push toward the door. "Ten minutes, then I'm tossing you over my shoulder and taking you whether you're ready or not."

Maggie's green eyes turned dark, the swirls reminding Kieran of something akin to funnel clouds. He swore the temperature in the room dropped about ten degrees, but she did what Michael said.

"And you," Michael said, staring pointedly at Kieran as he grabbed an apple. "Stop feeling guilty. I can see it in your eyes."

"She's scared, Mick," Kieran said, looking around the kitchen at all of the baked goods. The aroma alone was enough to make him consider spending an extra hour on the weight bags tonight, let alone the three plates of apple pie and vanilla ice cream she'd placed in front of him.

"I know," Michael said on an exhale, his voice softening. He was arguably the most even-tempered and rational among all the Callaghan sons with the possible exception of Shane. Only his wife had the ability to smash through his implacable façade with unerring precision. "And the fact that she is terrifies me. It's why we have to do this.

She'll worry herself sick."

Kieran nodded. He understood it, but that didn't mean he had to like it. He might never forget the way Maggie looked at him. It actually hurt enough to have him absently rubbing at his chest.

"Don't worry," Michael said as if reading his thoughts. "She still loves you."

Kieran sighed. "Yeah, I guess. Forgive and forget, right?"

Michael laughed and clamped his younger brother on the shoulder. "Don't be an idiot. Maggie doesn't forget. *Ever*."

* * *

"Hey, mom, look!" Matt's excited shout had Faith gripping the steering wheel hard and looking around for the source worthy of such an outcry. Only a few minutes ago the boy had appeared sound asleep. "The deer on the crossing signs! They have red noses, like Rudoph!"

A wave of relief washed over Faith O'Connell as she realized the cause of his outburst was not life-threatening. "You scared me half to death, Matt," she chastised. "What's rule number one?"

"Don't startle the driver," he exhaled wearily. "But mom – red noses! Is that cool or what? Hey, do they have reindeer in Pennsylvania?"

Faith smiled at her son's barely contained excitement. She'd worried how the move would affect him, but so far he seemed to be taking it all in stride, treating it like it was some huge adventure. It did her heart good to see her mature, quiet, thirteen-almost-fourteen year old acting like a young boy again, even if she knew it was short lived.

"I don't think so," she said, appearing to give the matter serious thought. "But I do think they have great big deer that look just like them."

"Cool," Matt breathed, searching the acres of forested land on either side of the highway as if he expected to see one jump out at any moment. "Holy shit, mom!" he exclaimed only a few short minutes later. "You're right! Look!"

"What did I tell you about cursing?!" she scolded, but even she found it difficult to bite back a colorful expletive when she spotted the fourteen-point buck grazing on the rocky incline off to the right, not even fifty yards from the seventy-mile an hour traffic on the Northeast Extension of the Pennsylvania Turnpike. At least three does were visible on either side of him.

"Mom!?" he yelled again, causing her to wrench her eyes back to the road and slam on the brakes when the flow of traffic slowed significantly in front of them. What the hell? When did the speed limit suddenly drop down to fifty-five?

"Oh, wow," Matt said, his eyes widening as he

looked to the front. “It’s a tunnel! Right through the mountains! We’re going to drive through a *mountain*, mom! How freaking awesome is that!”

“Pretty freaking awesome,” she agreed with only slightly less enthusiasm, removing her sunglasses as the warning signs commanded and turning on her headlights. Faith gripped the steering wheel tighter, fighting against the instant claustrophobia of being in such an enclosed space. The man-made arch loomed up over them, the yellow lights casting an eerie glow over everything as they made their way through and the song on the radio changed from an upbeat tune into a buzz of static. She didn’t realize she was holding her breath until they came out on the other side a scant one mile later.

“Wow.” Matt looked out the passenger side window down into the steep ravine, then up at the peaks that rose above them as they climbed steadily higher. Far below, small towns that once housed the local coal miners and their families looked like something out of a Norman Rockwell painting.

“So you’re liking Pennsylvania, huh?” Faith smiled, finding Matt’s good mood infectious.

“Oh yeah,” he grinned back. “At least, so far.”

He was growing up so fast, she thought. He’d be fourteen by the end of the summer, but no one would know that just by looking at him. He already towered over his mother by a good eight inches, his gangly frame the only glaring evidence that he was still a few years from full manhood. But it wasn't just his size that made him appear older. Matt was more mature than most boys his age, having to grow up faster than she would have liked. He hadn't had it easy.

More than anything else, Faith was hoping this move would be good for him. For both of them. A fresh start in a new place; it was exactly what they needed.

All of their most prized possessions were in the back of the light blue Taurus, now pushing the two hundred thousand mile mark and showing its age. It wouldn't win any beauty contests, but with a little help and a lot of luck it ran well enough. It had gotten them this far, and for that she was grateful.

As if mocking her, the radiator light started blinking on the dash, informing her that their current ascent up the mountain was pushing its limits. At the next widened area she'd pull over and refill the overflow tank with the gallon of water she always kept in the back along with an impressive supply of paper clips, rubber bands, bungee cords, and, her personal fix-it tool of choice - duct tape. She patted the console appreciatively, murmuring a few encouraging words. As if responding to her heartfelt plea, the light blinked off again.

"Tell me again about the house," Matt asked for the hundredth time, all traces of sleepiness gone. Faith didn't mind. She was every bit as excited about the prospect of having their own place as he was. And after nearly fifteen hours of driving, she welcomed the topic.

"Well, it's going to need a lot of work," she cautioned, just as she had every other time he'd asked.

"Yeah, but we're good at that kind of stuff," Matt said with the arrogance of a young teen.

"Yes, we are. It's a small place, little more than a cottage, really. Made of stone. Two bedrooms, two bathrooms, living room, kitchen."

"And a basement, right? Rooms actually under the house?"

"Yep," she grinned. Most of Matt's young life had been spent in areas of the south barely above sea level, where few homes actually had basements. And they'd never come across such a thing in the trailer parks they'd lived in over the past ten years.

"And a porch? And a yard?"

"Yep. Even a detached garage and a shed."

"Sweet." He settled back again, eyes wide as he took in the unfamiliar landscape, no doubt imagining all the wonders of their new home. In the back of her mind, so was she.

Chapter 2

"Kier, can you head over to the property on Sycamore later?" Shane asked as he lifted Ryan from his car seat so that he could run around a little. The boy was a true Callaghan – always moving, always looking for something to get into.

Kieran grabbed the box of baked goodies provided by Maggie and followed his brother into the massive home owned by the family of Shane's fiancé, Lacie. Shane managed the assortment of properties owned by the Callaghan Corporation, as well as handled all the legal dealings of the clan.

"Sure. What's up?"

"The new owner's due to arrive sometime this week. With everything going on it completely slipped my mind. The place has been empty for years, and I haven't had a chance to make sure the electric and plumbing are safe and operational."

Kieran frowned. "Wait. You mean that ratty old cottage? Someone actually bought that?"

"Yep."

"I hope he's a real do-it-yourself type. That place needs a major overhaul."

"Not 'he', 'she'," Shane corrected. "Single mom."

Kieran's frown deepened. "You're kidding, right?"

"Nope."

"We've got to have a better property available," Kieran said, shaking his head at the thought of a woman living in such a place. It went against every male instinct he had. "Something more suitable for a single mom."

"We do," Shane confirmed. "But the buyer was very specific about what she was looking for."

Kieran couldn't help the frown that creased his brow as he wondered what kind of woman would buy that type of property. Maybe she was one of these people who professionally "flipped' houses – bought old ones in poor shape for a song, fixed them up, then sold them for a profit. That had been one of Shane's reasonings for buying the old place originally.

Kieran was as surprised by the fact that he was selling it in its current condition as he was with the buyer. Then again, the past couple of months had been pretty rough on Shane. Several months ago he'd discovered his *croie*, only to have her kidnapped at the hands of a psychotic family friend. Factor in the tricky extraction of her brother from Afghanistan after being missing and presumed dead for nearly three years, and Kieran could definitely understand Shane's lack of attention to some things, however uncharacteristic of his highly-organized brother.

"What do you know about her?" Kieran asked, his curiosity getting the better of him.

"The buyer? Not much. Single mom, like I said. Relocating from down South. Works for the Goddess."

When the newest location of the Celtic Goddess first opened its doors in the northeast a few years previously, owner/partner Aidan Harrison brought in staff from their other successful locations in Georgia and Chicago, as well as hiring quite a few locals. The Goddess was doing so well, surpassing so many expectations, that Aidan was currently adding on an entire new series of luxury suites as well. The remote mountain location and the panoramic view it afforded made it a natural progression, as well as a lucrative endeavor.

Something about the whole situation bothered him. Kieran rubbed absently at a spot on his chest, unaware that he was even doing so. The motion did not escape Shane's attention, though.

"Something on your mind, little brother?" he asked.

"Yes. No. Maybe." Kieran shook his head, not at all surprised that Shane had picked up on it. He was used to his brother's uncanny senses.

"Feeling anxious, huh?" Shane prompted knowingly.

"Yeah," Kieran admitted. "A little." He

exhaled and relayed all that had happened at Michael's earlier.

Shane looked thoughtful. "That might explain it," he said carefully, but his eyes watched Kieran, unconvinced.

"Yeah." Kieran wasn't convinced either. He was worried about Maggie, and the fact that she was unhappy with him at the moment didn't sit well, but he couldn't help feeling that there was something more to this strange apprehension he was feeling.

"So you'll check it out?"

Kieran blinked, mentally backtracking to figure out what Shane was talking about. Right. The cottage. Electricity. Plumbing. "Yeah, sure."

* * *

"How much longer?" Matt asked impatiently. They'd gotten off the very last exit of the turnpike extension a while ago, the roads getting progressively narrower and less travelled the farther northwest they went. They'd been on the road for nearly seventeen hours straight with only brief stops at interstate rest areas for bathroom breaks and tank fill-ups.

"Not much longer, I think," she said, not minding the question at all. It was the first time he'd asked the entire trip. He'd been her stalwart copilot, studiously informing her on their progress as he navigated them through one state after another, map in hand. It wasn't that difficult. Once they'd hopped onto I-95 North it was a straight shot up the coast till they hit Philadelphia and picked up the PA Turnpike. It was only since they had abandoned that that he seemed to have grown anxious.

In all honesty, she was feeling a bit anxious herself.

"Wow." This time it was Faith uttering the exclamation as they rounded the final ridge and saw the entire valley spread out before them.

"Is that it, Mom? Is that Pine Ridge?"

A grin slowly spread across her face. "I believe it is."

Matt let out a hearty whoop, making her laugh. "We're home!"

Home, indeed, Faith thought, feeling the depth of it in her soul.

* * *

After dropping Ryan off with his sister-in-law Taryn, Kieran headed out to the little stone cottage at the outskirts of town. It was a nice piece of property, or at least it had been at one time. A decent parcel with a small house set back from the road, but within shouting distance of the nearest neighbors. It would have been described with words like "charming" and "cozy" and perhaps even "rustic" in a professional real estate ad.

"Handyman special" was an understatement.

The place was not without appeal, however, Kieran thought as he got out of his sleek custom black Porsche. With significant amounts of money, labor, and time, it did have the potential to be very charming and cozy indeed. Kieran absently rubbed his chest again when the troublesome ache intensified. If it kept up, he might have to ask Mick about it, get it checked out.

The cottage and property showed classic signs of neglect. What was once a pebbled drive was now dotted with weeds and small saplings. The lawn was too high with wild grass and wildflowers, obviously forsaken by the teen Shane had hired to mow the place once in a while. Shutters hung drunkenly from wood-framed windows. A couple of the steps and boards on the small front porch were rotted and warped. Several shingles lifted in the slight breeze; undoubtedly there would be more in a good, stiff wind or one of the frequent thunderstorms that popped up this time of year. And that was just the outside.

Kieran wondered what Shane was thinking, selling a property in this condition, even with the current distractions in his life. While unusual for him to buy a property in such a state of disrepair, it was not unheard of. In those infrequent instances, the purchase was usually made as a joint venture with their cousin, Johnny Connelly, who ran a construction and home remodeling company in the next town. But Johnny clearly hadn't been working his magic out here, and Kieran had trouble believing his overly-cautious brother would let anyone buy it, let alone a single mom. Even if she was the female equivalent of Bob Villa or Ty Pennington she'd be in over her head with this place.

At first glance, the inside wasn't much better. A thick layer of dust and cobwebs covered everything. It was minimally furnished – at least Kieran supposed it was furniture beneath the heavy drop cloths scattered here and there. What looked like a couch in the living room. A rickety table and two chairs in the kitchen. Nothing in the bedrooms.

Not surprisingly, the electricity was not turned on, though the place did seem to have running water. He turned on the spigot in the kitchen, letting it run for several minutes until the rusty brown started turning clear again. Thank goodness for small miracles, he muttered.

At least the cottage seemed to be structurally sound overall. The interior would need a lot of patchwork, and a few sheets of drywall here and there, but nothing too overwhelming, he admitted reluctantly, then wondered why it mattered so much to him.

He knew why. Jack Callaghan had raised his boys the old-fashioned way. Women were exquisite creatures that were to be coveted and cared for. He had a very strong protective streak in him when it came to things like that. Oh, he knew it wasn't exactly a politically correct viewpoint, but such things were hard-wired into him, right alongside his sense of honor and loyalty and Irish pride.

He respected a woman's right to have the same choices as a man, but he also felt a responsibility to look out for them, some deep-rooted belief that it was simply the right thing to do. It was what his brothers consistently referred to as his "knight" complex, though in truth, they were all guilty of feeling the same thing to some degree.

Kieran rubbed at his chest again. The strange unease he'd felt all day was intensifying. He looked up into the late afternoon sky expecting to find the hint of an approaching storm – it felt just like that, like a warning that something powerful was headed his way – but found nothing except cloudless blue all around. The sensation seemed much stronger here than it had earlier at Maggie's or Lacie's.

He tried to shrug it off, believing it to be his own conscience rebelling – first at helping Michael distract Maggie, and now at the thought of a single mom moving into a place like this.

Most of the time he kept his views to himself, at least tried to, but this was just going too far. Deciding that something had to be done, Kieran got back into his Porsche and returned to the Pub with the intent of telling Shane he simply had to find another property.

Maybe then this anxiety would ease.

* * *

Faith felt a stab of excitement when she made the right onto Sycamore Lane. According to the realtor, the property was all the way down at the end on the right hand side. She cruised past the houses, reciting the numbers on the mailboxes aloud, Matt's soft echoes synchronized with hers.

A sleek black Porsche passed them going in the other direction, earning a murmur of appreciation from Matt. Faith felt a brief but intense shiver of anticipation, a warming tingle that began deep in her belly and radiated outward.

"Ready?" she asked, shoving the odd sensation out of the way when she stopped the car at the massive evergreen that marked the property end of number 1780 and the beginning of 1782. Beyond that tree lay the culmination of dreams over the last ten years: a home, a real home.

Matt took a deep steadying breath. "Ready," he answered with his irresistible grin. Faith held that picture of him in her heart, knowing that in only a few years he'd be off on his own.

Faith edged the car forward, turning into the pebbled drive and continuing all the way up toward the cottage. They sat there, the two of them, wide-eyed and silent as they got their first look at their new home in the approaching twilight. Faith scanned the overgrown lawn, took in the sagging and cockeyed porch as well as the drunkenly hanging shutters.

"It's perfect," Matt said, his voice filled with awe. A single tear slipped down Faith's cheek.

She couldn't have agreed more.

* * *

"I'm still mad at you," Maggie sniffed when Kieran entered the Pub kitchen. He might have been the size of a Mack truck, but all Maggie could focus on was the puppy dog look in his big blue eyes. She steeled herself against them. Of all the brothers, Kieran was the only one who could make her heart melt in motherly affection with the slight hint of dimples and the boyish charm that defied his manly form.

Apparently she wasn't the only one susceptible to his charms. Her sisters-in-law were just as affected. Michael often quipped that it made Kieran the most dangerous of them all. Looking at him now, positively contrite, his eyes begging forgiveness, she had the nearly irresistible urge to ruffle his naturally unkempt hair. It was only through a sheer force of will – strengthened and continually tested by facing the same roguish charm on her own little boy's face – that she managed not to smile and retain a peeved expression.

"I know," he sighed soulfully, sitting next to her anyway. He crowded her with his big body, taking his time as he extracted a bag of bite-sized Reese's Peanut Butter Cups and put them on the table between them.

Maggie's eyes narrowed. She watched him intently as he opened the bag and slowly unwrapped one. He popped it into his mouth and closed his eyes, feeling Maggie's gaze as he chewed, then swallowed.

He flicked his glance sideways, as if he had just remembered she was there. "I'm sorry. Would you… like one?"

Maggie's tongue unconsciously peeked out and licked along her upper lips. Reese's peanut butter cups were her greatest weakness, and he knew it, the shameless devil. He must really feel bad, she thought, trying to ignore the heavenly scent of milk chocolate mixed with peanut butter.

Without waiting for her to answer, he extracted another and unwrapped it, placing it on the table and nudging it toward her while looking at her through half-lidded, cautious eyes, as if he wasn't really looking at her at all. After a moment or two of indecision – pride vs. desire – desire won out and she snapped it up, giving him a defiant look.

Kieran smiled, and she felt the impact all the way down into her toes. God help her if her son inherited this quality, too. She'd be beating the girls off with a stick in a few years.

* * *

"Mick says everything's good," he said conversationally, pulling out another peanut butter cup for himself.

"I told you everything was fine," she snapped, but there was no bite in her tone, and he knew he was in her good graces again. He'd take an 'I told you so' over bad news any day.

"Yes, you did," he agreed. The next piece went to her. "But you know Mick, how he worries." He didn't mention that she had been worried, too. The sheer amount of baked goods she'd made attested to that. Lacie's mom had taken one look at the massive treat-filled box and promptly forecasted a record in sales at her church's bake sale the next day.

"Yeah," she said, softly. "Thanks, Kier."

Before he knew what hit him, Maggie wrapped her arms around him – at least as far as she could – in a hug, even going as far as to place a chaste kiss on his cheek. "I'll repay the favor one of these days," she promised, her eyes twinkling mischievously.

Kieran thought that sounded ominously like a warning, and the unease in his chest flared momentarily.

Before he had a chance to dwell on it, Shane walked in and spotted them. He gave Maggie a quick kiss on the cheek and nodded to Kieran.

After passing along Lacie's thanks for all of the baked goods to Maggie, he turned to Kieran. "Hey. Did you get a chance to check out that property?" he asked, swiping a Reese's and grabbing some milk from the fridge. Kieran filled him in on what he had found. Shane listened to Kieran's detailed description on the state of the place. Maggie sat up, listening intently.

"I agree it is not an optimal situation," Shane said, frowning slightly, "but she was very specific, Kier."

"But why?" he asked, rubbing at his chest again. "I'm telling you, Shane, the place is not fit for human habitation in its current state."

"Maybe it's a question of money," Maggie suggested quietly, causing both men to look at her. "Well, it just makes sense, doesn't it?" she asked. Her eyes dropped to Kieran's hand and he abruptly stopped rubbing his chest. He turned to Shane, meeting his eyes, knowing she'd hit the nail on the head.

Kieran scowled at him. "Are you kidding me?"

Shane shook his head. "No. Maggie's right."

"Since when is money more important than people, Shane?" Kieran asked angrily. "Shit. It's not like we need the money. If she's that hard up, give her something else at a reduced rate or something."

Shane shot him a scathing look. "Don't you

think I tried? You know better, Kieran. I offered at least three other places in town. She refused. It was the cottage or nothing. She wouldn't have even qualified for that if I hadn't personally co-signed the mortgage application."

That was unexpected. "Why would you do that?"

Shane averted his eyes. "I don't know. Just a feeling."

Kieran felt a little better knowing that his brother didn't feel right about this either, but there was definitely something else at play here. He couldn't put his finger on it, but he felt it. He looked at Maggie, saw the colors swirling hypnotically in her green eyes. Then turned his gaze to Shane, and knew that he, too, felt it.

"You want her in Pine Ridge," he guessed, knowing even as he spoke the words that they were true. He felt like a moron. Of course Shane wouldn't allow something like this to happen unless there was a damn good reason for it. "Why?"

Shane exchanged a glance with Maggie, then shrugged. "I don't know. But when her offer came in, I couldn't put it down, no matter how much I wanted to."

Kieran knew better than to push. He trusted Shane's instincts implicitly. Like Kieran, he had a huge knight complex.

"Alright," he nodded slowly. "I don't like it, but if you say there's something there…"

"There is," Shane confirmed, but offered no more.

"We'll keep a close eye on this one, though, yeah?"

Shane smiled. "I was hoping you'd say that. Maybe we can head up there tomorrow, work a little magic before she arrives?"

Kieran nodded and agreed, feeling considerably better. He already had a mental list of things started as he began to plan a trip to the local home improvement store.

Maggie smiled enigmatically, plucking another Reese's from the table. "It will all work out. Like I said, Kieran, you just have to have *faith*."

Kieran reached over and patted Shane's back as his brother was suddenly thrown into a violent coughing fit. Shane pinned accusatory blue eyes on Maggie. She met his gaze head on, her own green eyes swirling madly and a completely unapologetic grin on her face.

"I think I'd like to go, too," Maggie announced brightly, but Kieran was already shaking his head.

"No way, Mags. Mick'll have my ass if I get you anywhere near that place in your current condition." She looked so crestfallen that he quickly added, "But maybe once we get it cleaned up a bit and a little less hazardous…"

* * *

"No electricity, Mom," Matt reported, methodically flipping switches in each of the rooms as they made their first pass through the cottage. A brief flashlight inspection of the fuse box showed that everything – while dusty and covered in cobwebs - looked fine, and that the electricity probably just hadn't been turned on yet.

"Guess we arrived a little earlier than expected," she mused. "I can call tomorrow. In the meantime, looks like our first night will be candlelight and a cold dinner. You up for that?"

"Heck, yeah." He grinned so wide her heart swelled. Her son had the ability to do that to her.

"But first I think we need to do the important stuff." His expression became guarded, no doubt thinking she was going to make him work. "I think we need to establish which bedroom is yours and which one is mine."

They took their time touring the small cottage. It didn't take long. The downstairs consisted of two large rooms – kitchen and a living space – as well as a full bathroom. The upstairs had two bedrooms, both with breathtaking views of the mountains and another full bath shared between them.

All the while, Faith was mentally designing the redecoration. The only exception was Matt's room. He had complete autonomy over his own space – within reason, of course.

Tomorrow she would begin sketching the images already forming in her head and compiling a list. They'd prioritize together and squeeze what they could out of their budget. Both had agreed before the move that the first order of business would be to purchase beds, or at the very least, mattresses.

Since they were both very hungry, they decided to postpone unloading and cleaning for a later time. Instead, they chose to spread out a blanket on the back patio and eat the sandwiches they'd picked up in town – oddly called 'hoagies' around Pine Ridge – outside under the ever-darkening dusk. The air was cooler than they were used to, but still quite pleasant. Cleaner. Less humid. It was quiet here. Their property was outlined in trees, affording them privacy.

"This is great, Mom," Matt said, wolfing down his sandwich with the hunger of a growing boy. Faith gave him half of hers and popped open Cokes for both of them.

"Yeah, it is, isn't it?"

"We're going to be okay."

"Yeah," she said, warmth blooming within her as a welcome peace settled around them. "We are."

Chapter 3

The sounds of birdsong and tires on the gravel drive woke Faith the next morning. It took a few moments to shake off the sense of disorientation. Matt was next to her on the floor, snuggled in his sleeping bag. Sunlight filtered through dirty windows; the slightest movement seemed to rouse a cloud of dust motes, but not even that could dampen Faith's sense of joy.

For the first time, they had a place that was completely theirs. They were *home.*

Faith rose quietly and padded to the window out of habit, but there was little, if anything, capable of rousing a thirteen year old boy short of a nuclear bomb. She would let him sleep a while longer. There would be plenty to do today.

She was pleasantly surprised to see an electric company truck parked alongside the transformer near the entrance to the property. The uniformed worker fiddled around for only a few minutes before driving off. Flipping the nearest light switch, Faith gave a silent fist pump as the porch light glowed through the layers of accumulated dust and bug carcasses and confirmed that the electricity was now officially on.

After a short trip to the bathroom – she was definitely going to hit that first thing so she could take a bath later in the old-fashioned claw-foot tub – Faith managed to dig out her coffee maker. She was enjoying her first cup of coffee on the porch when Matt found her.

Coffee in hand, his overlong chestnut hair sticking out at impossible angles, he sat down beside her, his long legs extending well past the two steps and onto the walkway. Most kids his age didn't drink coffee, but Matt had developed a taste for it early on. Faith didn't have a problem with it. Matt was a good kid, and it certainly wasn't affecting his growth. He was already pushing five-foot-nine with size ten-and-a-half foot pads.

"Sleep well?" Faith asked with a smile.

"Yeah. Except for the snout full of dust, I'm golden," he grinned. She knew he was every bit as happy to be here as she was. "What's the plan for today?"

It was a morning ritual they observed every day – a five minute meeting where they shared what was on tap, a connection that kept them feeling in touch and on the same page.

"Cleaning for me," she said, sounding much more pleased with the prospect than one would expect. "Bathroom first, then kitchen, I think. The beds are supposed to be delivered sometime today, too, so no more snouts full of dust tonight."

Matt nodded, his soft gray eyes, so like hers, looking thoughtful. "Mind if I start on the outside stuff?" he asked. "I found an old push mower in the shed last night and some clippers. I can siphon some gas out of the car; it should only need a gallon or so."

"I think that's a wonderful idea," Faith said brightly. "At some point we'll have to go into town and pick up some supplies, but I think we have enough packaged stuff for a decent breakfast. Besides," she added, "I'm really anxious to get started. How about you?"

"Yeah," he grinned. "It'll be nice to cut our own grass for a change." Matt often picked up odd jobs around whatever neighborhood they were in to earn a little extra cash. He was already pretty skilled at general handyman work.

* * *

"Is that the kid you hired?" Kieran asked as he pulled the big pickup into the driveway and spotted the unfamiliar teen.

"No," answered Shane.

"He doesn't look familiar," Lacie added. She'd convinced Shane to let her tag along and help with some general cleaning and tidying while he and Kieran took care of the heavy work and repairs. It hadn't been a hard thing to do. The last couple of weeks had been especially hard on her, and Lacie welcomed the opportunity to keep busy. It allowed her to work through things, she said, and Shane was more than willing to agree to anything that kept her by his side. After nearly losing her to a family-friend-turned-psycho, he was feeling extremely overprotective and hard-pressed to deny her anything.

As soon as he spotted them, the teen looked up from the ancient mower and stood tall, his posture wary but not aggressive. "Can I help you?" he called out as the two much larger men approached.

With the observation skills of the Ops men they were, they took in everything about the boy in a matter of seconds. Tall, lean, the kid was going to be big by the time he finished growing; it was something they understood all too well. Rich brown hair extended beyond the rag he'd tied around his head to keep the sweat at bay; gray eyes half shuttered, displayed both curiosity and caution. The kid's stance was relatively casual, holding a confidence rarely seen in one so young.

Kieran liked him immediately.

"Shane Callaghan," said Shane, extending his hand. "My fiancé, Lacie. My brother, Kieran. You the new owner?"

The boy puffed his chest out proudly as he accepted Shane's hand with a surprisingly firm grip, then Kieran's, and gave a respectful nod to Lacie. "Yeah. Matt O'Connell."

Kieran suppressed a knowing smile. It was a

long time since he'd been at that awkward phase when he wasn't really a kid anymore yet not quite a man, but some things a man never forgot. "We thought we'd ready the place up for you, but it looks like you arrived earlier than expected."

Matt gave a slight nod. "Got here last night."

"You stayed here?" Kieran asked, remembering the state the house had been in yesterday afternoon.

"Yeah." There was no mistaking the pride in the kid's voice. He didn't seem bothered at all.

"Well, since we're here, would you like a little help?"

Matt considered them, then his eyes wandered over the truck. The back of the pickup was loaded with equipment and supplies. "S'okay with me," he shrugged nonchalantly. "But you better check with my mom."

Matt pulled another rag from his back pocket and wiped the sweat from his face and neck. It was still pretty early in the day to work up a sweat like that. Kieran wondered how long the kid had already been at it.

"Come on. She's inside."

The strong scents of bleach and wood soap assaulted them as they neared the house. A battery operated radio played from the back of the house, and a woman's voice could clearly be heard singing along, slightly off-key but with lots of heart.

They found her in the kitchen. Her knees were on the floor, the upper half of her body swallowed up by the double-doored cabinet beneath the sink. The lower half of her body, along with her very attractive rear end, moved in rhythm to the song as she scrubbed and sang. Lacie put her hand over her mouth to stifle the giggle, but the men had better control and somehow managed to keep their smiles from extending past a few twitches at the corners.

"Mom," Matt called, looking a little embarrassed. She didn't hear him. "Mom!" he called louder, startling her. There was no mistaking the loud crack as she jumped, knocking her head on the underside of the sink basin. Everyone winced in sympathy.

"What?" Faith asked, extracting herself from beneath the sink, rubbing at the spot on the back of her head. She didn't seem nearly as angry as she might have been under the circumstances.

"Sorry," Matt mumbled. "We've got company."

* * *

Already? She thought. She'd hoped that her new neighbors might be a bit less intrusive than those in their old neighborhood. Faith sat on the floor, needing a moment to let the brightly colored lights currently flashing in front of her eyes to fade. They just didn't make sinks like that anymore, she thought wryly.

The first thing she saw was a pair of size

fourteen steel-toed leather work boots. Her gaze moved up muscular, denim clad legs. And up, past lean male hips and a ripped, massive torso encased in a cotton T. And up, to beautifully sculpted male features, jet black hair, and luminous blue eyes.

Faith gulped. If this is the kind of stuff she saw by hitting her head, she'd definitely have to do it more often.

Full male lips quirked in amusement.

"Mom," Matt said, breaking into her obvious hallucination, "this is Shane Callaghan and his brother, Kieran, and his fiancé, Lacie."

Faith shook the cobwebs from her head, turning to face the other man. He had the same black hair and blue eyes, but wasn't quite as large as the first one. "Shane Callaghan. We spoke on the phone. The seller, right?" Three male hands reached out to assist her, but it was Matt's she chose for a hand up.

"That's me," Shane said with a friendly smile.

"Hi." Faith returned Shane's smile with one of her own. Tugging off the heavy duty rubber gloves, she took the hand he offered, then Lacie's, then Kieran's. "I'm Faith."

* * *

Kieran Callaghan prided himself on the complete and total control he had over his mind and body. But the moment Faith put her hand in his, he could scarcely recall his own name.

Part of it had to do with the sudden rush of sparks and tingles that radiated outward from the point of contact, making him feel as if he had just grabbed an electric fence. For as unexpected as it was, it was not unpleasant; rather, it felt as though some hidden, heretofore unused part of him had just jolted to life. The growing unease that had been accumulating in his chest, getting heavier and heavier over the past couple of days, simply … vanished.

Well, *damn*.

In addition to the strange physical response, Kieran was caught mentally unprepared as well, for the image of the single mother he had been envisioning was about as far removed from this woman as he could get. He had been expecting an older woman, late thirties maybe – an opinion that had been enforced after encountering Matt. But Faith was not old, not by any stretch of the imagination. Unless she had discovered the secret of perpetual youth, she was no older than him. Younger, by the looks of it. She was small, sexy, and quite possibly the most beautiful woman he'd ever seen.

Damn didn't even come close to covering it.

"You've already met my son, Matt, I see." Kieran felt like he was in the Twilight Zone. There was no way in hell she was the single mother of the teen currently towering protectively over her shoulder. He blinked at her words, and was dimly aware of Shane clearing his throat and Faith attempting to reclaim her hand.

"Sorry," he murmured, stammering out an apology. He reluctantly released her hand. "I didn't expect you to be so..."

Matt scowled, but Faith's features softened. He could tell he embarrassed her, given the shy way she averted her gaze and the pretty pink color blossoming in her cheeks, and he immediately felt bad. It wasn't like him to totally zone out like that.

"It's okay," she said kindly. "You're not the first." She made a point of scanning him from head to toe. "But you might just be the biggest."

Her smile was dazzling, and he found himself chuckling with the others as the awkwardness passed. "Fair enough."

Faith's eyes moved away from him and back to Shane. For a moment, it felt as if the sun had been hidden behind some clouds. Surely it was a trick of his imagination.

"So to what do we owe the honor of your visit, Mr. Callaghan?" she asked. "I hope there's not a problem." Her voice was light, but Kieran didn't miss the way her pretty gray eyes clouded with concern.

"Call me Shane, please. And no, there is no problem. We were just hoping to make the place a little more habitable for you before you arrived."

"That's very kind of you," she said.

Kieran forced his addled brain to start

functioning again. “We’ve got the truck loaded with a bunch of stuff – lumber, hardware, a couple of fixtures.”

Faith’s smile faltered a bit. She glanced at Matt again and shifted her weight slightly. The two exchanged a knowing look before she spoke. “That’s really nice of you,” she said hesitantly, “but we haven’t really had a chance to go through thoroughly and see what we need.”

“I walked through yesterday,” Kieran told her confidently, confused by her apparent sense of discomfort. “Trust me. You need this stuff, and a whole lot more.”

* * *

Faith’s unease grew. It had taken nearly everything they had to get this far. Things were going to be really tight for a while, and they were going to squeeze every possible dime out of what they had left, at least until she got that first paycheck. Even then, it would be a struggle. For their own home, they had both decided it would be worth it.

But she did have her pride. She wasn’t about to share all that with a stranger, no matter how good looking he was. “I appreciate the thought, Mr. Callaghan -“

“Kieran,” he corrected immediately.

“Kieran,” she said, only to appease him. “It’s

not that we want to appear ungrateful, but we can't accept any of that. "

"It's all in the agreement," Shane interrupted smoothly.

"It is?" Faith blinked. She had read the contract six times, each and every legal word of it. What exactly had she missed?"

"It is," Shane assured her. "Page seventeen, Clause four, subclause B. 'It is the Seller's responsibility to ensure that the residence is habitable and up to code.' I'm paraphrasing, of course, but that's the gist of it."

"Oh," Faith said, her brows knitting together. "I'm afraid I don't remember seeing that."

"No?" Shane asked with a bemused expression. "Hang on – I've got the papers in the truck."

Faith shifted uncomfortably as Shane jogged outside. "I wish I could offer you something," Faith said to Lacie and Kieran, feeling somewhat embarrassed, "but I'm afraid I haven't had a chance to get to a store yet and our electricity was just turned on this morning…"

"It's fine," Lacie assured her with a smile that was as genuine as it was warm. "We weren't expecting you to be here, so we brought a couple of coolers with us." She looked around the decent sized kitchen with appreciation. It had definitely been built at a time when the kitchen was the hub of all family activity. "This is a great kitchen, by the way."

"It is, isn't it?" Faith agreed. Real wood cabinets, carved from what looked like dark cherry wood. Authentic marble countertops. A double basin stainless steel sink. The appliances – a gas stove and a refrigerator – were close to being considered of historical value, but they were sturdy and appeared to be in working order.

Like the rest of the house, it just needed some TLC. From the first moment they'd pulled onto the property, it felt like home.

* * *

Kieran forced his gaze away from Faith with some difficulty and took the opportunity to look around. The place didn't look as bad as it had yesterday. Maybe it was because Faith had managed to uncover some of the beauty beneath the layers of dust and dirt. Or maybe it was just because she was here, and her presence made everything seem a little brighter.

Shane returned with a slim, soft-sided leather case and proceeded to extract a small stack of papers. He hummed slightly to himself as he searched for the one he was looking for.

"Ah, here's the problem," he said, managing to look sheepish. He held up what looked like one page, then separated it into two. "These pages must have been stuck together. I'm so sorry about that."

Kieran narrowed his eyes. Shane was looking

just a little too innocent, and Lacie made a point of looking away. His brother had a memory like a computer. He did not make mistakes like that. Suddenly, Kieran felt a new surge of appreciation for his brother. He must have reworked the papers and added in that clause after the fact.

* * *

Faith scanned the "missing" page he handed her, her eyes growing wider the more she read. When she finished, she looked up and blinked. According to the paper in her hand, Shane Callaghan was going to pay for everything needed to repair the home.

"I don't know what to say," she said, blinking away the tears that were filling her eyes. It was simply too good to be true. She'd fallen in love with the place from the very first pictures, but had known it would take a lot to fix it up. Years, in fact, given that their limited funds and current budget would require them to do so in small increments.

Lacie seemed to understand. She moved closer to Faith and touched her shoulder. "Tell them they can start playing with the power tools before they die from anticipation," she whispered loudly.

"What do you say, Faith?" Kieran asked when several long moments passed and she still had said nothing.

He looked so eager that Faith couldn't help but

laugh through her stunned shock. "Well, apparently I already signed my permission. And we would really appreciate the help," she answered finally. "Thank you."

"Awesome." Kieran's smile could have lit the entire valley of Pine Ridge for a week. He turned to Matt. "Come on. I've got a portable laser miter in the truck..."

Faith wasn't sure what a portable laser miter was, but given the grin on Matt's face, it was something good. She watched as her son eagerly followed the two much larger men out of the house, grinning as if Christmas had just come early. Beside her, Lacie rolled up her sleeves, her eyes glittering.

"So where do we start?"

Chapter 4

The next few hours were a blur. The men made several trips out to their truck, carrying in various kinds of equipment, much of which looked more apt to be on a space shuttle than in a century-old stone cottage. For the most part, they stayed out of the kitchen where Faith and Lacie were hard at work, but she caught occasional glances as they moved past the doorway. The velvety rumble of their bass voices and deep-throated laughs were audible over her small, portable radio as the two brothers ribbed each other (and occasionally Matt) good-naturedly.

She couldn't be certain, but there were several times she thought she felt Kieran's eyes on her. It started as a tell-tale tingle running up and down the length of her spine, followed by a flare of awareness, but each time she turned around to check, he seemed otherwise occupied.

Matt was in his glory. Usually wary around others, he seemed to have taken to the Callaghan brothers immediately. Faith cringed when she saw Matt using some of the scarier looking tools. Lacie caught her worried glances and assured her that Shane and Kieran wouldn't let anything happen to

Matt.

It pulled at Faith's heartstrings. Matt was the center of her world. She would do anything for him. The one thing she hadn't been able to provide, however, was a positive male figure in his daily life. Matt's father never recognized his son. Faith's own family had disowned her when they found out she was pregnant at the very young age of fourteen.

Looking at him now, how he was soaking up their praise and attention like a dry sponge, Faith couldn't help but feel that she had cheated him somehow.

"Matt seems like a great kid," Lacie remarked, breaking in to Faith's thoughts. "How old is he?"

"He'll be fourteen at the end of the summer," Faith answered hesitantly, bracing herself for the slew of uncomfortable exclamations and questions that usually followed – 'Wow, you look so young!' 'How old were you when you had him?' 'Where's his father?'

To her surprise, Lacie didn't ask any of those things. "He's very capable for a fourteen year old," she said instead. "Most of the young teens I know would be whining and moaning about the work he's doing out there. And I haven't seen him texting anyone *once*."

Faith laughed; she couldn't help herself. "Oh, he does that," she admitted. A working cell phone was the one luxury she budgeted for. She wanted Matt to be able to contact her anytime, anywhere.

"He's been texting his friends back in Georgia about all the "cool stuff" in Pennsylvania since we crossed the border." She relayed their delight at the red-nosed deer signs and the tunnel through the mountain. "And he is so excited by the prospect of real snow. We've never had a white Christmas."

"I guess not, if you lived in Georgia," Lacie smiled, her eyes twinkling. "It gets pretty hot there, I imagine."

"Yes," Faith agreed. "And sticky. Nothing like this."

"Oh, don't worry. Come July it'll be humid enough."

With Lacie's help they managed to bring the first floor bathroom and kitchen up to acceptably clean levels. Lacie remarked on the quality and beauty of the aged wood that made up the cabinetry and trim as it was revealed beneath the layers of accumulated dust and grime; Faith couldn't help but feel a burgeoning sense of pride. Technically, she'd been in the house less than twenty-four hours, but it already felt like home to her.

Faith peeked out to check on Matt several times. They were the only times she saw him, except for when he came in to the kitchen to refill their water bottles from the tap. It felt a bit odd; she had expected today to be a two-person team effort, her and Matt against everything else.

She wasn't complaining, however. The sounds of laughter and the uncharacteristic but often-seen ear-to-ear grin on Matt's face as he worked with the two brothers was music to her ears. And if she caught a few sneak peeks of the rippling muscles of Kieran Callaghan in the process, so what? She'd be hard pressed to find another man who looked as good as he did, so why not enjoy a few surreptitious glances while she could? Chances were, she wouldn't get the chance to see all that in action again.

It wasn't only Matt that was enjoying their unexpected (but greatly appreciated) guests. Faith found herself laughing and smiling, too. Lacie, while soft-spoken, was good company. She was a great source of information on the area and its people, having been born and raised in Pine Ridge. She told Faith about her family, about her older brother Brian who had just returned from Afghanistan and her younger sister Corinne attending the local university. Faith had the distinct impression there was a lot Lacie wasn't saying. But, as Lacie wasn't digging for any personal information, Faith wouldn't either.

The two women shared an instant connection, and Faith was grateful that she had made what she considered to be her first real friend in her new home.

They stopped for lunch a little after noon. Hammers stopped pounding, saws stopped running, and two massive coolers were hauled into the kitchen. Lacie hadn't been kidding when she said they brought their own stuff. Faith and Lacie unloaded item after item until nearly every clean surface was no longer visible beneath it.

Faith thought for sure they'd never be able to consume that much food.

She was wrong.

Each of the men managed to put away roughly the same amount of food in one sitting that she consumed in a week. Even more surprisingly – so did her son. She could only shake her head when Kieran handed the boy his third hoagie, informing him with a masculine grin that growing boys needed to eat. She didn't want to embarrass Matt; but she felt a little uncomfortable. The Callaghans didn't seem to mind sharing their food, but she didn't want to take advantage of their kindness and generosity. Perhaps helping repair things around the house was part of the deal, but feeding them certainly wasn't.

* * *

Faith didn't eat very much, Kieran thought, watching her surreptitiously from beneath half-lidded eyes. Like all of his brothers, he had perfected the ability to observe without being observed. While everyone else dug in with hearty appetites, Faith hung back, accepting only an apple and a bottle of water, and that was only when Lacie pressed her. He had the distinct impression she wouldn't have had anything otherwise.

She wasn't overly thin. On the contrary, she had some fine curves that would catch any man's interest. So why did she seem so reluctant to join them in a meal? She'd obviously been working her ass off, just like everyone else. Surely she had to be hungry, too.

A loud knock sounded at the door, and Faith peeked out the window. "Looks like our stuff's here!" she said to Matt, and just like that, her slight frown turned up into a wide grin and her eyes lit up with excitement. When the others went to stand, Faith waved her hand at them. "It's okay – you guys stay and finish eating. This won't take long."

"Is your mother on a diet or something? She hasn't eaten anything." Kieran leaned over and spoke quietly to Matt when Faith excused herself to answer the door.

Matt shrugged, chewing the mouthful he had. Just that quickly, his expression changed to one that looked suspiciously like guilt as he put down the unfinished half of his sandwich. Kieran frowned. The kid was putting it away like a champ a few minutes ago. What had changed?

"Had enough?" he asked.

Matt nodded. "Yeah," he lied. "But can I save this for later?"

"Sure," Kieran nodded as Matt wrapped up the sandwich with care and put it into the fridge. It did not escape his notice that there was nothing else in there. Then again, they had just arrived, and Faith had admitted earlier they hadn't had a chance to do any shopping yet. Still, the empty fridge bothered him.

"Do you think your mom will mind if we leave the rest of this stuff here?" Kieran asked suddenly. "No sense letting it go to waste."

Matt's eyes widened. "You don't want it?"

"Nah," he reassured the kid. "Plenty more where that came from."

Kieran helped Matt wrap up the leftovers and put them in the fridge. At least he knew they'd have dinner tonight. Maybe Faith was self-conscious about eating in front of other people, or maybe she felt bad that she hadn't had anything to offer them.

It was ridiculous, of course, but she seemed like the type of woman who would care about that kind of thing. Besides being beautiful, she was also a proud woman. Her initial reluctance to accept help demonstrated that clearly enough. And she obviously cared a great deal for her son. Kieran had caught her worried looks and frequent peeks all morning. Of course, that may have been because he was watching her so closely, too.

The woman had an unexpected way of commanding his attention; there was no doubt about that. He'd had to put an extra effort into focusing on what he was doing lest he lose a finger or some other important body part while operating various power tools. Even now, he couldn't help himself from listening to what was going on in the other room. He could hear Faith's soft voice, along with two deeper, obviously male ones.

He honed in on the exchange, his protective instincts surging as he moved closer to the archway separating the kitchen from the living area. As far as he could tell, the delivery men had made only two trips from their truck to the house. Two mattresses and two box springs sat propped up by the door. Surely that wasn't all?

"If you'll sign here, Mrs. …."

"Miss," Faith automatically corrected as she signed the papers. The delivery man's grin grew. He was the younger of the two; Kieran put his age somewhere around twenty-five or so. The guy was decent looking enough, he supposed. Brown hair, brown eyes. Well-toned.

Kieran's eyes narrowed. The guy – the name stitched on his shirt said *David* - was looking at Faith with far too much non-professional interest. Faith must have noticed, too, because she shifted uncomfortably. After handing the clipboard to him, she took a deliberate step backward.

"Are you sure you don't want us to put those bed frames together for you?" the other guy asked. He lifted his cap and smoothed back his hair as he nodded toward the tangle of thin black steel rods now leaning against the wall. He was older, with clearly defined lines around his eyes and a fair smattering of gray around his close-cropped hair.

His gaze toward Faith was decidedly more fatherly than *David*'s. Kieran didn't have the sudden, irrational urge to kill *him*.

"I'm sure, thank you," Faith said politely.

"It's much easier with an extra set of hands," the younger guy pushed, coming dangerously close to invading Faith's personal space. Kieran only just managed to silence the low warning growl rumbling around in the back of his throat. Faith had already said no. Why was this guy still here?

Dropping all pretense of not listening, Kieran placed himself in the archway. Faith didn't respond to the man's latest offer. Judging by the way her pretty eyes were flashing with irritation, it was not the first time he'd asked. She stood patiently by the door to see them out. Unfortunately, they didn't seem all that anxious to leave.

Faith took another step back when *David* got a little closer than was socially acceptable. He was not a large man, not by Callaghan standards, but he was a good deal bigger than Faith. Faith's shoulders stiffened. With a slightly defiant tilt to her chin, she held her ground. For his part, Kieran did not like the way the guy was openly appreciating her assets.

"You know, tomorrow's my day off," the little rat bastard was saying. "I'd be glad to stop by and give you a hand. Looks like you could definitely use some help." His attempted sexy grin only managed to look smarmy. Faith opened her mouth, presumably to decline his offer, but before she could say a word, Kieran spoke up.

"That won't be necessary." Kieran crossed his massive arms over his equally massive chest, allowing his form to fill the archway, his deep voice booming throughout the small space as he set his laser-like stare upon the would-be do-gooder.

Matt, who had also been following the exchange, squeezed thru and stood beside him with a smirk. "Yeah, we got it covered, man."

David looked like he was about to say something else, but upon seeing Kieran, changed his mind. Apparently the guy had some brains after all. "Maybe another time," the delivery guy muttered before the two of them glanced once again at Kieran and made their exit. Faith's expression was a little harder to read. She looked relieved, but he couldn't be sure.

"Thanks," she said somewhat shyly.

Without another word, Kieran nodded, then turned on his heel and stalked back outside, fighting his own powerful urge to get close up in Faith's personal space. Matt followed closely behind.

"That happen a lot?" Kieran asked, once he was sure they were out of earshot.

"Yeah," Matt frowned. "Guys are hitting on my mom all the time. Most of them are pretty cool when she shuts them down, but some get kind of pushy."

"Turns down a lot, does she?" he asked

casually.

"No," Matt said with a grin. "She turns down them *all*," he clarified.

Kieran's dark mood took a definite upswing.

* * *

"I think we're in the way," Lacie observed as Shane, Kieran, and Matt progressed through the house, patching and fixing as they went. She pulled off her cleaning gloves. "I'm ready for a break anyway. How about we head into town for a bit? You said you needed some supplies, right?"

Faith pulled off her gloves, too, and wiped the back of her hand over her sweaty forehead. Everything about her felt grimy. "I do, but I can't go looking like this."

Lacie regarded her. "This is Pine Ridge, not Paris," she chuckled. "Although I think I could make good use of a wet washcloth and a hairbrush."

With some gentle prodding, Lacie persuaded Faith to accompany her into town, if for no other reason than to have something to offer her hard-working guests. She was from the South, after all, and Southern hospitality was more than just a catch-phrase; it was a part of her heritage.

"What about Matt? Maybe he should come too."

Lacie looked doubtfully over to where the three men were working. "Guys, Faith and I are going to head into town for supplies." She received a few grunts in return and laughed.

"Matt, you want to come with?" Faith called out.

Matt shot her a suitably horrified glance. Kieran paused what he was doing long enough to turn around. "Matt's a great help here if you can spare him."

Faith was pretty sure Kieran Callaghan officially became her son's hero in that moment. While he dutifully helped her when necessary, one of Matt's least favorite things to do was shopping. So much so, in fact, that she occasionally threatened it as a punishment when he was being particularly surly. The only thing that was more effective was taking his phone away for a few days, but she hated doing that in case he needed to get in touch with her.

"They'll be fine," Lacie assured her as they made their way out to the car. "Matt couldn't be safer with those two."

For whatever reason, Faith believed her. She liked Lacie, a lot. And every instinct she had said the brothers were good, decent men. She took a deep breath to settle her maternal nerves and changed the subject. "So you and Shane are engaged?"

"Yeah," Lacie said, positively glowing with happiness. "We're getting married in August."

"Congratulations."

"Thanks. I can't wait!" Lacie got a particularly bright look on her face. "Hey! You could come! I'll send an invitation to you and Matt."

Inwardly, Faith grimaced. She liked Lacie. The two had hit it off immediately, and that was something very rare; Faith didn't usually feel as naturally drawn to someone as she was to Lacie. In some ways, she felt a kindred spirit in the mild-mannered Kindergarten teacher. But weddings meant dressing up and buying gifts, and she couldn't afford either of those things right now. She mentally searched her limited wardrobe in vain for something even remotely suitable to wear and came up empty.

"It's going to be very small and informal," Lacie went on, then caught herself and laughed. "Though I guess when the Callaghans are involved, nothing can ever truly be considered *small*."

Faith had to grin at that. They did seem to have a huge presence that extended beyond their large physiques. It brought to Faith's mind the irrational thought that the wedding would be another excuse to see Kieran again, but she pushed that thought away as quickly as it came. She had no business thinking anything of the kind.

Lacie rummaged around in her purse for a bit, extracted a small notepad, removed the attached pen, and jotted something down. "I tend to be a bit disorganized, sometimes," she explained apologetically. "I find that if I don't write it down, I sometimes don't remember until it's too late."

That was something with which Faith could empathize. She had a similar notebook in her bag, though hers was filled with as many sketches as it was enumerated lists and notes. Sometimes an idea struck at the oddest times and if she didn't capture the gist while it was fresh in her mind, it was harder to reproduce later on.

"Shane is so organized, poor guy. My disjointed brain drives him crazy sometimes."

Faith chuckled at that. Shane did seem to be the type to be exceptionally well-prepared for any situation, but in a competent, good way. She hadn't detected any of the less desirable anal retentiveness so many control freaks had.

Faith didn't realize she'd voiced her inner thoughts out loud until Lacie bellowed a laugh. She felt the heat rushing into her cheeks when the men's heads snapped up suspiciously with the instinctive knowledge that such a full-hearted sound could only come at their expense.

Thankfully, they hadn't heard exactly what she'd said and Lacie didn't seem at all offended.

"Thanks. Shane is… well, let's just say he's everything I could have hoped for and then some."

Faith smiled, feeling genuinely happy for her. She couldn't find it in herself to begrudge the other woman a happy ending, not when they were so obviously in love.

"Kieran's a good guy, too," Lacie pointed out.

"They both seem very nice," Faith said carefully. As much as she liked Lacie, she didn't know her well enough to sense if there was any hidden meaning in that last statement. She'd been on the fix-up list so many times she'd become a bit paranoid. People generally meant well, but once they found out she was young and single they felt obligated to "help". Sometimes she felt like she had a bulls-eye tattooed on her forehead. So far Lacie had not shown any signs of gossipy nosiness, just natural curiosity. And she had been nothing but kind and helpful, so Faith decided to give her the benefit of the doubt and take the statement at face value.

"I still can't believe how much you're doing for us. With your help, we've already accomplished more in one morning than Matt and I could have in a whole week."

More like several, Faith added silently, given how long it would have taken to be able to afford all those supplies. The shingles and lumber alone would have put her back several hundred dollars, not to mention all the nails and screws and tools they would have had to buy or borrow to get the job done. She had her trusty collection of secondhand tools that she'd managed to collect over the years out of necessity, but it sure as heck didn't contain portable laser miter saws.

"I'm glad you're letting us help," Lacie

countered. "Most people wouldn't appreciate us barging in and taking over like that. You must think we're terribly pushy."

"Not at all," Faith was quick to reply, but an inner part of her squirmed. If it had been anyone besides Lacie, Shane, and Kieran, she probably would have been a bit more bothered than she was. She was normally a very private person, and did not accept help easily. It was nearly impossible not to like Lacie, however. And the appearance of the two men who seemed to know what they were doing was just too good to pass up.

"And we *do* appreciate it," Faith said sincerely. "Matt's been in seventh heaven all day."

Faith had given Lacie the perfect opportunity to ask about Matt's father, but she didn't. That raised her yet another notch in Faith's opinion.

"I think the guys are enjoying it, too. They can't wait till their nieces and nephews get a little older."

"Big family?" Faith guessed as Lacie directed her toward the town proper.

"You could say that. There are seven Callaghan brothers. Five of them are married with kids, but the oldest isn't close to being ready to use a power saw just yet."

Faith performed a few mental gymnastics. Seven brothers, five married, and one engaged. Lacie spared her the embarrassment of asking. "Kieran's the only remaining eligible bachelor."

Faith hated the little flutter she felt beneath her ribcage at that disclosure. She was *not* interested. And she was glad she wasn't interested, because she knew she had the equivalent of a snowball's chance in hell of catching the eye of someone like Kieran. Even her uninterested, don't-need-a-man self couldn't help but admit the man was a walking, talking fantasy. Gorgeous, strong, kind, good with kids …

Giving herself a mental shake, Faith forced herself away from those thoughts. She couldn't afford to think things like that just because a man was nice to her. Yet she still found herself asking, "And how's that going for him?"

Lacie laughed. "Honestly? I think he's seriously considering joining the priesthood." Faith looked over at her and caught her twinkling eyes. "Not really," Lacie admitted, "but I wouldn't blame him. He's got women throwing themselves at him all the time."

"And he doesn't like that?" Faith gave her a sideways glance. That didn't sound like any man she had ever known.

Lacie thought a few moments before answering. "No," she said finally. "I don't think he does. Callaghan men aren't like other men," she added carefully.

"How so?"

Lacie gave her a devilish grin. "You'll find out soon enough."

Faith wasn't quite sure what to make of that, so she remained silent.

With Lacie's help, Faith managed to procure nearly everything on her "first-run" list, as she called it. Food, paper products, additional cleaning supplies. Faith carefully considered each purchase before it went into her cart. She had to count every penny.

Thankfully, Lacie seemed to understand. Faith didn't know much about the local school system, but as a young, elementary school teacher who most likely hadn't been vested yet, Lacie was probably on a fixed budget herself and could relate. She seemed to know where to find the best deals, and willingly shared her knowledge with Faith.

Chapter 5

When Faith and Lacie returned a few hours later, the men were just cleaning up, which involved dousing themselves with water from an outdoor spigot.

Faith had to concentrate on her steps when she saw a shirtless, wet Kieran laughing with his brother and her son. The sight made her stumble at least once. *Dear Lord*, she thought, catching her balance, if she looked closely enough she was pretty sure she could see an *eight*-pack in those abs.

It did not improve her concentration any when they slipped on clean white T-shirts and helped the women carry things into the kitchen. The thin white cotton clung to Kieran's skin, still damp from the hose, and tiny prismatic droplets of water dangled teasingly from the ends of his blue-black hair.

"Will you stay for dinner?" Faith asked, once she swallowed past the huge lump in her throat and found her voice again. She figured it was the least she could do. They had spent nearly an entire Saturday making her and Matt's new house livable.

"Thanks," said Shane with a friendly smile,

"but Lacie and I have dinner plans."

Kieran didn't say anything right away. "What about it, Kieran?" asked Matt hopefully. "My mom's an awesome cook." Faith was surprised. Not because Matt was praising her culinary skills, but because he rarely warmed up to anyone as quickly as he had to Kieran.

Kieran's eyes met Faith's, and her heart stuttered. They were at once tremendously powerful and completely unreadable.

"I think your mom's done enough for one day. How about I take you guys out for pizza instead?" Matt turned hopefully to Faith. Pizza was one of his favorites, but eating out was something they usually reserved for special occasions.

"That's very thoughtful of you," Faith said hesitantly, "but you've done so much already."

"It's no problem. You'd be helping me out, actually."

Faith didn't see how taking them out for pizza could be helpful in any way, but Matt took Kieran at his word without question. "Come on, Mom. Please?"

The word "no" hovered on her lips. Going out in public looking and feeling the way she did – tired and in need of a good shower – was the last thing Faith wanted to do at that moment. Shopping at the farmer's market was one thing, but a restaurant?

There was also the issue of money – or, more accurately, her shameful lack of it. The trip north and today's purchases had all but obliterated their petty cash.

As if reading her mind, Kieran turned those amazing blue eyes back to her and said, "I need to head back to my place and get cleaned up first, but then I'll come back to pick you up. It'll be my treat."

When Faith worried her bottom lip with her teeth, he turned to Matt, and added slyly, "Did I mention I have a Porsche?"

Matt's eyes nearly bugged out of his head. He regarded Faith with a look of such longing she felt the pull on her heartstrings. "A *Porsche*, Mom."

Faith felt herself weakening. She really should say no, but it was next to impossible when Matt looked at her like that. It wasn't like he was asking for anything extravagant, either, just some pizza. He had been working hard all day, and this *was* kind of a special occasion.

Besides, spending a few more hours with Kieran wasn't exactly a hardship. He had been so patient and kind with Matt. If she was honest with herself, she had to admit that she had enjoyed his company, too. It was nice to be with someone so easy going and pleasant.

As a general rule, she avoided that kind of thing – especially with single men. She had neither the time nor the inclination to get involved with anyone. But this wasn't really a date, she rationalized. It was more like a friendly, welcome-to-the-neighborhood kind of thing. She could handle that.

Maybe.

"Okay, but only on the condition that you let us treat you."

Kieran frowned. "I asked you. You can't treat."

His downcast expression was so boyishly adorable that she found her fingernails digging into her palms to keep from touching him. That was enough to startle her into cognizant thought again. Faith had never had such a strong reaction to anyone before, and it set off blaring alarms in her head. She quietly turned them off with a mental note to examine them further later on.

"Technically, I asked you first when I asked you to stay for dinner. And I'm afraid it's the only way we can go."

He looked like he wanted to argue, but apparently he thought better of it. "Okay. I guess I can leave my man card at home for one night." He grinned and winked at Matt, who laughed. "See you in about an hour?"

Faith nodded, unable to completely stop the smile from curving her lips.

Guiseppe's was everything a traditional Italian pizza parlor should be. Along the side of the building, a red and green striped awning hung over a patio dotted with tables. Inside, dangling lights were suspended over high-backed booths and red and white striped tablecloths. Huge framed posters of Italian cities, buildings, and maps hung on the walls, and the delicious mix of spicy aromas had Faith's mouth watering within minutes.

"I think I gained ten pounds from the aroma alone," Faith murmured, making Kieran laugh. She didn't miss the appreciative glance he gave her, feeling it all the way down to her open-toed sandals.

"I like a woman who can appreciate good food."

"Easy for you to say," she muttered, attempting to hide her blush behind the menu and internally racked up a substantial calorie count. "You have what, about two percent body fat?" She looked longingly at the tray the waitress carried past filled with thick, Sicilian style pan-fried crust. "You could probably eat one of those and burn it off before we leave."

Kieran flicked his eyes over her in such a way that heat blossomed in places that had no business being that warm. "Nothing you need to worry about either," he said with an enigmatic smile before turning to his own menu. Faith wasn't sure what to make of that. Was it a compliment? Or was he politely telling her to mind her own business?

Faith deferred to Matt to order on their behalf, then sat back and looked around. There was a decent crowd, fun but not overly rowdy. It was a nice place, and the prices were reasonable. Anything was more than she had budgeted for, though, so she'd have to get extra creative for a week or two, but it was worth it to see the smile on Matt's face.

Matt and Kieran handled most of the conversation. When Matt found out Kieran was a seventh degree black belt, Faith swore she saw stars in the boy's eyes. For a while they talked about the programs offered at *BodyWorks*, and Kieran invited them to attend the free demo on the following day.

"Kieran!" Faith turned to see a very pretty young blonde woman balanced on sky-high heels waving and making her way over to their table.

"Natalie," Kieran acknowledged with a polite nod. Was it her imagination, or did she see a flicker of irritation in Kieran's expression? Was this one of the women Lacie had alluded to?

Natalie tore her eyes away from Kieran only long enough to take in Faith and Matt and summarily dismiss them as unimportant. "I had a wonderful time the other night," she said silkily. *Suggestively*. Faith's eyes widened as she felt the rush of color rising up into her cheeks. Matt gaped at the substantial amount of cleavage revealed as Natalie leaned in a bit closer.

* * *

Wrenching his gaze away from Faith, Kieran

cursed silently in his mind. This was exactly what he had been hoping to avoid. After spending the day around Sean, Lacie, Faith, and Matt, he'd had no desire whatsoever to return to his lonely room at the Pub. He didn't go out on his own much anymore, either. It just wasn't worth the hassle of being approached every ten minutes when women realized he was flying solo.

Of all the women he dreaded running into, Natalie topped the list. While unarguably stunning, she was about as far removed from what Kieran was searching for as possible. Self-absorbed, vain, and spoiled were just a few of the words that leapt to mind, all within the first five minutes of their ill-fated date less than a week earlier.

Kieran did follow through with a nice dinner, but ended the evening as soon as respectably possible. He had thought he'd been quite clear in his polite but firm assertion that he would not be calling her again. He believed honesty was the best – if not the always the most welcome – policy, and wanted to avoid any false expectations.

But, he thought as her cloying perfume wound its way into his sinus cavities, he obviously had not made it clear enough. Or, it was more likely that she just did not know how to take "no" for an answer. As she had so often alluded during their few hours together, she was used to getting what she wanted. At some point, unfortunately, she had decided that she wanted *him*.

Kieran stole a glance at Faith, saw her feigning great interest in the laminated maps of Italy on the backs of the menus, discussing the different regions with Matt. Head bowed, her dark waves cascaded over her shoulders as she tried to politely pretend she wasn't listening. Even from where he sat he could see the pink blush stealing across her cheeks. Her discomfort made the unfortunate interruption even more so.

In that moment, he knew what *he* wanted. And it was not Natalie.

"Wanna do it again sometime?" she pressed when Kieran didn't seem likely to take her not-so-subtle bait.

She emphasized her point by leaning over the table, right in front of Faith, showcasing her fabulous cleavage even more. Faith shrunk farther back in the booth, obviously uncomfortable. Because his eyes had been trained on her, he didn't miss it, and it annoyed him. They'd been having such a nice time together. Matt was funny and had a quick and clever wit. And Faith was absolutely breathtaking when she was relaxed and smiling.

"Maybe your friend would like to join us," Faith suggested quietly. She offered a polite smile. Matt had not yet learned how to mask his feelings quite as well, though his scowl wasn't as noticeable as it might have been.

One look confirmed that Faith was pulling back into herself again. *Damn it!* She had just started to relax around him. He didn't like the tension in her shoulders or the way she wouldn't look at him. He wanted to see her eyes sparkling – she had the most amazing soft gray eyes that shone like polished silver when she smiled.

Natalie looked thrilled with the idea and made a move to slide in next to Kieran, but he was not as amenable. "No, I'm sure she wouldn't," Kieran said, flashing a warning glance at Natalie. Their eyes met for a moment, and Kieran's were not nearly as kind and courteous as they had been. On the contrary, they were frosty and laced with warning. "Your friends are waiting for you, Natalie."

As pouts go, Natalie's was classic, but Kieran's message apparently got through. The waitress arrived with their food and Natalie stalked off to a different table to sulk. Kieran didn't look her way for the rest of the evening, but he could feel Natalie's eyes on them. Given the few uncomfortable glances he saw Faith make in that direction a couple of times, he was sure she was aware of Natalie's less-than-cordial glares shot toward them during their meal.

"Sorry about that," Kieran apologized into the awkward silence that had descended upon them with Natalie's exit. The comfortable, relaxed atmosphere they'd been enjoying only a few minutes earlier was gone.

"No problem," Faith said with forced lightness.

Any hopes he had of rekindling the easy comradery were quickly dashed. Faith made a point of avoiding his gaze and kept her conversational contributions to a minimum. Thankfully, Matt didn't seem to feel the same sense of discomfort; they managed to maintain a nice dialogue throughout the remainder of the meal.

"I had fun tonight," Kieran said later as he hung outside Faith's front door, reluctant to leave. "Thank you."

"We did, too," Faith responded politely. Her soft gray eyes flicked to his for just a moment, and he saw the blatant little white lie in them. He silently cursed Natalie again.

"I'm sorry about Natalie," he began, hoping to explain, but Faith cut him off by raising her hand. "Don't be. She seemed very, uh, interested. I hope we didn't make things too awkward for you." She bit her bottom lip, looking embarrassed.

Kieran blinked, bemused. *Jesus*! Is that what she thought? "What? No, of course not. I - "

"Good," she said quickly, looking anything but relieved. "Thanks again. Goodnight." Then she hurriedly stepped inside and closed the door, leaving him standing on the porch wondering what the hell had just happened.

* * *

"He likes you," Matt said, startling her. She

hadn't even realized she'd been standing just inside the door. Matt had already changed into a pair of pajama bottoms, so she must have been in a daze for a couple of minutes at least.

"I think Kieran is the type of man who likes everyone, Matt," she said, brushing aside the tiny thrill that ran through her at Matt's words, even as images of the immaculately coiffed and voluptuous Natalie wormed their way into her mind. If that was the type of woman that Kieran Callaghan courted, then she had even *less* than a snowball's chance in hell of catching his interest. Faith was the anti-Natalie.

"Don't read anything more into it." There was no place in her life for silly things like that. She was a grown woman, a single mother with a teenage son. And Kieran was a nice guy.

A really hot, incredibly sexy, gorgeous, muscular, nice guy who helped them out.

Because he was a nice guy.

"He didn't like Natalie," Matt smirked, attempting to mimic the seductive way the young woman had spoken to Kieran.

Yes, he did, Faith thought as she held back a dejected sigh. At least once, anyway. Maybe more, based on the look of desire in the woman's eyes. Though it had appeared that Natalie was a whole lot more impressed with Kieran than Kieran had been with her. Faith probably shouldn't have taken as much pleasure in that thought as she did.

Lacie's words came back to her again. Kieran had lots of women interested, and for good reason. Did this kind of thing happen all the time?

Maybe he was that way with all of the women he dated. She'd known men like that. Men who prided themselves on hooking up with as many women as possible, but having a set threshold of encounters to avoid things from 'getting complicated'.

Somehow that didn't quite ring true with the impression she'd formed of him throughout the day, but she had no reasonable basis for that. She'd known Kieran for all of what, twelve hours? How could she possibly know what he was like? She'd been wrong before, and with men she'd spent a lot more time around than a mere half day. So what if he had affected her more in that short span of time than anyone else had in the last fourteen years?

It was a depressing thought. Pine Ridge wasn't that big. Was she bound to run into Kieran groupies wherever she went? It was only their second night in their new town and already she had managed to make an enemy. The notion settled in her chest like a heavy stone.

"She was very pretty," Faith sighed. And young. Really young, not just young-looking like people told her she was. And blonde. With the toned body of a Zumba instructor. She probably drove a sporty little red convertible, too. *Bitch*, her snarky side added on for good measure.

"Not as pretty as you," Matt said sincerely. Faith felt the tears start to well up in her eyes and had to look away. Someday all too soon her sweet son would understand what drew men's attentions. Blue collar single moms who didn't have the time or money for things like salons and fitness memberships weren't at the top of the desirable date list. But for now, she would gratefully accept her son's heartfelt compliment.

"You should go out with him," Matt said firmly, apparently having thought about it and deciding the issue.

Faith's mouth dropped open. "Excuse me?" Never had she heard anything remotely similar come out of her son's mouth. He was usually very protective, and had a trademark scowl reserved for any man who exhibited the least amount of interest in her.

"You should go out with him," Matt repeated with exaggerated patience. "I like him. He's cool."

"First of all, you barely know him. And second, I don't have time for that kind of stuff," Faith said. She bit her lip to avoid adding number three – Kieran hadn't asked.

She was still reeling as much from her son's declaration as the fact that he seemed to genuinely take to Kieran. It certainly wouldn't hurt for him to have a positive male influence in his life. Faith knew as well as anyone how difficult the next few years could be, and based on what she'd seen so far,

Matt could certainly have picked a lot worse for a role model.

"But I don't think I'd have a problem if he wanted to take you to a game or something," she amended.

To her further surprise, Matt grinned. "I was hoping you'd say that. Kieran's doing that martial arts demo tomorrow in town, and he did say we could stop by. Can we go?"

It was amazing how fast 'you should' became 'can we', she mused, but she felt some measure of relief. Dealing with her son's desire to attend a martial arts demo was more in her comfort zone than her desire to… Faith slammed a heavy brick wall down on that avenue of thought before it could make it any farther along what was certainly a dead-end.

"What time is the demo?" she asked. "I was hoping we could get a few more things done before I start work on Monday."

"Kieran said you'd probably say that," Matt said. "So he said if you brought me down, he'd bring me home and then he'd help with whatever."

"He did, huh? When did you guys decide all this?"

"When you went to the ladies room. So can we?"

As if on cue, Matt's cell phone buzzed. He glanced at the screen and then looked impatiently back at Faith. "Can we?"

"Who just texted you?" Faith asked, having a sneaking suspicion she already knew the answer.

"Kieran," Matt said unapologetically. "Well?"

Faith exhaled. Kieran had Matt's cell number, too? He hadn't asked for *her* number. Then again, she wouldn't be surprised if Matt had already provided Kieran with her number, too, given the way he was acting.

She promptly popped that little bubble of hope the moment it tried to surface. So what if he did? It wasn't like Kieran would call her.

Matt looked at her expectantly, waiting for an answer. She should tell him no, that they had far too much to do around the new house and property. But the truth was, it was good to see Matt so excited about something. He rarely asked for anything, and a ride into town wasn't an unreasonable request, especially when she had planned on heading that way anyway to check out the farmer's market again to scope out prices on used furniture and second-hand items.

And she would get to see Kieran again, an inner voice pointed out.

"I guess," she said finally, laughing when Matt whooped and started texting Kieran immediately. "He says the demo starts at noon and lasts till two."

Faith nodded. She could rise early and get some sketches done, then take Matt into town. With any luck, they wouldn't cross paths with more Natalies in the process.

Chapter 6

"This place is awesome," Matt declared the moment they pulled into the parking lot and saw the state-of-the-art structure that was *BodyWorks*. Three visible stories of brick and dark glass that somehow fit perfectly against the scenic mountain backdrop. The outside, however, was nothing compared to the inside. Black marble and gold abounded in the entry way along with huge ferns and plants creating a lush, cordial atmosphere.

Faith had to agree with Matt's initial assessment. The interior was beautifully done; it was understated and ultra-modern yet warm and welcoming. She would have expected to feel woefully out of place in a fitness center, but strangely enough, she didn't. There were people of all ages, all sizes, all walks of life milling about. Some wore expensive-looking designer fitness wear; others sported the same cotton tees and shorts she bought from the end-of-season clearance rack at Walmart.

"Can I help you?" said a friendly-looking woman from behind the black marble Member Services check-in desk. The recessed lighting made the highlights in her hair shimmer like spun threads of gold. Young and extremely attractive in a form-fitting black *BodyWorks* polo embroidered with the name *Phoebe* and black boy shorts, her million watt smile nearly blinded them. Faith self-consciously tugged on her plain white, short-sleeved cotton blouse.

"We're here to see the martial arts demo," Matt said, his eyes wide as he tried to take in everything at once. "Kieran invited us."

The young woman nodded. "Faith and Matt, right?"

Faith nodded, nonplussed. How could this woman possibly know their names?

"Great! He wanted to know the moment you arrived." The woman pressed a button on the console and spoke into the small microphone near her flat screen. "Mr. Callaghan, your guests are here." She paused briefly, and Faith realized she was listening to the very tiny receiver tucked around her right ear. "Yes, sir." Pressing another button, Phoebe looked up at them and grinned again. "Mr. Callaghan will be down shortly. Paul will take you down to the café."

Paul stepped forward. Like Phoebe, he wore a black *BodyWorks* polo embroidered with his name, but instead of shorts, he sported thin men's workout pants.

"Hi." Every bit as attractive and fit as Phoebe, his grin was equally devastating. He gave Faith a knowing grin. "First time?"

She nodded. Paul laughed easily. "I know. A bit overwhelming, right? Don't worry. You get used to it."

"Oh, we're just here for the demo," Faith told him, expecting Paul's friendly façade to fade once he realized they would not be the source of his next commission, but he remained as pleasant as ever, leading them over to the café. The subtly lit board boasted the Celtic Goddess name, along with a dizzying assortment of organic, healthy fare choices.

"What can I get for you?" he asked expectantly.

"Oh, uh, nothing, thanks," Faith stammered. There were no prices listed, and she heard her mother's voice echoing in her mind: *If you have to ask how much it is, you can't afford it.*

Working for the Goddess as she did, Faith knew that even the smallest item was out of her price range; she could only imagine how expensive some of those exotic (but delicious) sounding smoothies were, let alone the healthy cuisine that smelled so heavenly. There was a reason the Celtic Goddess was as wildly successful as it was. As well as being out-of-this-world good, it was well-known for being completely organic. Whoever ran this place was smart to incorporate it into the overall package.

"Are you sure?" Paul asked, his smile slipping a bit. "It's on the house."

Matt looked hopefully at Faith, but she shook her head slightly. She had no intention of abusing Kieran's generosity any more than they already had. "Thank you, but we're sure."

Paul frowned, looking uncomfortable. Faith didn't understand why until Kieran appeared a few moments later. She caught her breath. He looked amazing in his *BodyWorks* outfit, the form-fitting black showcasing his magnificent physique and making his incredible blue eyes stand out even more than usual.

Kieran was all smiles as he greeted them, but less so when he turned to Paul. "You didn't get them something?"

Color rose upward from Paul's collar as he shook his head. "He offered, several times," Faith said quickly, not wanting to get Paul into trouble. "But we had something just before we came." Paul shot her a grateful glance.

"Wow, Kieran. This place is awesome," Matt said.

Kieran's easy grin returned. "Glad you like it."

"Are you like a manager or something?" Matt asked, his voice full of hero worship.

"Or something," Kieran chuckled. Faith didn't fail to notice the hint of a smirk on Paul's face. She thought back to the woman at the reception desk, at the way everyone referred to him as "Mr. Callaghan" and the obvious air of respect they had for him. Her knees nearly buckled at the obvious answer. He didn't just work here. He *owned* the place.

"Come on, I'll give you a tour before the demo starts."

When Faith hung back, assuming he was talking to Matt, Kieran reached out for her hand with a half-grin. It did nothing for her sudden lack of muscle control from the waist down. "You, too, Faith."

Kieran's much larger hand swallowed hers. The immediate jolt that raced through her system left her heart thudding in her chest. She glanced up at Kieran. His eyes widened as if he had felt it too, and then met hers. For a brief moment she saw his surprise. Faith tugged her hand back quickly, offering a quick apology.

"I'm so sorry," she said awkwardly, rubbing the palm of her still-tingling hand on her soft cotton capris. "I didn't realize I'd built up a static charge." It didn't help that instead of abating, the feeling only seem to intensify as he regarded her. The wonder remained in his eyes, but it was joined by a grin that slowly crept over his features and made him … utterly devastating. Faith caught her breath – again – and averted her eyes.

* * *

Kieran had heard his brothers describe the

phenomena several times over, but nothing could have prepared him for it. That moment when everything changed. An epiphany.

Kieran Callaghan, the last remaining eligible male of the clan, had just recognized his *croie*.

Unfortunately, Faith didn't seem to be as familiar with the phenomena. She thought the lingering tingle she must also be feeling was the result of a "shock" brought about by the build-up of static electricity. His grin widened further when Maggie's words came back to him in a rush: *You've just got to have Faith.*

Kieran chuckled inwardly. Maggie's eyes had twinkled devilishly then. He should have known.

* * *

Faith hadn't planned to stay for the demo. It wasn't that she didn't like martial arts, but as a woman with limited time and limited means it had been a good opportunity to kill two birds with one stone: Matt could spend a few hours enjoying something he loved, and she could return to the farmer's market for some hopefully low-cost decorating supplies and maybe some bargains on fresh fruits and veggies. Most vendors tended to slash their prices toward the end of the day to avoid having to cart things back to wherever they'd come from.

She'd gone from room to room that morning,

sketching the designs that had been developing in her head. Everything from color schemes and fabrics to incidentals. It was a gift, a special talent that had her mentally rearranging every room, every house, every place she visited. Except *BodyWorks*. This place, she had decided right off, was already perfectly done. Her designer's mind was serenely quiet here.

The rest of her was not. Watching Kieran Callaghan in action was mesmerizing. Hypnotic. He was big, yes. But he was also incredibly lithe, graceful, and, she realized with a start, incredibly lethal. It seemed strange that that particular word would pop into her mind for such an easy-going man so obviously generous with his time. But the truth of it resounded through her like a perfectly pitched bell.

Faith was not the only one in awe. When Kieran made his final bows to his fellow instructors and the spectators, Faith noticed that nearly everyone else had been as mesmerized as she had been. And when Kieran winked in her direction, she felt the heated gaze of a dozen envious females, not to mention the curious stares of quite a few men.

Apparently anyone who warranted the attention of Kieran Callaghan automatically warranted the attention of others as well.

Faith was uncomfortable with the sudden interest, and tugged Matt out of the large room rather hurriedly. It was good to have such a tall son, she thought gratefully as they waited beside the massive potted plant in the corridor. Only the tip of her head was visible over the ever-broadening shoulders of her teenager.

* * *

It took a while for Kieran to make his way out of the demo room. People were converging from all sides. The demo had had exactly the response he'd hoped for. Judging by the amount of people hanging around the sign-up tables and asking questions, he'd be adding more classes. Though that had been his intent, it was now relegated to the back of his mind. There was only one thing consuming his thoughts now.

Getting to his *croie*.

She was fast, he had to give her that. One moment she was there, and the next, she'd simply disappeared. The natural hunter in him sat up excitedly. The thought of a brief chase coming on the heels of what had been a flawless demonstration had adrenalin coursing through his veins. Especially when he knew he was guaranteed success. She might elude him temporarily, but he would always find her.

He spotted Matt easily enough. With that burnished brown hair and gray eyes he stood out. Apparently a lot of younger girls noticed him, too.

Kieran chuckled, seeing their interested double-looks and murmurs to their friends. Matt, however, seemed oblivious to it all. Kieran remembered those days with a slight pang of nostalgia.

There! Faith was behind Matt, trying to fade into the shadows. That puzzled him for a moment. Why? Perhaps she didn't like crowds. Then he realized it was probably a good thing she was off to the side. It kept her from getting caught in the throng moving to the next demo as part of the open house.

She *was* on the small side. He wondered vaguely if her petite stature would be a problem, then dismissed it just as quickly. If she really was his *croie*, as he suspected, then they would fit together flawlessly in all things.

"That was the most freaking awesome thing I've ever seen," Matt said, his eyes bright with excitement.

"Thanks," Kieran said modestly. "How about you, Faith? Did you like it?"

She peeked around Matt's shoulder. "I've never seen anything like it," she said truthfully. "You were … amazing." The color crept up in her face and she turned shyly away even as the beast in Kieran's chest purred with her praise. He had never been the sort to consciously try to impress a woman with any display of prowess, but standing before Faith, he had the nearly irresistible urge to preen.

Outwardly, he smiled, pleased, and kept the

preening to a minimum. "How about some lunch?"

"Oh, no, thanks," Faith stammered, that restless look back in her eyes again. "We really should be going."

Kieran frowned. "Why?"

"I wanted to get to the farmer's market while we're in town," she explained. "I was going to leave after I brought Matt in earlier, but I got caught up in your demo…" She shifted her weight from side to side. Quite a few people were trying to get his attention, and at least half of them were clearly unhappy that he was devoting so much of it to her. Too bad.

"Okay," he said slowly, not liking the idea of her leaving one bit. It was a natural reaction. Now that he knew who she was to him he would always want to be near her whenever possible. It was pure instinct, generated on a level far beneath layers of conscious and rational thought. "I have to stick around for a while, but I can take you over later."

"I couldn't ask you to do that," she said, and he was beginning to sense her rapidly rising sense of discomfort as the small crowd around them grew.

"You didn't," he said firmly but quietly. Faith *was* uncomfortable in crowds, he realized. And unfortunately, his interest in her was drawing more attention with every passing second. His first instinct was to grab Faith and whisk her away to someplace more private, but that would only exacerbate the situation. She was getting ready to bolt, and he had to do something. If she left with Matt now, he would have no excuse to see her again later.

And he *needed* to see her again today, if for no other reason than to confirm what he already knew.

"Tell you what. Why don't you let Matt hang here with me while you hit the Market?"

He turned to Matt. Enlisting an ally was good strategy. "You don't really want to troll the farmer's market, do you?" he asked, appealing to Matt's innate male aversion to shopping and hoping the kid took notice of the attractive teenage girls currently milling about.

Matt looked hopefully at his mother, who in turn looked back to Kieran, her eyes narrowing somewhat. Had she seen through his not-so-subtle ploy?

"You're very busy," she said, glancing nervously around them.

"My entire team's here," Kieran informed her with a casual shrug. Then he lowered his voice and winked. "Sometimes it's good to be the boss."

* * *

Matt continued to stare at her with hope in his eyes. She might have been hurt by her son's blatant preference to spend the afternoon with Kieran in a testosterone-laden environment instead of sorting through stacks of second-hand wares looking for the best possible deals, but she couldn't find it in herself to do so. Truth be told, she didn't blame him one bit. If there were no other considerations, she'd rather spend the afternoon watching Kieran than haggling with the local vendors, too. But she was a woman with responsibilities, not a mooning teenage girl crushing on the popular jock.

"Alright," she breathed, reaching for her wallet as she mentally calculated how much she could afford. "I'll leave you something for lunch - "

Kieran's hand closed around hers, and this time the effect was even more powerful than before. Rather than a sharp, unexpected shock, she felt a heady warmth radiating outward from the point of contact.

"No, Faith," he said softly but firmly. "Matt is my guest. I'd like to treat you as well, if you'll let me."

His breath smelled like peppermint, cool and fresh. It was in distinct contrast with the warmth of it, which she felt very clearly throughout her entire body when he leaned down to speak into her ear. The same thought she had before loomed in her mind once again: Kieran Callaghan was a dangerous, lethal man in boy-next-door clothing.

She somehow managed not to melt into a puddle at his feet. The very thought gave her the strength she needed to ensure that her backbone remained in place. No matter how much she might outwardly resemble those young, college-age groupies anxiously awaiting Kieran's attention, she was a twenty-eight year old mother barely making ends meet. She could not afford to indulge in any silly girl fantasies, and especially not with a man as unattainable as Kieran Callaghan. He was so far out of her league it would take a space shuttle to get to his realm.

That's when it hit her. Kieran Callaghan could never be interested in a woman like her. And that made her safe. Hadn't Lacie alluded to something like that? That Kieran was tired of being chased by women? She thought back to the pizza parlor the night before. Kieran had been so relaxed and easy-going. Until Natalie showed up. Then he'd grown tense.

Faith felt a stab of sympathy for him. He really was a nice guy. And here she was, offering him the perfect out.

She ignored the pang of disappointment. This wasn't a fairy tale, after all. Kieran might be many women's idea of a modern day Prince Charming, but she was as far away from a Princess as she could get. Even Cinderella in her early days looked like a finishing school deb next to her.

It was disappointing, yes, but also liberating. The realization that she could provide him with an excuse to avoid some of that – albeit through her son – was grounding, too.

Calmed, she offered him what she hoped was an understanding smile. "Thanks, but I'll take a raincheck."

* * *

Kieran considered her thoughtfully. He'd seen the wheels turning. Sensed when she'd made a decision. Unfortunately, he had no idea exactly what she'd been mentally debating or what the resolution was, but something told him he wouldn't like it. He knew there could only be one possible outcome where he and Faith were concerned, but that didn't mean that *she* did.

His brothers had a hard time of it when they had met their *croies*. Trials by fire, so to speak. Maybe he would, as well. The thought was not a pleasing one, but there was no other option. He would simply have to tread carefully and try to minimize the damage. If he was careful and gave it some serious thought, he might be able to learn from his brothers' mistakes and ensure he didn't make the same ones. Perhaps there were some useful benefits in being the last to find the woman meant for him and him alone.

He fought his natural urge to pull her to him and simply refuse. Taryn had put a name to it, calling it the 'inner caveman instinct'; apparently it was a trait shared among the men of his family. Instead he said, "I'll hold you to that. How about I bring Matt home later? That way you don't have to cross town again when you're done."

"I couldn't ask you to - "

"You aren't. I'm offering. Besides, I was going to stop by tonight anyway. I found some more stuff leftover from when we renovated the Pub that you might be able to use."

Faith bit her lip. Several people were getting rather impatient, clearly unhappy that Faith was consuming so much of Kieran's attention. Given the way she was practically dancing on the balls of her feet, she was anxious to be out of there as quickly as possible. It worked to his advantage; rather than continue to argue with him, she nodded in concession. "Okay. Thanks."

Kieran smiled, relieved that she had finally decided to stop fighting him on every little thing. "Cool." Placing his hand on Matt's shoulder, he said, "Don't worry, Faith. I'll take good care of him."

Faith nodded, a resigned look on her face that made Kieran want to kiss her senseless, and disappeared toward the exit.

It took a while to work their way toward the café. To his great surprise, Matt would accept nothing more than a smoothie.

"Come on," Kieran coaxed, seeing the hunger in the boy's eyes, even hearing the protesting rumble as Matt's stomach loudly voiced agreement. "Growing boys need to eat." But no matter what he said, Matt politely refused.

Sensing that he was making Matt

uncomfortable, he changed the subject. He would have to pick his battles, he realized, with both mother and son. "So, you liked the demo?"

The tactic worked. Matt's eyes brightened. "Yeah."

"Think you might want to sign up?"

The brightness faded just as quickly. "Nah. It was cool to watch, though."

"Not interested?" Kieran prodded, but he had a feeling lack of interest wasn't the problem. He'd seen looks like that before, knew when someone wanted something badly. Matt simply shrugged with feigned disinterest.

"If it's a question of money, don't worry about it," Kieran told him. "We'll work something out." He had no intention of taking any money. As far as he was concerned, Faith and Matt were already part of his family.

Matt bristled. "It's not." He eyed Kieran warily. "And don't go talking to my mom about it, either," he said, a warning edge to his voice. Kieran lifted an eyebrow. So. It was like that, was it?

"Okay," Kieran agreed, drawing the word out slowly, but met Matt's glare. The boy showing pride was one thing – Kieran could respect that – but there would be no question of who was in charge. Matt held Kieran's gaze longer than most men – it was a testament to the kid's character – but eventually he did lower his eyes. Quietly releasing an exhale of relief, Kieran relaxed.

It lasted for all of a minute. "Maybe you and I can work out a deal," Kieran offered.

"What kind of deal?"

"Well…" Kieran's mind was whizzing through ideas, discarding them almost as quickly as they came to him. "The kid my brother hired to do mowing and stuff around some of the properties up for sale isn't working out. You saw the state your place was in. You interested?"

"Maybe," Matt hedged.

"You proved you know what you're doing yesterday," Kieran continued. "You'd be doing us a favor and putting a couple of bucks in your pocket."

"How much?"

"Minimum," Kieran said casually, making it up as he went along. "But there are benefits."

"What benefits?"

"One free class a month."

"Here?"

"Yeah."

"Any class?"

"Yeah."

The kid was thinking about it, he could tell. Kieran kept quiet, let him work it out. "And if I don't want to take a class?"

Kieran shrugged. "Then don't. But you'd be missing a great opportunity."

Matt looked down into the now-empty glass, considering it. "I'll think about it, okay?"

"Good. But if you're interested, your mom's

got to give her permission."

Matt nodded in agreement. "I'll talk to her about it tonight."

Chapter 7

Several hours later, Kieran took Matt home. With a quick “Hey, mom” in greeting, Matt made a beeline for the kitchen. Kieran had trouble making it past the living room. Dressed in well-worn, torn jeans and an oversized raggedy shirt, Faith stood before him, hair escaping the confines of her ponytail, dollops of paint adorning her arms, her legs, and her face. He felt a twinge deep in his chest; it was such an adorable image. The unease he’d witnessed at *BodyWorks* was gone. Clearly she was much more comfortable in her own environment. He could work with that.

“Painting, then, are you?” he said, unable to completely hide the smile that tugged at his lips.

“That’s one of the things I like about you,” Faith said, shooting him a smile of her own and a teasing glance. “Your exceptionally keen grasp of the obvious.”

“Yeah, well, you know,” he said, puffing himself up with feigned bravado, “I was a SEAL. I’m trained to be observant.”

Faith laughed softly, sending rivulets of sunshine directly into his chest.

"What I don't understand," he continued, affecting a look of puzzlement, "is exactly which parts of yourself you were painting with."

She looked down and checked herself out, as if just realizing some of the medium had gotten on her. When she looked back to him, her eyes sparkled with mischief. "Don't tell me you've never heard of full-contact body painting before?"

He laughed, though he couldn't help the ache in his groin at the thought of finger painting *her*. "And here I've been doing it the boring way. Your way seems much more fun."

* * *

Faith couldn't stop the heat from rising in her cheeks. Even though she knew Kieran meant nothing by it, it was impossible not to let her overactive imagination run rampant every now and then, especially when he looked at her with those hypnotic blue eyes as if she was the only woman on earth.

She shook herself free, a bit miffed with herself for falling under his spell. She'd spent all afternoon convincing herself that she could be the unassuming friend who didn't have grand expectations. It eased her mind, as well. She didn't have to worry about her appearance quite so much, or saying the right thing at the right time. She'd never been very good at that kind of thing anyway.

His words finally sank in. "You were a SEAL, huh? That's pretty impressive." It certainly explained a lot – his lean, muscular build, economy of movement, and overall quiet intensity.

Kieran shrugged modestly. "Family tradition."

"So you're not anymore?" Except for his hair, which was longer than standard military length, he looked like he could still be one. Faith hadn't known too many servicemen, and none well enough to ask, but it didn't seem like the kind of thing you could do for a couple of years and simply walk away from. Obviously, given the fact that Kieran was the same age as she was, he hadn't made a lifetime career out of it.

"No."

The single word hung in the air; Faith didn't miss how he averted his eyes. Clearly it was not something he wanted to discuss. That was okay; there were plenty of things she didn't like talking about either. She mentally catalogued that for future reference, putting it in the 'topics to avoid' category.

Thankfully, Matt re-entered the room at that point, stuffing the remains of last night's pizza into his mouth. Faith looked at him, amused. "Hungry?"

"He wouldn't let me buy him lunch," Kieran said. Judging by the way his lips thinned when he said it, he wasn't happy about it. Well, too bad. She was inwardly proud of her son, who she knew could scarf down half his body weight in one sitting. It showed remarkable restraint and a sense of manners she couldn't help but feel good about. She might not be able to buy her son all the extras some kids had, but she'd do her damnedest to give him other, less tangible things like pride. Self-respect. Dignity.

"I know you mean well, Kieran," Faith said gently. "And please don't take this the wrong way, but we would prefer to pay our own way, if you know what I mean. You've done so much already."

* * *

Kieran nodded. "I get it." But he didn't have to like it. His natural inclination was to want to take care of them, and it would be an effort to curb that enough so that she would not be offended.

It was bad enough to see the slight flash of hurt in her eyes when she'd asked him about being in the service. He hadn't lied. Technically, neither he nor his brothers were part of the service any longer. Kieran wouldn't be able to offer any more details than that, however, until she became his wife. The thought sent a rush of longing, heat and need rippling through him.

His eye caught the sketch pad laying on the edge of the covered sofa. As an artist himself, his curiosity got the best of him. He picked it up and glanced through it, sucking in his breath at the black and white sketches that looked like they had come straight out of a book.

"Did you do these?" he asked.

Faith saw what he had in his hands and a blush stole up her cheeks. "Yeah. They're nothing. Just some ideas."

"They're really good," Kieran said truthfully. Faith had a natural talent for perspective. He flipped through page after page, seeing her visions for what this tiny, run down cottage would someday become. Is this what she saw when she looked at this place? No wonder she loved it so much.

"Thanks," she said quietly, but she looked down at her shoes as if suddenly embarrassed. She had no reason to be. Her sketches were amazing. "Are you an interior designer? Is that why Aidan hired you? To work on the new suites?"

* * *

The color in her cheeks darkened. Kieran must have known she worked for the Goddess, but not what she did. Housekeeping services was a far cry from interior designer.

Thankfully, she was spared from answering that question when Matt stood and looked over Kieran's arm. "Looks good, mom," he said in between mouthfuls as he polished off yet another slice of leftover pizza.

"Where did you study?" Kieran asked.

“Study?” Faith blinked.

“Yeah. For art and design.”

Whoa. “You think they’re that good?”

“Hell, yes,” he said emphatically. “If this is what you see when you look around this place, you have a gift. Show these to Shane and he’ll probably start asking you to check out properties with him for potential. And my cousin Johnny – he does some historical renovations – would hire you on the spot.”

Faith blinked again, but smiled as Kieran’s compliment rattled around inside and filled her with the strange urge to giggle in joy. She never willingly shared her sketches with anyone besides Matt, not since her parents had eschewed her for wasting her time on something as impractical as art when she was younger. Kieran was the first to openly compliment her talent, and the effects of it nearly had her bouncing on her toes. There was a good possibility he was just saying those things to be polite, but they were awfully nice to hear, just the same.

“Would you like something to drink?” she offered instead.

* * *

Kieran regarded her with fascination. The transformation that had occurred was nothing less than stunning. Her eyes sparkled, her face glowed, and she seemed … buoyant. He tried to think of what he might have said to elicit such a powerful response, because he wanted to make a point of doing so repeatedly.

If he didn't know any better, he might think she wasn't used to hearing such praise. But with talent like this, she had to be. Didn't she?

"Yeah, anything cold would be great," he said.

He stalled as long as he could, taking his time as he unloaded his truck and showed Faith what he'd managed to find. Judging by her reaction, he might have thought he'd created an unlimited spending account at the home center for her, rather than delivered an unimpressive truckload of odds and ends. He would have gotten a hell of a lot more if he thought for one minute she would have accepted it.

"This is a lot of stuff," she said, shifting uncomfortably as Kieran carried things into the shed. "Are you sure you don't need it?"

"It's all leftovers," he assured her. "The Pub reno is complete, although after seeing your sketches, maybe you should come by and take a look."

He didn't want to leave. He wanted to follow her into the house and spend a few hours removing the paint from specific parts of her anatomy before crawling into bed with her and claiming that which he now knew was exclusively his. He knew from his brothers' experiences that now that he had discovered his *croie*, it would be impossible to find satisfaction with any other woman, not that he'd want to. He was officially off the market. And so was she.

"Thanks for dinner," he said, grasping desperately for a few extra moments any way he could get them. A cold drink had turned into a meal. The vegetable stew she'd had simmering in the crock pot and the crusty loaf of homemade bread had been mouthwateringly good.

"You're welcome."

"You'll let me know? About Matt?" He and Matt had presented a thorough and well-executed offensive at dinner. The kid was a natural. Plus he knew how to capitalize on Faith's weaknesses – her unease of leaving Matt alone for the entire day while she worked, the allure of having him under watchful eyes and knowing that he was doing something constructive with his time.

Oh yeah. She didn't stand a chance against the two of them when they joined forces. It was a heady feeling.

She exhaled and furrowed her brows, crossing her arms over her chest as she leaned against the doorframe. Kieran found himself envious of the door frame.

* * *

"It's a very tempting offer, Kieran," she said

slowly. "But I worry that we are taking advantage of your kindness."

"Oh, well, yeah," he grinned mischievously. "There's that, of course."

Faith looked up but saw the teasing in his eyes and bit back a smile. It was impossible not to like Kieran. He had this force about him that just drew her in, made her want to lose herself in it and absorb it all in. No wonder so many hopeful females had set their sights on him. Whoever captured Kieran's heart would be a lucky woman, indeed. The thought shouldn't have been as depressing as it was.

"But it benefits us, too," he added. "Matt's a responsible, hard-working kid with a good head on his shoulders. They're not that easy to find these days."

"I can understand why you want him to do yard work and stuff," she said, subconsciously biting her lip. "But what about the classes?"

Kieran shrugged. "The kid's a natural, lots of potential. With a little direction and self-discipline, he can be amazing." Faith's eyes glowed with pride. "Plus he's going to make me look good. Other kids see him, what he can do, and I'll have them lining up to join. Gets them away from their computers and keeps them off the streets, plus it's good for business."

Faith saw the masses of people at the open house and didn't think he was having any kind of trouble getting business, but she understood what he was saying. Still, she hesitated.

"How about we give it a trial period?" he prompted. "One month. If anyone's not completely satisfied with the situation – for any reason – we chalk it up as a learning experience and move on."

One month. That would put them halfway through the summer. Four weeks where she wouldn't constantly be worrying about where Matt was or what he was doing while she was at work.

Not that Matt was a bad kid, but he was a teenage boy. It wasn't in his nature to sit around idly all day and twiddle his thumbs. He would definitely benefit from an outlet for all his youthful energy. And if he earned a little pocket money in the process? It might be a good motivator, a real-world way to enforce the lessons of responsibility she was forever bombarding him with in voice and deeds.

"Okay," she agreed, making her decision. "One month."

From inside the house, she heard Matt's excited whoop and laughed.

* * *

Kieran wasn't quite sure what came over him in that moment. Maybe it was the sound of her heartfelt, genuine laugh. Maybe it was the way her eyes sparkled when they lit up. Whatever the reason, Kieran impulsively stepped forward and brushed a kiss across Faith's cheek.

It only lasted a moment; a split-second at most. A friendly, purely chaste kiss as kisses went. But it was enough to nearly bring him to his knees. That excruciatingly brief contact was more than enough for each of his highly acute senses to process it. From the unbelievable softness of her skin to the light, clean, natural fragrance that simmered beneath the lingering aromas of paint and wood soap. Nor was it possible for him to ignore the soft feminine murmur of surprise.

"Thanks, Faith," he said softly, forcing himself to walk away before he did something else. But nothing could stop him from glancing back and seeing her silhouetted against the inside lights, her hand poised at her cheek where his lips had touched her.

Chapter 8

The few doubts Faith had about the situation faded a little more with each passing day. It didn't take long for them to settle into a comfortable routine. She left for work early in the morning. Kieran, or sometimes Shane, would drive out to the cottage to pick up Matt and take him to whatever properties required attention that day. Matt learned a lot about the area that way. Both brothers seemed pleased with the quality of Matt's work as well, increasing his responsibilities as he proved himself.

After the day's jobs were complete, Matt would go to *BodyWorks*, where he and Kieran would grab some lunch and Matt could shower and change. Kieran would spend some time teaching Matt the basics and then would leave him to practice or spar with some of the other instructors while he attended to business.

Faith would pick him up from there on her way home. Each night, over dinner or while working on the house, Matt would recount the highlights of his day to her: where he'd gone, what he'd done. She'd never seen her son happier; he was adjusting well, and the smile on his face at the end of each day went a long way in reassuring her that she'd made the right decision.

She was pretty happy, too. She liked her job. Most of the staff at the Pine Ridge branch of the Goddess had been friendly and welcoming. She'd had far worse jobs in her time; catering to the upscale and wealthy guests who stayed there certainly had its perks, especially since she did her job so well. Tips alone surpassed the salary of some of the jobs she'd had.

At night, she and Matt would work side by side, transforming their cottage into a real home. Even with the leftovers Kieran had supplied it was a challenge, given their meager budget, but they were both determined and creative. Faith had learned the invaluable skill of sewing early on, and was able to create curtains and decorative slip covers using bargain-table materials for minimal cost. Since they were doing nearly all the work themselves, progress was slow, but there was something to be said for the pride that came from their efforts.

Twice, Lacie had driven up to chat and putter. Faith appreciated her visits. Lacie was the first and only female friend she'd managed to make since relocating, and she enjoyed their hour or two of "girl time". So much so, in fact, that they agreed to make it a regular, weekly event.

* * *

Kieran didn't get to see Faith nearly often enough during the first couple of weeks, having to rely on only those few minutes each day when she came to pick up Matt. It was hard; he had to keep himself busy so he would not drive up there each night like he wanted to and take their relationship past the friend stage to the next level.

Faith wasn't ready. She became skittish whenever he got too close. It wasn't ideal, but he was a patient man. He understood that Faith needed some time to get herself situated, to find her place in Pine Ridge, and to accept him as something more. He and Shane had several discussions on the topic, and Shane agreed that slow and steady was the way to go.

In the interim, Kieran made good use of his time. Matt, while not overly talkative, was a wealth of information on all things Faith.

For instance, Kieran discovered that Faith's birthday was approaching, and that Matt was saving up his earnings, thrilled that this year he would be able to get his mother something nice. He also learned, with very little effort, that Faith loved flowers, cried easily at especially sad or romantic movies (a trait that horrified her son), and preferred thoughtful gifts to expensive ones.

What Kieran had not been able to unearth had been anything substantial about life prior to Pine Ridge, or, more importantly, Matt's father. Matt tended to clam up if asked either directly or indirectly about either.

Some things Matt didn't seem to mind talking about, though. He told Kieran they had never had a "real" house before, having lived mostly in trailer parks. He also occasionally made mention of an older man that had taken him fishing once in a while and had taught him how to shoot, but Kieran didn't get the impression the man had been a relative.

Kieran couldn't help but wonder who and what they had left behind. Instinctively, he knew the basis for Faith's reticence lie there, and until he knew what that was, he had to tread carefully. So far, he had managed to restrain himself from asking his older brother Ian to run a bio on her. Ian had a knack for anything digital. With a few keystrokes and a bit of time, Ian could create a comprehensive dossier on anyone, living or dead.

He wasn't sure why he hadn't asked Ian for the information. Maybe on some level he was afraid of what they might find. Or maybe, he wanted the information to come from Faith. He hoped that eventually, she would trust him enough to confide in him.

* * *

"So can we go?" Matt asked, shifting his weight impatiently from one foot to the other.

"You got ants in your pants or something?"

Faith teased, the ancient phrase bubbling up from her childhood. It was something her father would say when he'd look down from the pulpit and see her squirming on the hardwood pew.

Matt scowled as only a teenager could. "Come on, Mom. You said we could go if we got everything done and we did."

Surely not, Faith thought as she wrapped the paint brush in aluminum foil and placed it in the fridge. It was a handy trick, one that kept the brush soft in between coats without requiring her to clean it each time. But a quick glance around told her that Matt wasn't kidding. He'd mowed the lawn, trimmed the hedges, and built several of the flower bed boxes she'd requested out of old scrap lumber they'd found in the shed.

She'd spent the entire morning painting the outside trim and shutters that Kieran and Shane had repaired, greatly improving the exterior appearance of the place.

"I still need to clean the bathroom and do the dishes," she told him, wiping the back of her hand over her sweat-covered brow.

"Done," Matt informed her.

She raised her eyebrows and glanced at the counter, now conspicuously empty of the morning's breakfast dishes. Then she walked into the first floor bathroom. It wasn't that her son was in the habit of lying to her, but some things needed to be seen to be believed. The clean scent of lemons and bleach tickled her nostrils, and the old fixtures literally gleamed.

"Wow. You must really want to go to this, huh?"

"Yes, Mom," Matt said, infusing the words with as much "duh" as he could safely get away with. "Kieran says it's awesome."

And if Kieran said it, Faith thought with a smirk, *it must be true.* According to Matt, the sun rose and fell based on Kieran Callaghan and his brothers. It wasn't a bad thing, not really. She had hoped that Matt would find some positive male role models, and he had. All week he had been polite, accommodating, and suspiciously obeisant.

"They've got rides and games and food," Matt said, launching into excruciating detail of each. "Come on, Mom. I'll even pay." Matt proudly reached into his pocket and extracted his week's earnings.

She sighed, sensing defeat. And the Tusquannock County Fair *did* sound like fun. "Okay."

"Yeah?"

"Yeah. But I need a shower first."

Matt looked like he wanted to argue, but wisely kept his mouth shut and nodded before walking back outside, cell phone in hand, obviously texting Kieran to tell him the good news.

Faith shook her head as she stepped into the shower. Truth be told, she was feeling a sense of anticipation as well. She hadn't seen much of Kieran all week, except for the few minutes at the end of the day when she picked up Matt. He always greeted her with a friendly word and that devastatingly handsome grin, leaving her feeling a touch giddy inside as she drove home.

It was silly, she knew. Kieran had no interest in her like that, nor did she have any in him (or so she kept reminding herself). He was simply one of the first friends she had made in Pine Ridge, a kind, generous, and thoughtful man. Thanks to her job and the amount of work they were putting into their home, she hadn't had much opportunity to make others. It was only natural that she was looking forward to seeing him again.

Plus Lacie would be there with Shane, too, according to Matt. Matt said the Fair was the site of the annual Callaghan family reunion. That was three friendly faces, more than enough to rationalize an appearance.

She washed her hair, treating herself to a conditioning rinse. After a slight hesitation, she also opted for the moisturizing, scented body wash instead of her traditional (and much less expensive) bar soap. Donning jean shorts and a forest green tank, she pulled her hair into a ponytail and regarded herself in the mirror. She wouldn't win any beauty contests, she mused, but then reminded herself that she was not trying to impress anyone.

Matt was waiting for her downstairs, shifting

his weight eagerly from one foot to the other and back again. “Ready?”

“Yes,” she answered, laughing at his youthful exuberance. “Let’s do this.”

“Will you stop texting already?” Faith said, standing in line with Matt before the Toxic Hammer. The ride consisted of two bullet-shaped, caged vehicles that spun in a vertical circle while revolving laterally. With their similarly-colored hair and eyes, and the fact that Matt towered over her, they looked more like brother and sister than mother and son. Both were receiving more than their fair share of appreciative glances from the late teen – early twenties crowd.

Matt grinned and pocketed his cell as their turn came and they climbed into the cage.

The ride was brief but violent, and Faith was exceptionally glad that they had refrained from indulging in any of the succulent treats they’d passed beforehand. She stumbled slightly as she stepped out of the cage, leaning on Matt for support. It was another hand – a much larger one – that reached out to steady her.

Still trying to get her bearings, she found herself staring at a muscular chest shrink-wrapped in a plain men’s black t-shirt. Tilting her head up, she found Kieran’s smiling face about the same time she heard him. “Steady,” he said, grinning.

"Stop laughing at me," she grumbled good-naturedly, directing the comment more toward Matt, who seemed to find her lack of balance hilarious. He looked at Kieran and stopped laughing long enough to snicker, "I told her she shouldn't ride that. She didn't quite meet the height requirement."

The corner of Kieran's mouth quirked.

"I can still put you over my knee," Faith threatened, though the amusement glinting in her eyes took much of the heat out of the threat.

"Matt," Kieran said, his voice suddenly deep and commanding. "Do not disrespect your mother."

Matt's smile faded immediately, and Faith looked up at Kieran in surprise. "At least not until you're sure you're faster than she is," he added with a wink.

Matt and Faith insisted on riding nearly every ride, dragging Kieran along with them. Matt was less than subtle in his attempts to pair Kieran and Faith together on the two-person cars.

Afterwards, when they'd had their fill of thrill rides, Kieran was more than happy to guide them through some of the tasty delicacies NEPA (Northeastern Pennsylvania) had to offer. On Kieran's suggestions, they had sampled handmade pierogies, potato pancakes, kielbasa, sausage and pepper sandwiches, splurging on waffles & ice cream and funnel cakes until they couldn't eat another bite.

"Why don't you come back to the pavilion with

me?" Kieran coaxed again when they had run out of rides and food stands. It wasn't the first time he'd asked. Each time, Faith managed to find another excuse.

The heavy mixture of deep-fried and spicy foods rolled uncomfortably in Faith's stomach. After hearing a couple of Lacie's and Matt's stories of some of the yet-unmet Callaghan clan, she was quite sure that Kieran, Shane, and Lacie were about all the family she could handle at any given time.

"It's a family reunion, Kieran," she reasoned. "We wouldn't want to intrude."

"Don't be ridiculous. The more the merrier. Plus everyone's dying to meet you."

His words only served to reinforce her belief that this was not a good idea. If they were as close-knit as Lacie made them out to be, she was sure they would have heard about her and Matt. No doubt they wanted the chance to see for themselves the woman and boy occupying so much of Kieran's free time. She didn't blame them, really. They were just looking out for their own. She'd probably be doing the same thing – if she still had a family.

Yet she had no desire to be a part of it. Even without meeting them, they intimidated her. The Callaghans, she'd learned soon enough, were a powerful family in the valley and surrounding areas. The thought of being subjected to their close scrutiny made her uncomfortable. She was getting used to Kieran and Lacie, but if she was truthful, even the soft-spoken Shane scared her a little. Sometimes, when he looked at her, she had the feeling he was seeing a lot more than she wanted him to.

And, really, there was no reason why she *should* feel obligated to meet them. Most of them already knew Matt, and it wasn't like she was important or anything. She and Kieran were just friends, after all. There was nothing romantic between them (she immediately quashed the pesky pang of despair at that thought), and so they needn't worry unnecessarily.

It would just be awkward and uncomfortable all around. She and Matt were still outsiders, after all, and she hated drawing the kind of curious attention a huge family gathering would bring. Pine Ridge wasn't that big; eventually, she'd run into them, but hopefully it would be in small and infrequent doses rather than all at once.

"Please, Faith," Kieran said, entwining his fingers with hers as he tugged her toward the pavilion. As she looked into his big blue eyes and felt the pleasant hum reverberate through her body at the simple contact, all of her perfectly reasonable and logical rationalizations flew right out the window. Faith could not come up with a single reasonable excuse not to accompany him to the pavilion, not without hurting Kieran's feelings.

"All right. But just for a little while." Kieran's face split into a grin so wide she had to smile. As he tugged her excitedly toward the massive pavilion at the heart of the annual Callaghan/Connelly family reunion, her much shorter legs struggling to keep up with his and Matt's longer-legged pace, she shored herself up with the protective shields she'd developed over the years, hoping she wouldn't need them, dreading that she would.

* * *

"Who's that with Kieran?" Lexi asked, spotting him as they neared the pavilion.

A few sets of eyes followed her gaze. "Oh, that's Faith," said Lacie, the smile evident in her voice. "She's really nice. You'll like her."

"What is she, nineteen?" Taryn asked, narrowing her eyes to get a better look as her protective instincts flared. Kieran was such a sweetheart, she and her sisters-in-law often took it upon themselves to ensure he wasn't taken advantage of. "A bit young for him, isn't she?"

Lacie laughed. "No. She's the same age as he is, but she does look young, I admit."

"And who's that with her?" Nicki asked, her agent's eye immediately picking up the similar, unusual hair color. "Her brother?"

"No," Lacie said, her voice quieter. "That's her son, Matt."

Several pairs of shocked eyes turned toward Lacie. "You're joking, right?" Taryn said.

Lacie shook her head, but was unable to say anymore before they were within hearing range.

* * *

The familiar sense of unease around large crowds hit with the force of a tsunami when Faith realized just how many Callaghans and Connellys there were. Even Matt, having already met several of them, seemed a little overwhelmed. The two of them stayed close together as Kieran introduced them, rattling off names faster than she could process them.

Faith tried to keep track, she really did. Six brothers, all older than Kieran but bearing the same blue-black hair and trademark Callaghan eyes. Six wives (she considered Lacie was close enough to being married to include her), one for each of the brothers. The patriarch of the family, Jack Callaghan. Three cousins – the Connelly branch – with their spouses, plus the shared grandfather to both sides, Conlan O'Leary. Children were everywhere, ranging in age from around seven years to only a few weeks old.

Out of this initial introduction to the Callaghans and their kinsmen, several things became blatantly clear. One, they were every bit as close as Lacie made them out to be. Two, they were loud and boisterous. And three, they were a prolific bunch.

Everyone seemed nice enough, offering smiles

and welcomes. No one grilled her beyond asking how she was settling in and what she thought of the area so far, but Faith sensed their curiosity. Kieran remained in close proximity, his hand lightly behind her shoulder or lower back, and she drew a lot of strength from that. Lacie seemed to pick up on her discomfort and stayed relatively near as well.

"Hang around for a bit?" Kieran asked Faith hopefully when the men started gathering for their annual football game.

"We really should be going," Faith said, aware of the curious glances being cast her way, no doubt wondering exactly what her relationship was with Kieran. He had been very considerate in his introductions, though even she had been a bit surprised by the constant contact, thankful though she was for it. It was making them wonder, too, and she was sure that it had to do with the fact that of this huge clan, Kieran was the youngest, and only single, male. Any woman in which he showed even the slightest interest was fair game for analysis and inspection.

"Please?" he asked, his face so hopeful that she found herself nodding. She chastised herself vehemently – and silently – as she watched him walk away with that devastating half-smile plastered on his face. If she had any hope of retaining her sanity, she was going to have to work on developing an immunity to such things.

A few minutes later, she found herself

wandering over to watch as ten men took to the field, seven Callaghans and three Connellys, five on each team. Around the perimeter of the field, Faith noticed that others were gathering to watch as well. It was no surprise, really. When you had that many gorgeous, muscular men concentrated in one small area, it was bound to draw some attention. She had to admit, she was enjoying the show herself.

She kept a close eye on Kieran, inwardly cheering whenever he managed to break free of a tackle or take someone down. He was one of the biggest of the bunch. There were two or three that were about his size – a golden-haired blonde and his brother from the Connelly side, and the one she thought might have been called Jake – but only one that was bigger. Kane. She had no trouble remembering his name; that man was intensity personified. When introduced to him earlier, she'd had the odd sensation of standing next to a thunderstorm.

Regardless, they all moved with a fluid, masculine grace that was mesmerizing to watch.

At one point Kieran looked over at her and waved. The next moment he was hit so hard the gathered crowd moaned for him en masse. Faith flinched and winced as he went down. Within seconds, though, Kieran was back on his feet and shouting back at Kane.

"Be ready, old man!" he taunted, earning himself several chuckles and head shakes from the others. Kane smiled and beckoned him with two fingers. "Give it your best shot, pup."

"Boys," laughed the woman called Rebecca. Faith had a hard time imagining how such a small, soft-spoken, gentle woman could end up with a force of nature like Kane. Several other women joined her in knowing nods.

One of the men not participating in the game – Lacie had introduced him as her brother Brian – was talking with Matt. At least her son seemed at ease, she thought with some comfort. It wasn't that they weren't nice – she couldn't imagine a nicer group of people. Faith just couldn't shake the feeling that she didn't really belong here. The sense that she was being discreetly inspected didn't help, either.

The men returned from their game, sweaty and dirty but grinning like idiots as they allowed their wives to tend to their various scrapes and bruises.

"This is their favorite part," confided Maggie to Faith with a smirk. "Tough guys, all of them, but they love for us to pamper them." She winked. "Almost as much as we love doing it."

Faith watched as the men made their way to their wives. All except Kieran. He walked over to one of the many water coolers, grabbed a wet rag and attempted to clean himself off. Faith wasn't sure if she should offer to help him or not, but the sight of him trying to reach a spot in the middle of his back made up her mind.

"Come here," she commanded, taking pity on him. Faith swung her leg up and over, balancing on the railing of the pavilion so she could reach between his shoulder blades. Kieran grinned and handed her the wet cloth.

"Thanks," he said, gratefully.

Faith suddenly became aware of the interested looks of his family. She blushed dark red and handed the cloth hurriedly back to Kieran before leaping from the railing. "You're welcome."

She shoved her hands in the back pockets of her jean shorts, cursing the fact that they still tingled from where she had run her hands across his back. Talk about awkward.

Matt chose that moment to approach her. "Mom! Ian says I can help with the fireworks, but only if you say yes. Can I?"

Fireworks? "Oh, Matt, I don't know about that," she hedged, biting her lip. She didn't want to embarrass her son in front of everyone. "What do you know about fireworks?"

"We won't let him do anything too dangerous," Ian said, joining them. He had a mischievous glint to his eyes and Faith instinctively knew he was the smooth-talking trouble-maker. Every family had one.

Faith raised a doubtful eyebrow, giving him her full-fledged mother glare that let Ian know that she knew he was full of shit. His response was to grin even wider. Maybe it didn't work as well on grown men who towered a foot or so over her and had families of their own. Go figure.

"I won't let anything happen to him, Faith," Kieran promised quietly. "You have my word."

Against her better judgment (she seemed sorely lacking in the willpower department today), Faith nodded.

"Don't worry, Faith," Ian said, sharing a fist bump with Matt. "We'll bring him back with all of his parts."

"And if we don't," the one called Sean added over his shoulder, "Mick can reattach them."

Faith paled, despite the fact that she knew they were teasing. "He really will be alright, you know," assured Lacie. Nicki laughed, and Faith was almost hypnotized by her super light silvery eyes. "You know men. Explosive incendiaries are like a rite of passage. A male bonding ritual, if you will."

Unable to watch, Faith excused herself to visit one of the fairground's restrooms. The port-o-potties would have been closer, but she welcomed the chance to walk for a bit and stretch her legs. It felt good to be swallowed up by the crowd, just another anonymous face. The intense scrutiny at the pavilion was starting to wear her down.

It was clear to see that they were very protective of Kieran, and she couldn't blame them. Lacie had already warned her how desirable Kieran was, and Faith had seen enough with her own eyes to substantiate that claim. What none of them seemed to understand, however, was that she was not trying to "catch" Kieran. She was simply his friend, and wanted nothing more from him.

Liar, her conscience scolded as she slowly made her way back to the pavilion, keeping to the shadows as a force of habit. She did want more. Just as she wanted a lot of things she knew she could never have. It didn't make a difference, though. She'd made her bed a long time ago, and now she had to lie in it, as her father had so often said.

A pang of disappointment went through her, but she stifled it immediately. She had no cause for self-pity. She was blessed with a wonderful son, a steady job with good benefits, and a roof over their heads. They were healthy and happy, adjusting to their new life and making new friends. She should be grateful for all of the gifts she had been given, instead of longing for those she hadn't.

Chapter 9

"Kieran said she works for the Goddess," Taryn said to Lexi, looking out toward the walkway where Faith had disappeared into the crowd. "Do you know her?"

"No," Lexi said, sipping her tea as her baby daughter Kate snuggled in her lap. "But then I wouldn't unless she was part of the kitchen staff. Aidan?"

Lexi's longtime friend and business partner, Aidan Harrison was the owner and CEO of the Celtic Goddess chain. "I hadn't met her personally before tonight, no," he answered carefully.

Lexi looked at him, her surprise evident. Aidan made it his personal business to meet with everyone who worked for him. "Why not?"

He shrugged. "Marco's been handling it. She's a transfer from our Georgia location."

"Marco?" Lexi mused, trying to put a face with the familiar name. "Head of Environmental?"

Aidan nodded. Lexi frowned. Something didn't sound right. "Kieran thought she was hired as an interior design consultant or something like that."

"No."

"Then what does she do, exactly?" Nicki asked.

"Environmental handles upkeep and maintenance."

"You mean she's a maid?" Taryn blurted out. Aidan, looking slightly uneasy, nodded.

"So what?" Lexi asked. "What difference does it make what she does? Lacie said she's really nice and Kieran likes her and her son."

"I'm still having trouble processing that," Taryn said, outspoken as usual. "How could she have a son that old? I mean, she looks so young. What was she, like, ten when she had him?"

"Fifteen, actually." Faith's quiet voice spoke up from behind them, startling them all. "Though I was fourteen when I got pregnant, so you're not too far off."

Expressions on the faces of those in the pavilion ranged from embarrassed to mortified. Taryn was the first to speak. "Faith, I'm so sorry. I didn't mean to - "

"Don't worry about it," Faith said with a tight smile. She'd had more than enough practice at this over the years, and had heard far worse words spoken in conjecture over her and her son, sometimes right to her face.

It had taken longer for someone to say something than she'd thought, and they had been quite polite about it, all things considered. It still hurt. It always did. Maybe some small part of her had hoped that things might be different here, but human nature was the same everywhere, it turned out. At least there was some comfort to be had in consistency.

Regardless, Faith had no desire to remain any longer. The lighthearted, fun atmosphere had taken a decided downturn, and her presence was making things awkward for everyone. "When Matt comes back, will you tell him to meet me at the car?"

"You can't leave now! You'll miss the fireworks!" Lacie said, jumping to her feet.

But Faith was already walking away. Lacie jogged to catch up to her. "Faith, please don't go. Watch the fireworks with us. Kieran will wonder what's happened to you."

Kieran was a smart man. He'd figure it out. And it was for the best. For the past few hours, Faith had felt out of place, and now she was just ready to go home and put it behind her. "Thanks, Lacie, but no. Please tell everyone I said goodnight, okay?"

Faith disappeared back into the darkness, the pavilion silent behind her.

* * *

"Where's Faith?" Kieran said, jogging up to the pavilion and looking around after the phenomenal display had gone off without a hitch. Matt, smiling broadly, and proudly still sporting every one of his fingers, came up beside him.

"Matt, Faith said you should meet her at the car," Lacie said quietly. Matt's smile faded and a dark look came over his features. He nodded, said a quick thanks to Kieran and the others before taking off toward the parking lot.

"What's going on?" Kieran asked.

"She's gone," Lacie said, gratefully stepping into the protection of Shane's arms. It was impossible not to note the tension in the pavilion.

"I can see that," he said impatiently. "Why?"

Lexi bit her lip, shifting the now-sleeping Kate over to her daddy. "I'm sorry, Kier. We messed up."

"Messed up? How?"

With help from an apologetic Taryn, they explained what happened. Kieran remained quiet, but his features grew uncharacteristically hard. By the time they finished, Kieran looked at each of them. "Funny," he said, his voice even softer than usual. "I never figured any of you for snobs."

"You know better than that, Kier," Jake said warningly in his deep voice, but Kieran ignored him. He stalked off toward the parking lot, pulling out his mobile before they could say anything else. He didn't want to hear it. The only person he wanted to talk to was Faith.

He dialed Faith's number, not surprised when it went right to voice mail. Good thing he had an ally.

"*Where r u?*" he texted Matt.

"*On r way home*," came the immediate reply.

"*Ur mom ok?*"

This time there was a slight pause in the response. "*idk*". *I don't know.*

Shit.

"Faith, it's Kieran. Please open up." Kieran waited patiently at the front door. He hadn't planned on driving up to her cottage tonight. His logical side told him to give Faith time to cool down first. His illogical side – the side that reminded him that she was his *croie*, said "Fuck that."

The door opened part way. Even in the muted light of the porch he could see that she'd been crying.

"May I come in?" he asked softly.

"Matt's already gone up to bed."

"That's okay. It's you I wanted to talk to anyway."

After a brief pause, she stepped back and opened the door wider so he could enter.

"You okay?" he asked.

Her chin lifted. "Of course. Why wouldn't I be?"

So it was going to be like that, was it? "Faith," he breathed. "Talk to me."

Faith took one look at him and exhaled. She wasn't happy about it, but she was smart enough to sense that he wasn't above planting himself on her porch until she agreed to talk to him.

“Would you like some coffee?” she asked resignedly. Her arms were crossed protectively in front of her, something she did when she felt a little uncertain, he’d noticed. He didn’t like seeing her this way, especially not when he was around. He wanted her to feel safe and secure in his presence. The fact that she didn’t bugged him, and made him want to fix it.

At least she wasn’t shutting him out completely. He decided to count that as a small victory.

“I’d love some, thanks.”

He followed her into the kitchen, glancing around as he did so. Over the past week she’d finished painting the living room walls and trim. He had to look twice at the ratty old sofa; it was now covered in a deep green and hazelnut print with cream and chocolate colored throw pillows. A few sketches hung on the wall, charcoals that looked like originals; drafts of the cottage and the grounds as seen through Faith’s eyes. The hardwood floor had been cleaned and polished until it shone, reflecting the soft hues of the small light she’d left on just inside the door. He could only imagine the number of hours she’d put into it; the transformation was stunning.

“The living room looks amazing,” Kieran said sincerely. “When did you have time to do all this?”

Faith shrugged, but she seemed appreciative of the compliment.

The kitchen wasn't overly large, so Kieran had no trouble staying in close physical proximity to Faith as she prepared a pot of decaf. It helped. He felt better just by being near her. He hoped that he was able to do the same for her on some level, even if she didn't consciously recognize it.

He watched her closely, studying every nuance of her features as she absently puttered about, gathering her strength. With every passing moment, she became more entrenched in his heart.

"You didn't need to come all the way out here, you know," she said, handing him his coffee a few minutes later.

They'd have to agree to disagree on that, because he certainly felt the need to see her, to be with her. There was no way he could have gone back to the Pub knowing what happened and how she'd left. Deep in his chest, his heart ached.

Forcing his hands around the cup so he didn't pull her into his arms, he shrugged. "You weren't answering your phone. And I wanted to see you."

Faith sat down across from him, a serious expression on her face. "Why?"

"Do I need a reason?"

She pinned him with her soft gray eyes. "Yes."

It wasn't that he didn't have an answer; he just didn't think she was prepared to hear it, and he could sense the walls she'd put up to protect herself. So he went with a partial-truth variation. "You left without saying goodbye."

Faith blinked back the moisture pooling in her eyes. Kieran had to fight the sudden urge to wrap his arms around her and comfort her.

She offered him an apologetic smile. "I'm sorry, Kieran. I didn't realize it would bother you so much."

Slightly mollified, Kieran took a drink from his mug. "They told me what happened."

It was Faith's turn to shrug. "It's okay. Most people wonder, I think. I overreacted."

"No, you didn't. If I had been there - "

"They didn't realize I was there, Kieran. I shouldn't have been eavesdropping." She smiled slightly. "What's that old saying? 'Those who eavesdrop hear nothing good of themselves', or something like that?" She exhaled. "It really is okay, Kieran. It is what it is. You can't be twenty-eight with a fourteen year old son and not have people wonder."

She paused, sipping her coffee. "Well?"

"Well what?" he asked.

"Aren't you going to ask?"

"Ask what?"

"Where's Matt's father? Do I even know who he is? Was I raped? Those are the most common questions."

Kieran's jaw clenched. "There's only one question I need to know the answer to. Is there another man in your life? Someone you care about? Are married to? In love with?"

Faith's eyes widened. "Besides Matt? No, there is no man in my life."

"Then none of that other shit matters," he said firmly. "Everything that's happened has brought you here, to Pine Ridge, and that's all I care about."

* * *

Faith felt a hollow ache deep in her chest. She wanted to believe him. Wanted to believe him so badly it actually hurt. But she'd been down that road once before. She'd fallen in love with a handsome, popular man once, making the mistake of thinking that he'd felt the same way. Some lessons you only had to learn once for them to stick.

"Someday," he said, his voice softening as he laid his hand over hers, "I hope you will have enough faith in me to share parts of your life you won't share with anyone else. And when that day comes, I will do the same. Until then, can we agree to just take each other at face value?"

His hand was so large and warm over hers; his eyes so blue, looking at her so earnestly. Face value. Asking for nothing more than what they already shared. Not delving into inglorious pasts or asking awkward and humiliating questions, making judgments. Yeah, she could do that.

"I'd like that," she said honestly.

Several days later, Faith sat in one of the employee break rooms of the Celtic Goddess, absently fingering the remains of her apple with one hand while she sketched with the other. Normally she would just work through lunch, but the Pine Ridge location was much more adamant about employees taking a break if they were scheduled to work for more than four consecutive hours. She had given up lunches a long time ago, a sacrifice to her necessarily tight food budget, and her body had adjusted. It was a good thing, too. The bigger Matt got, the more he ate, and she had promised herself a long time ago that her son would *never* go hungry.

Her hand moved automatically, drafting the images from her head without conscious thought, recreating the décor of the opulent new suites the way her mind's eye saw them. She didn't think anything would ever come of it; her sketches were for her and her alone. It gave her hands something to do while the more alert parts of her brain concentrated on something infinitely more complex: Kieran Callaghan.

She still felt the echo of warmth from his hand where he had held it over hers. Still envisioned the sincerity in the depth of those bottomless blue eyes. Still heard his deep, soft voice, telling her that he liked having her around.

She was paraphrasing, of course, but the overall gist was clear enough. The biggest question, the one that had been haunting her ever since, was, why?

Why would a man like Kieran care about her one way or the other? He owned and operated a highly successful business. Was stunning beyond belief. Had a large, close family that obviously cared for him. Women would give their right arms to simply be with him. What benefit could he possibly find in her?

No doubt his brothers' wives had been asking themselves the same question. The converse to that query – what benefit could Faith find in Kieran – unfortunately had several definitive answers, every one of which made Faith appear to be what her mother would call a 'gold-digger'. They were about as far apart on the equality scale as they could be and still live in the same town. Obviously, she wasn't the first one to have come to that realization.

She had nothing to offer him except her friendship. To be fair, he had asked for nothing more. Maybe that was the key right there. There were so many women that wanted him for something, something that would benefit them like wealth or power or the prestige of being on his arm. She hadn't asked anything of him, and maybe that was all he really wanted – a person he could hang out with, no strings, no pressure. Someone who didn't care about his money or his job or the fact that he looked like something right off the cover of a romance novel. All good things, to be sure, but they didn't matter to Faith.

Well, she thought ruefully, that wasn't exactly true. If Kieran hadn't been so gorgeous or successful, she might allow herself to acknowledge some of those unfamiliar feelings simmering inside her, the ones she kept tightly lidded and hidden away, even from herself. As it was, he was as unattainable as it got.

"Those are incredible," said a soft-spoken voice from behind her, startling Faith from her musings.

Faith looked up to see Lexi Callaghan peering over her shoulder, checking out her sketches. She had managed to capture a perfect balance of the cultures defining the Celtic Goddess, created with a series of raised layers of flooring, steps, and columns that had a decidedly Greek feel, mixed with the old-world charm and appeal of ancient Ireland.

"Thanks," Faith murmured as she hurriedly closed the cover of her sketchbook. With the exception of her son, she didn't allow anyone to look at her etchings. Kieran had seen them that once, too, but she was more apt to overlook that. He had seemed to like them, though he hadn't mentioned them since, either, so maybe he'd just been being polite.

"We met the other night," Lexi said, looking disappointed when she tucked her sketchbook away. "I'm Lexi Callaghan." She extended her hand. Faith looked at it for a moment before taking it.

"I remember," Faith said. It would have been

hard to forget the woman who had inspired the Celtic Goddess franchise. Flowing golden blonde hair. Eyes that glowed like a tiger's eyes, a beautiful, clear amber flecked with gold. Roughly the same height as Faith, Lexi Callaghan had more grace and poise in her little finger than Faith had in her entire body. *This was what a woman worthy of a Callaghan was like*, she thought.

"Do you have a moment?" Lexi asked shyly, which was odd considering who she was and all. Faith definitely pictured someone that important displaying a lot more attitude – or exuding a boatload of confidence at the very least. Lexi looked almost as uncomfortable as Faith felt.

Faith glanced at the clock on the far wall, wishing she could honestly say no, but the darned thing said she still had ten minutes left in her mandatory break.

"Not much," she hedged, hoping that Lexi would understand. Unfortunately for her, Lexi did.

"I won't keep you long, I promise." The break room had gone strangely silent as the curiosity of several others was piqued the moment Lexi spoke her name aloud. It was not often that the head chef made her way into this particular area, where those without plush, private offices came to take a load off for a few. Aware of the glances they were getting, she added, "Do you mind if we go up to my office?"

Dread pooled in the bottom of Faith's stomach.

What choice did she have? Feeling cornered, she nodded. She picked up her sketchpad and tossed the apple core into the nearest waste bin, then followed Lexi out of the break room, avoiding the curious glances of the others.

What could Lexi Callaghan possibly want to talk to her about? Was this about the other night? Was she going to warn her off of Kieran?

Lexi's expression gave nothing away; she looked every bit as poised and beautiful as she had at the Fair. If Faith hadn't known better, she never would have pictured the young, denim-clad woman to be the world class chef behind the Goddess's success. There were no airs about her at all, and she seemed almost embarrassed by the people who called out to her as they passed. That made two of them.

Lexi's office, too, was a surprise. It was relatively small and simply furnished. The most imposing thing about it was the adjoining door into Aidan Harrison's office. Aidan Harrison was the owner of the entire Celtic Goddess franchise, a highly lucrative division of his father's worldwide restaurant empire.

Faith had glanced him once or twice, had even shaken his hand at the Fair, but she doubted he'd remember that. The man oozed success and power, both of which intimidated Faith and made her want to run as fast as she could in the other direction.

"Can I get you something to drink?" Lexi

offered, twisting the cap from a bottle of water. Faith noted it was the same brand sold in the local supermarket; she would have thought Lexi would have opted for something a bit more expensive or imported.

Faith shook her head; even if she had been inclined to accept out of courtesy she didn't think it would sit well with her stomach doing flip-flops.

Lexi sat on the small but comfortable couch and indicated that Faith should take a seat as well. She did, though she remained perched on the very edge.

"First, I want to apologize for what happened at the Fair last Saturday."

"No need," Faith said quickly.

"We'll have to agree to disagree on that," Lexi said, sounding sincerely regretful. "It's just that… "

"You care for Kieran," Faith interjected. "I can respect that."

Lexi smiled. "You do understand," she said with obvious relief, "but we should have been more sensitive. It's no excuse, but you kind of caught us off-guard, you see. Well, except Lacie, that is."

Caught them off guard? Had she broken some unspoken rule by showing up at their family event? Kieran had assured her it was alright, and she'd made a point not to eat or drink anything or take advantage of their hospitality. She'd been very careful not to say or do anything that might embarrass Kieran.

“I’m sorry. I’m not sure I understand.”

“I’ve known Kieran a very long time, Faith. He is my oldest, dearest friend. I was surprised – and maybe even a little hurt – that he hadn’t told me about you.”

“Why would he?” Faith asked honestly.

“Like I said,” Lexi said, shifting uncomfortably, “we’re very close.”

“Kieran’s a good man,” Faith said slowly. She couldn’t shake the nagging feeling that she was missing something important, but couldn’t for the life of her put her finger on it. “He’s gone out of his way to be kind and help us get settled in Pine Ridge – stubbornly so, I’m afraid,” she added. “Matt and I are grateful for that, but we’re not trying to take advantage of him, if that’s what you think.”

Lexi’s eyes opened wide. Before she could say anything, Faith stood. “I’m glad he’s got so many people looking out for him,” she said quietly. “I have to get back to work. It was nice seeing you again, Mrs. Callaghan.”

Faith let herself out of Lexi’s office, glancing briefly at the personal assistant eyeing her as she made her way out toward the bank of elevators. She forced herself not to run.

Chapter 10

"Faith!" Kieran walked out of *BodyWorks* into the parking lot with Matt. "Got a sec?"

He kept his pace relaxed, and Faith had to admit, he looked damn good. It was the fourth day in a row she hadn't gone into *BodyWorks*, choosing instead to text Matt from the car when she arrived. She'd told Matt it was because they were having some trouble with the alternator in the Taurus, and she was afraid to turn the car off for fear it wouldn't start again without a jump.

That was only partially true. Faith had been making a concerted effort to keep her distance from Kieran. It wasn't easy, and she wasn't willing to give him up completely, but hopefully reducing their face-to-face time kept her from being called to Lexi Callaghan's office again.

"Sure," she said, hoping he hadn't picked up on her slight hesitation. He was a smart man, though, so chances were he had probably already figured out that she was avoiding him.

"Matt told me they delivered the new roofing shingles. I thought maybe I could come by on Saturday and help you get them on."

Faith shot a glance at Matt, who suddenly seemed to find his shoes terribly interesting. Matt knew quite well that they had been invited to a barbecue being hosted by one of their neighbors. Neither of them wanted to go, but as Faith had already politely declined several such invitations, she didn't think she could do so again without hurting the woman's feelings. Mrs. Campbell was at least eighty, and had looked so hopeful when she explained how everyone else on the street would be there, that Faith hadn't had the heart to say no.

Her decided lack of a backbone was really starting to become a nuisance, she realized.

Now Matt was trying to enlist Kieran unknowingly, no doubt in an attempt to avoid said barbecue.

"I'm sorry," Faith said, meaning it. "We can't."

She'd much rather spend a day on the roof pounding nails than at a neighborhood shindig. Secretly she hoped that there would be enough people there that she and Matt could stay only long enough to be polite and then return to their cottage. And she really did miss Kieran, even if they would never be anything more than friends. She'd hoped by keeping her distance it might prove to his family that she really didn't want anything more than that.

It was a lie, of course, but a moot one.

"Oh," Kieran said, his face falling.

Damn it! It was hard enough to stay away from

the man as it was, but when he looked at her with those soulful eyes, her resolve melted away completely.

"It's not that we wouldn't love your help," Faith said, searching for some way to get rid of that crestfallen look (and eliminate her own ache at the sight of it in the process), "but we kind of got roped into attending this barbecue one of our elderly neighbors is hosting."

"Not Mrs. Campbell?" Kieran asked, leaning his forearms against the driver's side door. It placed him close enough that she couldn't mistake the unique but familiar scent of Kieran – clean, warm, spicy male. Or the obvious amusement that had so quickly replaced the hurt in his eyes. Did they always sparkle like that, or had not seeing him for a couple of days made her forget?

Faith nodded, trying not to let either get to her too much. It wasn't easy. She concentrated on their conversation instead, definitely not looking at the finely carved forearms and biceps just inches from her face. No man should be that attractive. It was *so* not fair.

"Yeah. How'd you know?"

"Elsa Campbell is a legend in these parts," he chuckled. "She knows everything there is to know about everyone, and apparently, she's set her sights on you. I'm surprised it's taken this long for her to get her talons into you."

Faith thought about the sweet, white-haired old

woman with the mischievous blue eyes. "I've been had, haven't I?"

"Afraid so."

Faith pinched between her eyes where she felt a headache coming on. It was one thing to be politely social, another to unknowingly sacrifice yourself to the town gossip.

"Any words of advice?"

Kieran seemed to give it a moment of serious thought. "You could try a little ipecac in some baked beans."

Matt, now ensconced in the passenger seat, snorted in laughter. Faith shot him a warning glance but found her own lips twitching as well. "That bad, huh?"

* * *

Poor Faith, Kieran thought. She had no idea what she was in for. He kept the teasing smile on his face, but inside he was squirming. Elsa was as notorious for her matchmaking as she was for her penchant for gossip. Five minutes with Faith, with her quiet, gentle demeanor, and Elsa would no doubt be networking faster than Ian's quad-chip processor.

The thought clawed at his chest. He was taking things easy for Faith's sake, but there was no way in *hell* he was going to let Elsa Campbell dangle her out there as bait for the hungry wolves.

* * *

"Damn," Faith muttered Saturday morning, breaking her own rule about cursing. But she had every reason to after looking out the kitchen window and seeing nothing but a cloudless blue sky and copious amounts of bright sunshine. The weathermen had been teasing all week about a possible low pressure system heading into the area and threatening outdoor plans for the weekend, but as usual, they got it all wrong. It was going to be a picture perfect summer day, well-suited to outdoor activities.

Double damn.

Her trepidation had only increased since talking to Kieran, a sense of unease that left her slightly anxious and tense. She really didn't like these kinds of things to begin with, and generally avoided social gatherings as much as possible. It wasn't a hard thing to do when you worked full time and were singularly responsible for a child. Down in Georgia folks had become so accustomed to her declining such invitations that they eventually stopped asking.

But this wasn't Georgia. And maybe, just maybe, some very tiny part of her actually wanted to feel like she belonged somewhere.

It wasn't like she was going to join the Ladies' Auxiliary or the Holy Name Society or anything. But it might be nice to know the names and faces of her neighbors. Elsa Campbell had hinted that they tended to look out for one another up here, and that might not be such a bad thing.

Besides Kieran and some of his family, the only other people she'd met had been the mailman and Elsa, and that was because Elsa had tenaciously shown up on her doorstep several times. First as the self-proclaimed "Welcome Wagon" lady for the area, and afterwards to offer a few personal invitations to various events. The informal barbecue at Elsa's seemed the most innocuous choice; Elsa had assured her that it was only for neighborhood residents and would be an understated, casual affair.

With a sigh, she slipped on her simple white cotton print sundress and a pair of Earth Spirits. Matt looked every bit as unhappy as she was to be going, but he had at least dressed in one of his nicer pairs of shorts and a clean short-sleeved shirt.

Elsa accepted Faith's contributions graciously – a massive bowl of southern-style potato salad and a pan of Mississippi mud brownies (sans ipecac or Matt's suggestion of chocolate Ex-lax) – and ushered them through her house and out on to the patio. Faith's heart immediately dropped when she saw the crowd assembled around the in-ground pool. At least half of them were young to middle-aged men, and nearly all of them were looking her way with interest.

She squeezed Matt's hand so hard he grunted.

"Leave me and I'll take you grocery shopping every day for a month," she whispered in warning.

In the first hour alone, Faith had been introduced to several "available" men. One of them was a gym teacher at the high-school, though after checking out Matt's height and build he was as interested in Matt's athletic inclinations as he was in Faith.

There was the bagger who worked at the Weis' market in town, nearing forty and still living with and caring for his mother (which, Elsa pointed out, proved that he was a good man).

The absolute worst had to be the divorced butcher, nearly as round as he was wide, whose breath reeked of garlic and dill spice.

There was the bookish-looking accountant that seemed nearly as embarrassed as she was. If worse came to worse, she decided, she would move towards him, especially since he confided quietly to her that he was, in fact, gay.

Somehow, Faith retained a pleasant smile and managed to nod in the appropriate places, but her head was already beginning to throb with what had the potential to become a migraine. She wondered exactly how long she'd have to stay before their departure would no longer seem rude.

Matt, at least, was faring better than she was. He recognized a couple of boys who also took Mixed Martial Arts classes at *BodyWorks*, and gravitated toward them. Shortly thereafter, the boys were joined by several young girls, who were naturally drawn to the “new kid”. Faith watched in fascination as her son smiled shyly and nodded, hands in pockets, at something the pretty brunette said.

He was a good-looking kid, she thought with no small measure of pride, though she wasn’t quite sure she was ready for the boy-girl stage yet. On the plus side, he was meeting kids he’d be going to school with in another few weeks, and Faith knew how much of a difference even one friendly face could make. They seemed like good kids, too, which helped ease some of her worry.

After enduring another hour of mingling and skillfully evading personal questions, Faith sought a few moments of solitude in the shadows of the tall arborvitae that bordered Elsa’s massive patio. Matt was now flanked by another brunette and a pixie-ish looking blonde, though he didn’t seem to mind so much. She saw a couple of the men looking around for her and sighed, wishing she could just close her eyes and become invisible.

“Didn’t go with the ipecac, huh?” Kieran’s deep, velvety voice teased her ear. Forgetting where she was, she spun around and nearly launched herself into his arms, the sound of his voice was so welcome.

“Kieran!” she exclaimed in hushed tones. “Am I happy to see you! What are you doing here?”

He chuckled, the low tones warming her from

the inside out. "Why, rescuing you, of course."

She blinked, then a low grin spread across her features. "Yeah?"

"Yeah. But I have to warn you – it may ruin your chances with a few of those fine eligible bachelors out there."

Faith glanced toward the patio and suppressed a shudder. "Hmm. Sounds serious."

His eyes darkened. It was incredibly sexy, and something deep inside her clenched.

"Oh, it is," he answered, his voice dropping an octave, and Faith wasn't sure he was kidding anymore. "But it will get those guys to stop sniffing around you. Are you game?"

She inhaled, taking in the deliciously masculine scent of Kieran. She hadn't realized she'd become so fond of it. Or of him. But after spending a very long afternoon playing Elsa's version of "The Dating Game", she realized that no one came remotely close to Kieran on the desirability scale, even if they were only friends.

"Absolutely," she nodded.

"Good girl," he said, pressing a quick kiss to her forehead that nearly had her swooning. "Stay out here for another five minutes, then make your way back to the patio."

"But where are you - " She turned, but Kieran was already gone. She shook her head. How did a man that large move so quickly and quietly? Must be something they taught to SEALs, she realized.

After all, they couldn't exactly send in soldiers like bulls in a china shop now, could they?

She remained hidden in the shadows, wondering what he was up to. Within a few minutes, she heard Elsa's twittering but very pleased voice.

"What a lovely surprise!" Elsa was saying. Kieran murmured something; from this distance Faith could only identify the deep, resonating timbre of his voice but not what he said. Whatever it was, it made Elsa laugh in delight.

A peek between the bushes revealed Kieran emerging from Elsa's house onto the patio, with the older woman holding on to his arm and beaming up at him. He, in turn, looked at her as if he was the luckiest man in the world to have her on his arm. Female heads turned en masse, all drawn to the finely sculpted figure that was her knight. The thought made her tingle in some very private places.

Kieran said hello to a few people. It appeared that he knew everyone there, but that made sense. He'd lived here his entire life, and Kieran Callaghan was not a man easily overlooked in any event.

He looked especially good today, Faith thought. When he'd surprised her earlier she'd been so happy to see him that she hadn't noticed what he was wearing, but from her hiding place amongst the arborvitae she was able to gawk her fill. Faded, well-fitting Levi's clung to his muscular legs. A navy blue button-down with the sleeves rolled up enough to glimpse his muscular forearms. And boots – black Harley Davidsons that had a very distinctive sound with each step, one that caught your attention and made you look.

There was no doubt about it. Her knight was one damn fine looking man.

Faith caught Kieran's discreet glances toward her location and realized that she must have been ogling him for some time. A soft blush colored her cheeks when she caught the amused, knowing look in his eye.

Kieran leaned down and said something to Elsa, making the older woman's eyes widen. Elsa followed his gaze to Faith and she beamed. Literally.

Feeling more than a few curious eyes on her, Faith made her way over to them, silently praying she didn't trip and do a header into the pool in the process. Kieran's intense gaze remained glued to her. Heads turned and conversations stopped as others looked back and forth between them.

Kieran grinned devilishly. What was he up to?

"You look stunning, Faith, as always," he said, capturing her hand and bringing it to his lips. "Are you ready?"

It was hard to form a cohesive thought with Kieran's lips on her skin like that. "Ready?" she murmured.

Kieran grinned wider. Oh, the devil knew exactly what he was doing. "Yes." He paused as an amused expression crept across his perfectly sculpted features. "Don't tell me you forgot?"

Elsa tut-tutted and clucked her tongue in mild admonishment.

"No, of course not," Faith improvised. "I'm afraid I just lost track of time."

"Well, of course you did, Faith dear," Elsa said, pleased, before turning to Kieran. "She's had the attention of quite a few young bucks, I daresay," she said, obviously for Kieran's benefit. Her eyes twinkled mischievously. Elsa Campbell was enjoying herself immensely.

"Did she now?" he murmured. The look in his eyes still held a hint of amusement, but there was something else there, too. Something dark and carnal that made Faith go all liquidy inside.

"Everyone has been very nice," she said demurely. His look darkened further, sending delicious little shivers up and down the base of her spine. Surely Kieran wasn't jealous? That thought – as pleasing as it was – was crazy. What could he ever have to be jealous of? The man was masculine perfection personified. And a hell of a good guy to be using his Saturday afternoon to come all the way out here to rescue her. Best she play along, lest she blow the chance he was giving her.

"But I'm afraid we did have other plans for this evening, Mrs. Campbell. I hope you don't mind."

"Not at all, my dear, not at all." Elsa was nearly giddy with excitement. Kieran flashed her a devastating grin and winked, making the older woman blush like a school girl.

"Let's grab Matt and we can be on our way." Kieran placed his hand possessively on the small of Faith's back (it was a nice touch, she thought), and led her over to where the younger crowd had congregated. Fifteen minutes later, they were back at Faith's cottage.

"I can't thank you enough," Faith said, finally breathing a sigh of relief.

"Well, actually, maybe you can," Kieran hedged, looking adorably boyish yet again.

Faith raised her eyebrow in a silent question. No doubt she owed him big time for the save, but how could she possibly help him? Thankfully, she didn't have to wait long to find out.

"There are supposed to be some meteor showers tonight," he said slowly. "I was hoping to take the boat out on the lake to watch, but it's a lot easier with two people, easy as sin with three, and everyone else is busy…"

It had been spectacular. There was no other way to describe it. The "boat" was actually a 60-foot custom built houseboat privately docked at the lake in nearby Birch Falls, complete with an open-sky deck for viewing. Kieran maneuvered the craft expertly, anchoring at a secluded area far on the uninhabited side of the lake.

At twilight, they sat in the windowed cabin and ate a sumptuous meal out of the fully-stocked picnic baskets Kieran had provided (and filled by Lexi with Celtic Goddess fare). When it got dark, they laid upon the deck and watched the meteor showers.

It was then that Faith first realized that despite her best efforts, she was desperately, hopelessly in love with Kieran Callaghan.

"When you rescue someone, you really go all out," she observed quietly, as she and Kieran sat on her front porch later. Over the course of the evening, it began to dawn on her exactly what he had done. He had gone to great lengths to make it look as though they were together. "Why did you do it?"

Instead of answering, he posed a question of his own. "Does it bother you?"

Did it? No. Except maybe to the extent that she wished it were true. "No," she answered honestly. "But it doesn't seem fair to you."

"Yeah? How's that?"

She looked at her hands folded neatly in her lap. Words didn't come easy to her, and no matter how hard she tried, she couldn't come up with any that would accurately convey her thoughts without making it sound as though she had a tremendous inferiority complex.

Faith O'Connell was a realist, however, and any way she looked at it, Kieran was well beyond her reach as anything but a friend. While she could see how a perceived romantic relationship between them would elevate her in the eyes of others and keep unwanted male attention at bay, she couldn't see how it benefitted Kieran, beyond the fact that it might have kept some unwanted female attention away from him. It certainly hadn't won any brownie points with his family; the night at the fair had driven that point home rather painfully.

With nothing to say, she simply shrugged.

* * *

Kieran cursed softly under his breath. She still didn't get it. How could he explain it to her without scaring her away?

"I like being with you, Faith," he told her finally. "I don't feel like I have to be anything more than myself when I'm around you." *And you are the other half of my soul.*

She sighed, a soft, almost sad sound. A sound that had Kieran clenching his hands at his sides so he wouldn't scoop her into his arms and show her exactly what she meant to him.

"I like being with you, too," she said quietly. "And for the record, I think you're a pretty great guy when you're just being you."

Kieran was slightly appeased. At least she'd admitted that much. It was a start.

"Thank you. For rescuing me and taking us out on the lake."

"You're welcome," he said. "I've been on that boat more times than I could count, but I've never enjoyed it as much as I did tonight."

She smiled then, a real, honest smile. God, how he wanted to kiss her. The urge to do so was nothing less than a fever of need coursing through his blood. Without even realizing he was doing so, he leaned over and brushed his lips over hers.

They were so soft, felt so good that he did it twice more. Light little brushes that only heightened his need. He deepened the kiss, slanting his mouth against hers, coaxing her with his tongue to open for him.

She did, and Kieran was lost. If there was any lingering trace of doubt about exactly who and what she was to him, it was laid to rest in that moment. The feel of his *croie*'s lips upon his, the exquisite taste of her, grasped him with velvet-sheathed talons and refused to let him go. His heart, his mind, his soul – they belonged to her now.

"Mom! You still out there?" Matt's voice rang out from inside the house. Faith gasped and ended the kiss; Kieran reluctantly pulled away. Even in the dim porch light he could see her lips, red and slightly swollen from his kisses, a look of dazed astonishment in her eyes.

"Yeah," she answered, having to try twice before the word made it out.

Matt poked his head out, oblivious to what had just happened. "I'm making myself a snack. You guys want anything?"

Faith shook her head, amazed. "Only a teenage boy could be hungry after eating half his weight in food a little while ago."

"That was *hours* ago," Matt informed her with an air of martyrdom.

Kieran snickered knowingly even as the new awareness thrummed and vibrated beneath his skin. "He's a growing boy, Faith."

"So he is." She stood up. Kieran followed her lead. "It's late," she said, avoiding his eyes. "Thanks again for tonight. We had a wonderful time."

Kieran narrowed his eyes at the obvious dismissal, but said nothing. If he could only see her eyes… Faith spoke volumes with her eyes.

Had she felt it, too? Given the way her hands were shaking, and her refusal to look at him, probably. But unlike him, she didn't understand. Just one more soul-searing kiss might explain it to her more than any words possibly could. Before he could test his theory, Faith stepped toward the door.

"Goodnight, Kieran," she said over her shoulder.

He sighed inwardly. There would be no more kisses tonight. "Goodnight, Faith."

Chapter 11

Those stolen kisses turned out to be even more powerful than he'd thought - just not in the way he'd hoped.

Over the next few weeks, it became clear that Faith was avoiding any situation that might place the two of them alone together. Under different circumstances, it might have been amusing.

She was spooked, he got that. Faith had yet to open up about her past, but given what he did know, he could guess that she'd had a difficult time of it. Kieran wanted her to trust him, to believe in *them*, and just telling her wasn't going to cut it. She had to come to that conclusion herself, and the only way to convince her that he wasn't going anywhere was simply to be there for her, no matter what.

It wasn't easy. Kieran did his best to give Faith the time and space she needed, but there was no way he could stay away entirely. While he might be able to suspend his baser urges, he needed to be near her. To see her. To hear her voice. To simply be with her. Thankfully, she didn't object too vehemently as long as someone else was around.

On some level, he suspected that she needed the contact just as much, even if she had trouble admitting it to herself.

He had hoped the situation might improve by the time Shane and Lacie's wedding came around in the middle of August. It was a small, intimate ceremony held in the gardens of Lacie's parents' home. Faith didn't seem too keen on attending (which he didn't understand since the two women seemed to get along so well), but feared hurting Lacie's feelings.

Faith selected seats for her and Matt far in the back on the bride's side, staying as far away from the Callaghan side as she could, presumably to avoid any contact with his family. Clearly, she hadn't forgotten the incident at the County Fair. Throughout the ceremony, she kept her gaze fixed on the couple, ignoring his repeated attempts to capture her attention. It didn't help that his sisters by marriage were shooting curious, furtive glances back at her, either.

"You look beautiful," Kieran said quietly after the vows were spoken, catching her hanging back in the shadows, alone. His eyes scanned the yard, spotting Matt talking to another boy about his age.

"You look pretty good yourself," she said with a soft smile, the one she seemed to reserve just for him.

"Dance with me." Without waiting for an answer, he tugged lightly on her hand and guided her toward the area where several couples were moving together to a slow ballad.

"I can't dance," she murmured in protest, but he knew instantly that it was a lie. She moved easily, gracefully against him, fitting in his arms perfectly, as he knew she would. Yet there was no denying the tension in her body.

"Relax, Faith," he breathed, pressing her closer. "I won't let anything happen to you."

Her sigh was barely audible as she melted against him. Kieran held her close for as long as he could, wishing there was some way to keep her there, bound to him indefinitely, but the moment the song ended, she began to pull away.

"I have to go," she murmured, avoiding his eyes. Placing his finger beneath her chin, he lifted her face so he could see her eyes. What he saw there made the breath catch in his throat – sadness. And a soul deep longing that had no place in the eyes of his heart.

"No, you don't."

* * *

But she did. Because when she was this close to him, it was too easy to forget what might happen if she allowed herself to acknowledge the feelings she had for him. The feelings she was finding it increasingly difficult to hide.

Held safely in his arms, she could almost

believe that everything was right with the world. He felt so strong, so solid, so certain. Yet there were some things even he was powerless against. Her ever-growing certainty that she was in love with him for one.

It was why she had been trying so hard to avoid being alone with him. Because she feared that she would not say no if he wanted to kiss her again. Or more. If not for Matt's timely interruption that night, who knew how far she would have allowed things to go? When it came to Kieran, her natural defenses were useless. But here, with his family watching closely, she could find the strength she needed to leave before those defenses were needed.

"Kieran!" Shane's voice called from nearby. "We need you for some pictures."

Kieran made no attempt to move. "Go," she encouraged with what she hoped was a convincing smile. "They're waiting for you."

After a few more shouts and a couple of creative threats, Kieran gave her a martyred look. "I won't be long. Please wait for me."

She reached up to adjust his tie and smoothed down his lapels. "You clean up pretty good, you know that?" It was an understatement. In everyday clothes, Kieran was gorgeous. In a wedding tux, he was devastating.

He smiled, then leaned down and brushed a quick kiss across her temple. "Please be here when I get back, Faith."

Without giving her a chance to respond, he was gone just as quickly. She muttered a near-silent curse as she watched him cross the lawn to join the others for the obligatory wedding photos. She couldn't leave *now*.

"Faith, right?" The low, raspy voice startled her. She turned to look at the lean, blonde man who had spoken.

"Right," she said, recognizing him. "You're Brian, Lacie's brother."

"You have a good memory," he observed.

"I could say the same for you."

One corner of his mouth quirked. "You could, but it's not quite the same. You are far more memorable than I am."

Faith couldn't tell if he was teasing her or not, but the mischievous glint in his eye hinted that he was. "I doubt that."

He chuckled softly. "You look like a woman in the grips of a fight-or-flight battle. Can I ask which one is winning?"

"At the moment, it's a dead heat."

"Then permit me to sway the odds. Come and have a drink with me."

Faith glanced over toward the flower-laden arch where the photographer was positioning the wedding party. "I'm not really much of a drinker."

"All the better. Won't take as much to get you nice and liquored up." Her eyes widened, and he winked. "Trust me. It'll help."

For some strange reason, she *did* trust him. With another quick glance reassuring her that Kieran was occupied and Matt was engrossed in conversation with his friend, she dutifully followed Lacie's brother across the yard, through the sliding glass patio doors and up to the fully stocked bar.

"The Callaghans are good people," Brian said, grabbing a variety of bottles and tipping them into a glass with dizzying speed. "A little intense sometimes, but good people."

Faith didn't know how she was supposed to respond to that, so she said nothing. Brian tipped the mixture into a silver container, added some crushed ice, and shook it.

"Lacie tells me you're from Georgia," he said, pouring the drink back into the glass. She nodded.

"I was at Marietta for a while," he told her. "Hot as hell down there, and those swamps stink to high heaven sometimes, at least to a boy who grew up in these mountains. Here, try this."

Faith eyed the concoction warily. "Go on," he coaxed. She lifted the glass to her lips and took a tentative sip. It was delicious. She took another and realized her tongue and lips were tingling. "What is this?"

"Secret family recipe. We call it the 'Virgin Slayer'. Crafted by my great-grandfather on his wedding night to ease the fears of his bonnie bride."

Her eyes grew into large silvery gray saucers as the first few sips sent the warm, tingly feeling down into other parts of her body. "Really?"

"Oh, aye," Brian grinned and winked. "'Tis the curse of the McCain men to be so well-endowed as to cause the swooning of many a high-bred virgin lass."

Faith couldn't help it. She giggled. Brian's eyes sparkled. "See? It's working already."

* * *

The photos took longer than expected. Kieran looked to the shadows where he had left Faith, but he was unable to catch a glimpse of her. The moment he was freed, he made a beeline for the spot, only to find it empty. His heart fell. He'd been so sure she'd wait for him.

The sound of laughter rang out from the patio, drawing his attention. He blinked and looked again, sure that he was seeing things. There, amidst a cheering circle of onlookers, Lacie's brother Brian and Faith were executing a perfectly synchronized rendition of "Cotton Eyed Joe".

Kieran could only gape in wonderment. He'd seen Faith smile before, and heard her gentle laugh, but had never seen her kick back and simply enjoy herself with wild abandon like she appeared to be doing. What happened to the woman so ready to flee just a short time ago? He was torn between being happy that she was having such a good time and being unhappy that she wasn't having it with him. It was the sheer intensity of his jealousy, however, that left him feeling winded.

"Oh, will you look at that," Lacie's mom said, coming up next to him and clasping her hands together with tears in her eyes. "I haven't seen Brian smile like that since he came back. Faith must be an angel."

She was, Kieran thought with a rush of stark possessiveness. But she was *his* angel.

It wasn't that he didn't like Brian; he did. He and his brothers had done their damnedest to pull him and what remained of his team out of Afghanistan a few months earlier. He'd seen firsthand the kind of hell Brian had endured, knew that it would haunt him forever. Begrudging him a few minutes of happiness made him feel like shit, but Faith was his *croie*.

As the song ended, Brian bowed low to Faith, and Faith offered a proper Southern curtsy in response. Those gathered around cheered loudly, and it was only then that they seemed to realize they were the center of attention. Faith turned a brilliant shade of pink. When she looked up and saw Kieran, she made a beeline for him.

The fact that she did assuaged most of the murderous thoughts he'd been having.

"I thought you told me you couldn't dance," he accused. "That was wonderful!"

"That wasn't really me," she said, her face flushed and her eyes twinkling. "That was the

'Virgin Slayer'". When Kieran raised his brow in question, Faith explained Brian's special drink and the dubious history behind its making. Faith sucked in a breath when Kieran tightened his fingers around hers, and leaned down close to her ear.

"Does that mean I'm going to get lucky tonight?" he asked in a husky whisper.

A noise – it sounded like a whimper - escaped her lips. Kieran looked deeply into her eyes and her breath caught. Kieran glanced down at where their hands were joined.

"Oh, look," he said with a roguish smile. "I already did."

Once Matt started school at the end of August, Kieran didn't get to see Faith every day anymore. She had declared Matt's school work a priority and his "job" and martial arts lessons secondary. Kieran understood that, even agreed with it, but also knew that there was much more to Faith's avoidance tactics than Matt's grades.

For Kieran, it was sheer torture, leading him to new levels of frustration, and he knew he had to do something. His body, his heart, and his soul recognized her for what she was. Being around Faith – seeing her pretty face, hearing her lovely voice, scenting her natural fragrance - had become a physical need for him. While he was trying to be patient and understanding, hoping that Faith would eventually realize what he already knew, he was getting desperate. He had to figure out something.

Soon.

Chapter 12

"Maybe I should, you know, hang around tonight," Matt suggested, eyeing her with concern etched in his youthful features. Faith sat at the kitchen table, fighting the urge to close her eyes and rest her head upon the smooth, cool surface. She impatiently wiped at the persistent sheen of perspiration across her brow and shivered slightly beneath the three layers of flannel.

"Matt, don't sneak up on me like that," she chastised gently. "And don't be ridiculous. You've been looking forward to this for two weeks."

"It's not a big deal," he shrugged, pinning her with a look way too mature for a fourteen year old.

"Neither is this."

Matt crossed his arms over his chest, just like she'd seen Kieran do when she wasn't being completely honest. She knew then that she must look even worse than she'd thought.

"All I'm going to do is have some soup and make it an early night. You'd give up an all-guys weekend at Jace's cabin for that?"

Jace and Matt had become fast friends, and the former had invited Matt up to his family's cabin for their annual "male retreat" over the extended Labor Day holiday. It was a great opportunity. The group consisted of Jace's dad and a couple of his uncles, several of whom were members of the Pine Ridge police force as well as voluntary firemen, Jace's two brothers, a few cousins, and two or three additional friends from school with whom Matt got along well. Up until about an hour ago, Matt had been very excited about the trip; it was practically all he'd talked about all week.

And, since it was to take place the weekend after Matt's birthday, Faith had agreed to let him go as part of his "present". They'd celebrated privately the night before with a special dinner and a small, homemade cake, but Faith knew this trip would be the best thing she could give him.

"You're sick." Matt shifted, caught between what he wanted to do and what he felt he should do. He was a good kid like that, and Faith felt a surge of motherly pride. But there was no way she wanted him to give up this weekend for her. The only way to get him to go was to convince him that she would be fine.

"So? Everybody gets sick sometimes. Like you said, it's no big deal. It's not even a bad one. A hot bath, extra rest, maybe some NyQuil, and I'll be right as rain by the time you get back."

"What if you need something?"

"I have everything I need," she assured him. "A brand new box of tissues, chicken soup in the freezer, half a box of Calgon and my fleecy pj's waiting for me. And if I do need anything, I'll call Mrs. Campbell. But I won't."

Matt shifted again, and Faith knew he was close. He needed this, needed the chance to bond with guys his own age. And she needed to rest. If she knew Matt was away having a good time with his friends, she wouldn't have to feel too guilty about not accomplishing anything around the house for a day or two.

"Go. Really. *I'm fine*."

The sound of a truck crunching along the gravel drive, followed closely by the pound of heavy teenage feet on the porch and the subsequent knock signaled the moment of truth. Matt's ride was here.

For good measure, Faith got up and walked to the door, though it took nearly every last bit of strength she had not to sway. She discreetly used the sturdy doorframe to keep her upright.

"Hi Jace," she said in friendly greeting to the boy, offering a wave to Jace's dad easing out of the massive King cab. She turned to Matt, who was appraising her carefully, looking for a reason to stay.

"Go," she coaxed. Jace already had Matt's bag and was loping back to the car. "Have a great time. And don't worry so much. I'm a big girl." She smiled. Matt exhaled, still not looking sure, but nodded. He was so close…

"You've got enough clothes? Underwear? Socks?"

"*Mom.*"

"Phone? Cash? Toothbrush?"

"*Mom.*"

"Right," she grinned as Matt's focus was taken off of her and he shot his friends a somewhat embarrassed smile. Mild humiliation in the form of an overprotective mom – a true classic - worked every time. Faith exhaled in triumph when Matt finally nodded, leaned in to give her a quick peck on the cheek, then jogged to the truck.

Karl, Jace's dad, chuckled. "Don't worry, Faith. He's in good hands."

She nodded. "I know. Mother's privilege."

"Hey, you okay?" he asked, his expression growing concerned when he noticed how pale she was.

"Yeah, I just picked up a little cold."

"There's some really nasty stuff going around."

"Yeah, but this is nothing."

Like Matt, Karl looked unconvinced. "If you need anything, give Carole a call, ok? She'll be going stir crazy with an empty house all weekend."

Somehow Faith doubted that. The woman was probably already pouring herself a glass of wine, sinking into a hot bubble bath, and picking up the latest romance novel. "I will, thanks."

She leaned against the doorframe and waved as the car backed up and made its way back up the drive. The moment it was out of sight, Faith closed the door and slid down. With her back to the wall, Faith closed her eyes and fell promptly asleep.

* * *

Kieran turned away from the massive flat screen he wasn't really watching anyway when his cell chimed, indicating a new text message. Picking it up, he checked the number and looked at the text.

K, u busy?

Thought u were away. Whats up?

Moms not answering.

Without hesitation, Kieran pressed the pad of his large finger to the call icon. Matt answered on the first ring. "Talk to me."

"Mom was sick when I left. I didn't want to go but she said she'd be fine."

"Sick how?" Kieran asked, looking for his sneakers.

"Like a cold or a flu or something. I texted her goodnight, just to, you know, check, but she's not answering."

"She probably just went to bed early."

"Yeah, she said she was going to do that, but…" Matt let the sentence hang.

"You want me to check on her?" Kieran asked. Without waiting for an answer, he pointed the remote at the bank of electronics and shut them all down with a quick tap of his thumb, then flicked off the lights, keys in hand.

A pause. "Yeah."

"You got it. I'll text you, let you know everything's cool, ok?"

"Ok. Thanks, K."

Kieran was already out the door.

There weren't any lights on when Kieran cruised up to the house, which was unusual. Faith always kept the porch light on and at least one on inside. He knocked softly, not receiving an answer. Trying the door, he frowned when it turned easily in his hand.

"Faith?" he called out. A slight noise near his feet had him looking down. Light from the dusk-to-dawn feature he'd installed on the garage flowed in, illuminating a figure on the floor.

Cursing softly, he bent down. "Faith? Faith, honey? It's Kieran." He touched her face, found it burning up with fever.

Her eyes fluttered open, and it took her awhile to focus. "Kieran? What are you doing here?" Her eyes widened and filled with fear. "Matt!? Is everything okay?"

"Matt's fine," Kieran soothed. "He was worried because you didn't answer his texts. He said you were sick."

Relief washed over her and she slumped again. "Just a cold," she murmured. "I guess I was too tired to make it to the bedroom," she said sleepily.

Kieran lifted her into his arms, ignoring her

weak protests. “Don’t. I’ll get you sick.”

“Hush, now,” he told her. It was a testament to exactly how sick she was that she did exactly that. Kieran tucked her against his chest, cursing again when he felt the heat of her skin burning into his neck.

He flicked on a small light before carrying her up the stairs, but it was unnecessary. Kieran knew the layout of this house as well as he knew his own. Still, he didn’t want to take any chances, not with Faith in his arms.

He flipped down the covers of Faith’s bed and set her down gently. She insisted on visiting the bathroom; he put an arm around her waist and assisted her as far as the door. Once she was inside and he heard the water running, he pulled out his phone.

First he texted Matt. *Moms ok. Sleeping. Got it covered.* Matt must have been waiting, because within seconds Kieran received a response: *thx k. i o u 1.*

Then he dialed his brother. “Mick…. Yeah, sorry to bother you… Hey, Faith’s sick…. Fever, chills… What should I do?... Uh huh… Thanks, man.”

Michael told Kieran that Faith had probably contracted the flu that was making its way around, and that rest and fluids were the best form of treatment. It was common sense, but Kieran didn’t always trust his when it came to Faith. Michael had understood that all too well. With a promise to call if things didn't improve by the next day, Kieran disconnected the call, feeling a little better.

"Faith? You okay?" Kieran knocked on the bathroom door when she seemed to be in there an extraordinarily long amount of time.

She opened the door, and he was hit with the scent of Listerine and minty toothpaste. She had also washed her face and combed her hair. "You should be in bed," he scolded gently.

Pale as she was, the blush was easily visible, and in a flash of comprehension, he realized that Faith had gone to the trouble for his benefit, not hers.

"Come on," he said, his arm slipping around her waist again.

"You don't need to - " she began to protest.

"Yes, I do. I told Matt I'd look after you. Don't make me go back on my word, Faith." As expected, Faith clamped her mouth shut. Kieran had brought out the Matt card early, wanting as little resistance as possible.

"Have you taken anything?" he asked, tucking her under the covers. He may have been overstepping the bounds they'd defined so far, but he'd had more than enough of those. Patience was all well and good to a point, but she was sick, and unless she somehow managed to find the strength to physically throw him out of her house (an impossibility on the best of days), he was staying.

Fortunately, she wasn't complaining too loudly.

"Acetaminophen," she admitted. "Just now."

"Good. Get some rest. I'll just hang out for a while."

"Kieran, you don't need to - "

"Rest. Don't argue with me. I'm bigger and stronger and not in the grips of the flu."

Faith's mouth twitched. "You're very bossy tonight."

"Sweetheart, you have no idea," he said, his voice softer.

With a much-martyred sigh, and a smile he was sure she had not meant for him to see, Faith sank back into the pillows and closed her eyes.

After assuring himself that Faith was resting comfortably, Kieran went back downstairs and did a little recon. It didn't take him long to find everything he was looking for; Faith was very organized. He found clearly labeled containers of homemade soups and stews in the freezer. Several boxes of tea in the cupboard, along with sugar and local honey. Extra bedding was in the hall closet.

Satisfied, he made up a makeshift bed for himself on the sofa and settled in.

* * *

Faith couldn't believe it when she woke up a full twelve hours later, still weak but feeling noticeably better than she had. She smiled, remembering how Kieran had come to take care of her the night before. He really was the sweetest, kindest man she had ever met. And gorgeous. And smart. And funny. In fact, if Faith sat down and envisioned her idea of the perfect man, Kieran would fit the bill quite nicely.

A small ache bloomed in her chest, but she stuffed it down. It didn't do any good to think things like that. She might as well wish for a mansion or a Mercedes or a vacation home in Aspen (which would be stupid, since she'd never been skiing once in her life and had no desire to start). The only thing that could come of wishing for such things was heartbreak and disappointment.

If life taught her anything, it was to be thankful for what she had.

She was happy now. Happier than she had been in a long, long time. She had Matt. He was happy and healthy, and she couldn't ask for a better son. They had their own house, nestled in a beautiful valley. A good, if not lucrative job at the Celtic Goddess, offering great benefits and enough to ensure their basic needs were met. She had a friend now, too. She and Lacie chatted almost every day.

And there was Kieran. Despite her not-so-subtle attempts to discourage him, he was always around, cheerfully helping out. Matt adored him. She didn't know what they would have done without him. It was painful to think of the time when he would move on to other things, so she shoved that thought aside, too. She was tired of fighting him; he was a force of nature. Trying to resist him completely was as futile as trying to defy gravity.

She would enjoy all of it, including Kieran, for whatever time she had.

Like that kiss they had shared. It had only been that once, but it had rocked her world.

She took her time getting out of bed. Her entire body felt stiff and achy. Discarding her sweat-soaked PJs – her fever must have broken overnight - she tossed back a couple more tablets and turned on the shower. The hot water felt heavenly against her aching muscles, and the fresh, clean fragrance of the soap made her feel almost human again.

Donning a fresh pair of pajamas – with Matt gone there was no need to bother getting dressed – she picked up her cell phone and frowned. There were a couple of messages from Matt, all from last night. Nothing since. She felt a tiny stab of disappointment, then reminded herself that Matt had been concerned enough to ask Kieran to check on her. He was probably having a good time and didn't want to disturb her.

Still, knowing Matt, he was worried. Faith typed in a quick message: *Feeling much better. Hope u r having a gr8 time. LM.*

LM was their code for Love, Mom. It saved him embarrassment in case one of his buddies was around.

Faith took her time heading downstairs, gripping the banister since she was still a bit lightheaded. She blinked when she got to the bottom. Neatly folded blankets and extra pillows were set beside the couch. She had no recollection of putting them there.

"You shouldn't have come down," Kieran said, startling her. She turned around to find him standing there freshly showered, looking more than a little yummy, holding a tray with scrambled eggs, toast, jam, tea, and juice. Her eyes grew to the size of saucers.

"Kieran!" Color rose in her cheeks as she realized what she must look like. Hair still damp from her shower in loose curtains around her face. Faded old flannel pajamas, so worn they should have gone out with the trash years ago but so comfortable.

"I heard you moving around. I was going to bring this up to you, but since you're here, I guess the couch is as good a place as any."

* * *

She blinked, looking at him as if he'd grown a second head.

"I mean, 'breakfast on the couch' doesn't have quite the same ring as 'breakfast in bed', but it's the thought that counts." He beamed at her. She looked beyond adorable in those pajamas, the faded images of Eeyore peeking out from all over. Though she was still too pale, there was a bit of color in her cheeks and her eyes didn't look quite so feverish anymore.

When she made no move to take a step in any direction, he said, "Go on, then. Or are you going to make me put this down and carry you over there?"

Faith opened her mouth to say something, but promptly shut it again when Kieran lifted an eyebrow in warning, leaving no doubt he would do exactly that. She turned around and shuffled into the living room dutifully.

"That's better," he said in approval. He loved her fire, her independence, but he certainly wouldn't complain about a little good-old fashioned cooperation once in a while.

"How are you feeling?"

"What are you doing here?" she said as she sat down on the edge of the couch. Kieran set the tray down on the coffee table and grabbed both of her legs around the ankles, swinging them up to the couch.

"Taking care of you," he said simply. He tucked a blanket around her legs and fluffed a pillow behind her back before pressing his hand to her forehead and nodding, pleased to feel her skin much cooler than the last time he'd checked. He stuck a thermometer in her mouth anyway.

"Why?" she asked, pulling it out.

He grinned boyishly, wrapping his hand around hers and guiding the digital probe back between her lips. "Because."

"Because why?"

"*Because I can.* Geez, you ask a lot of questions. Now keep this under your tongue until it beeps or I'll put you over my knee and put it somewhere where you won't be able to get it out quite so easily."

Faith's eyes grew as wide as saucers, uncertain as to whether Kieran was bluffing or not.

She kept the thermometer in her mouth.

"Don't you have anything better to do?" she asked several hours later. He removed the empty soup bowl and re-tucked the blankets around her. College football was on the small, old-fashioned box television, and Kieran settled back into the far end of the sofa to watch. There was nothing snarky about her tone, but Kieran flicked her a sideways glance anyway, on the verge of being annoyed. It wasn't the first time she'd asked.

"I'm starting to get the feeling you don't want me here," he said accusingly.

She turned bemused eyes on him. "How could you not have anything better to do than sit here and babysit?"

He turned his blue eyes to her, and unleashed all of their significant power amidst an expression of infinite patience. "Faith, do you *want* me to leave?"

She bit her lip and thought about it for several interminable seconds. Finally her eyes softened. "No."

Inwardly, Kieran did a fist pump. "Then no, I don't have anything better to do."

She looked at him doubtfully.

"I like being with you, Faith," he said, repeating the words he had spoken a lifetime ago. She had doubted him then, too. Before she could question him further, he added with a wink, "You let me have control of the remote."

The corner of her mouth quirked upward and Kieran breathed a sigh of relief, knowing he had bought himself a little more time. Eventually he was going to have to tell her exactly how he felt, but not yet. He had a feeling she wasn't ready to hear about *croies* and soul mates just yet.

Chapter 13

His comment reminded her that as big as he was, he was the youngest of his family. "What is it like, having six older brothers?" she asked, genuinely curious. "I can't even imagine it."

Kieran laughed. "That's probably for the best."

"Tell me about them."

Kieran flipped off the TV and gave Faith his full attention. "Well, you've already met most, if not all of them. Where do I start?"

"How about with the oldest?"

"That would be Kane. He's the oldest, and the scariest."

An image of the large man tackling Kieran at the Fair came to mind. He *was* big and scary. "The alpha among alphas?"

"Yeah," he grinned. "Something like that. He handles all the financial stuff for the family. We don't see him much. He's not exactly what you would call a people-person. He lives up in the mountains with his wife Rebecca, their little girl Aislinn and their two monster-sized canines, and only comes down into town occasionally. Then there's Jake, he's the next oldest."

"He runs the Pub in town?"

Kieran nodded. "He's married to Taryn."

Faith thought about it for a moment. "Taryn…purple eyes and dragon tattoo?" The one who openly wondered about Faith's age, she recalled, feeling the twinge of that moment again.

"Yep. Taryn's a bit outspoken, but she's a real sweetheart. Jake was the first of us to find his *croie*."

"*Croie*?"

"It's Irish for heart," Kieran explained. Faith's eyes softened, the way a woman's tended to do when she heard something incredibly romantic. "You mean like a soul mate? That's beautiful."

"Do you believe in soul mates, Faith?" he asked, watching her carefully. What was she supposed to say to that? In theory, such things were wonderful, but in reality…

She shrugged and sipped her tea. For a moment, she could have sworn his eyes flashed, but it was probably just a trick of the light. Thankfully, he didn't dwell on the subject.

"Their daughter, Riley, is a spitfire just like her mom, and their son, Rory already has Jake's scowl," he grinned. "Then there's Mick – Michael. He's a doctor, but his real skill lies in biochemistry. He's a genius. He's married to Maggie, and they've got the farm that grows all the organic produce for the Goddess. They've got one little guy, Ryan, and another on the way."

Faith nodded. She'd liked Maggie instantly, though she had a harder time recalling which one was Michael. They all looked very much alike, really.

"Ian – you've met him, too. He's the one who offered to hook up a security system for you."

Faith nodded past the look he gave her, the one that let her know he was still not pleased with her outright refusal to consider home security. As far as she was concerned, she didn't need one; that was the kind of thing you got when you had something worth stealing. A good old-fashioned baseball bat took care of the rest. She and Matt each had one within reach of their beds.

"He's married to Lex. Lex was my best friend in high school."

Ah, yes, she knew Lexi Callaghan, remembering the day that Lexi had called her up to her office. Thankfully, she hadn't done it since. The other women in Housekeeping Services shot curious glances her way for a week afterward. She hadn't mentioned that visit to Kieran, and wondered if Lexi had. Somehow she thought not.

"Lexi is the master chef at the Goddess."

"One and the same." The pride in his voice unmistakable. "Of course, we knew she was destined for greatness when she started baking us chocolate chip cookies after school."

"I thought she was from Georgia."

Kieran shook his head. "No. She moved away

in high school, but she grew up right here in Pine Ridge."

Judging by the clouds that momentarily rolled through his eyes, Faith guessed there was more of a story there somewhere, but Kieran didn't elaborate. She still had trouble picturing the down-to-earth, blue jean clad woman she'd met as the genius behind the Celtic Goddess cuisine. It was another reminder of how out of his league she was.

"Anyway, they've got two little ones - Patrick and baby Kate. Patrick started Kindergarten in the Fall – he's the oldest of the nieces and nephews and loves having Laci as his teacher. There's Shane – you know him, of course. And Sean, he and Shane are twins. Sean runs the garage in town. He's married to Nicki."

"Matt was quite taken with Nicki," Faith said, remembering the way her son's eyes had gone huge at her jet black hair and super-pale eyes. For as beautiful as she was, the woman held a distinctly mysterious, dangerous air.

"Yeah. I imagine most boys are," he chuckled.

"And you're the baby." Faith smiled.

"Guilty. And you already know everything interesting there is to know about me."

Faith didn't believe that for a moment. She suspected Kieran Callaghan was a man who could keep her interest indefinitely. Then she shut those thoughts down right away before she started daydreaming the impossible again.

"Your turn," Kieran said. "I showed you mine, now you show me yours," he said with a wicked grin.

"If I had what you do, I'd want to show it off too," she teased, surprised at her own boldness.

"You are beautiful, Faith." The depth of emotion in his voice stirred something inside, but he didn't allow her to dwell on it. "Enough stalling. I have ways of making you talk, you know."

The deep, suggestive tone of his voice made her body grow warm, and it had nothing to do with her lingering low-grade fever. "You're not going to let this go, are you?"

"Not a chance. I want to know you, Faith."

"You do know me," she murmured, knowing it was a lie. He only saw what she allowed him to see. With each passing day it became increasingly difficult to convince herself that she could be happy this way, being nothing more than a friend to him. But even then, he deserved to know the truth. It had to come out eventually, and it was better that he find out now, before she lost any more of her heart to him.

Faith blew out a breath. The time had come to be honest with Kieran, at least a little. He had earned that much. He looked at her with so much intensity in those beautiful blue eyes. And each time he did, it made her feel more and more like a fraud.

"What do you want to know?" she asked

resignedly.

His eyes widened slightly as if he was expecting more resistance. "Let's start simply. Do you have any brothers or sisters?"

"Yes."

Kieran waited expectantly for her to expound on that, but she didn't. "You're not going to make this easy, are you?"

Her brows furrowed. It had been so long since she'd spoken of her family to anyone, it took a moment to gather her thoughts. "I have three brothers and two sisters."

Kieran laughed. "Like the Brady Bunch? Three girls and three boys?"

"Exactly like the Brady Bunch," she said half-mockingly, "if Mike and Carole were Bible thumping zealots."

Kieran raised an eyebrow, pulling Faith's foot into his lap and beginning a slow massage. "Tell me."

"That's so not fair," she moaned. On top of everything else, the man had purely magical hands. "You didn't strike me as the type to play dirty."

"I gave you fair warning," he smirked. "There are definite benefits to knowing every muscle and tendon in the human body." He did some kind of squeeze/massage thing that she was pretty sure might lead to an orgasm if she'd let it. Her head dropped back against the pillows and her tongue loosened. Clearly there was a link from that spot in the middle of her foot and the part of her brain that controlled her mouth.

"I'm the oldest. Then there's Mark, Luke, Grace, John, and Hope."

Kieran's hands paused for a moment along her arch and looked at her in disbelief. "Gospels and Virtues?"

Faith smiled wryly. He resumed his rhythmic kneading, taking up the other foot.

"Are you close?" She was just about to moan an emphatic "yes" when she realized he wasn't talking about the effect his foot massage was having on her personal regions.

"No. I haven't spoken to any of them since before Matt was born." Even Kieran's magical touch couldn't completely erase the sense of disappointment, of failure. "I think about them often, though. Wonder where they are now, what they're doing. Did they marry? Go to college? Move away? Do I have nieces and nephews I don't even know about?"

She only allowed herself to think about those kinds of things late at night, when she was alone in her bed and there was no one to see the tears that inevitably fell when she remembered her family, and she never spoke of them out loud. Now here she was, spilling her secrets to Kieran in the light of day.

It was difficult. Moisture began to accumulate in her eyes and that cold, empty feeling started seeping into her chest again. Not wanting him to see her like this, Faith tried to pull her foot away, but Kieran wouldn't allow it.

"Talk to me, Faith. Why don't you keep in touch with your family?"

Kieran kept a firm but gentle grip on her ankle, and even had she not been sick, she didn't have a prayer of getting away from him if he didn't allow it. And, if she was honest with herself, she didn't want him to. His hands, his presence, felt good.

Faith took a deep breath and blew it out. She knew it would come to this eventually. He might as well know the truth. Maybe it might even be cathartic. "They disowned me."

"What?" His hands paused again.

"It's scripture. *'If your hand or your foot causes you to stumble, cut it off and throw it away. It is better for you to enter life maimed or crippled than to have two hands or two feet and be thrown into eternal fire.'* Matthew 8:18 – one of my father's personal favorites. I brought sin into the family, so they cut me off."

The words were laced with a sadness and pain she'd thought she'd come to terms with long ago. But now that she had started, she was determined to get it all out. "I was the minister's daughter, Kieran, and my dad was a very outspoken pillar of the community. To have his fourteen year old daughter come home pregnant and unwed was like a slap in his face."

"You are his *daughter*," Kieran said.

She took some measure of comfort in Kieran's simmering outrage. The fact that he couldn't understand her father's rationale confirmed what she had already guessed – that Kieran Callaghan was a good man all the way through.

"*Was*. I don't exist to them anymore."

"Because you got pregnant?"

"That's part of it. To be honest, my father never seemed very happy with me, but that was the straw that broke the camel's back. He and my mother wanted me to stand up in church every week, to use myself as an example of what happens when you stray from the Word and yield to the temptations of the flesh."

"That wasn't the worst part, though," she added quietly. "They wanted me to give Matt up for adoption so that a 'good God-fearing couple' might raise him."

Kieran released her foot and pulled Faith into his arms. "Ah, Faith. I'm so sorry."

She knew she should resist him, but she couldn't bring herself to do so. Kieran felt so strong and warm and solid. She couldn't ever remember feeling like this, so … safe. She knew he was a wonderfully sweet and caring man, and that it meant nothing beyond friendship, but at the moment she didn't care.

"I'm not," she said finally, sniffing a little. "They thought of Matt as a mistake, but he's not.

He's a Blessing, a Gift. If they can't see that, it's their problem. And if they hadn't thrown me out, we wouldn't have found our way here. And here is good."

Kieran's big hand stroked the length of her back, the gentle pressure keeping her tucked and sheltered against him. She curled her legs up, wanting to hide in the protection of his arms for a while longer.

"Fourteen and pregnant. What did you do?"

"Well, being the oldest of six, I already knew a lot about babies and kids and how to take care of them, just not how to do it alone and without food, money, or shelter. Thankfully, I found this great organization that took in girls like me. Pregnant girls who had been cast out by their families and had nowhere else to go. We all lived together in this big house. It was hard, but it was good, too. We had to hold down jobs, share the chores, and every one of us had to work on our GED. Matt and I stayed there till I turned eighteen, but then I aged-out and we had to leave."

"What about Matt's father?" he asked.

She closed her eyes. She didn't want to talk about Nathan. "What about him?"

"Didn't he try to help?"

Faith laughed, but it came out sounding more like a choking sound. "God, no." She recalled the night she'd gone to Nathan Longstreet's house in tears. She'd knocked on the door and asked to speak with him, only to see him emerge from the kitchen hand-in-hand with Carla Martin. How his eyes had widened in outright shock and fear, as if he sensed why she had come.

"Nathan refused to believe me, even though he knew I'd been a virgin." He'd been seventeen to her fourteen, and her first real crush. So tall and handsome, a promising quarterback for their high school football team. Going into his senior year, he already had several scholarship offers. She couldn't believe it when he actually smiled at her. And when he offered to walk her home one night after Bible study? She thought she'd died and gone to heaven.

"He'd just broken up with his girlfriend," Faith said quietly, lost in her own memories. "He said I was a good listener. That when he was with me, he felt… different. That I was unlike anyone he'd ever met."

Being so close to Kieran gave her the strength she needed. As much as she didn't want to tell him, she had to. "It started off innocently enough. He held my hand as we took the long way home. We had a secret spot where we'd sit and talk, a small clearing in the woods…" She wasn't even aware of the tears filling her eyes. "He told me how much he needed me, how I made him feel better, how I could make his pain go away."

"Did he rape you, Faith?" Kieran asked, his voice low and deadly.

She pulled back enough to look in his eyes. This was the part she had been dreading the most. If she could have laid all the blame on Nathan, it might have been easier. But she couldn't.

Her face had to reflect the absolute shame she felt down to her core. "No," she whispered. "I knew what we were doing was wrong, but I let him. I didn't say no."

"Oh, baby," Kieran said, pulling her close again.

"God, it hurt so much," she sniffed, the tears flowing freely. "He was so rough, and all I could think of was how it was nothing like I thought it would be. And then, suddenly, it was over. I barely remember him walking me to my door, smiling at my dad when he actually *thanked* him for walking me home."

"He avoided me like the plague after that. I was hurt at first, but I still had stars in my eyes and believed he'd come around. Right up until the time I saw him back with Carla. Then I knew."

"You didn't tell anyone who the father was?"

"No. But his dad knew. Nathan must have told him. Once word got out about me being pregnant, he went out of his way to be kind to me. I think he was grateful that I didn't ruin Nathan's chance for a scholarship by publicly naming him as the father."

"What about you, Faith? What about your chances?"

"I was a nobody, Kieran. And I don't think

anyone believed my family would react the way they did. People of God and all that." She smiled sadly. "Unfortunately for me, my father was more of an Old Testament kind of guy than New Testament. Fire and brimstone over turn-the-other-cheek, if you know what I mean."

"I'd get envelopes with money sometimes," she said. "Sometimes they made the difference in whether or not we ate or had a warm bed to sleep in. There was never a name or a note, but I knew it was from Nathan's father. Sometimes he'd come by and ask to take Matt fishing, or to teach him how to shoot. I couldn't say no. He never told Matt who he really was, though. Neither did I."

They were silent for a long time. Faith kept her head against Kieran's chest, feeling the strong, steady beat of his heart beneath her cheek. His shirt was wet from where she had been crying against it.

"Does Matt ever ask about his father?"

"He used to. Not so much anymore. It's hard to explain what happened without hurting him or making him feel unwanted. I never lied, but I didn't provide details, either. I think he kind of figured things out for himself as he got older."

"He's an amazing kid."

"Yeah, he is."

"And you are an amazing woman, Faith." He kissed the top of her head. "I'm sorry you had such a hard time of it, but it brought you here, to me, and I can't say I'm sorry about that."

The strangest sensation rippled through Faith, a kind of humming that was centered deep in her chest and radiated outward. It was soothing and pleasant, just like the way Kieran's hand rubbed up and down her back. It felt so good to be in his arms, to soak up the warmth from his body and feel the rise and fall of his chest. Suddenly exhausted, she let her eyes drift closed.

* * *

Kieran knew by the heavy, even sound of her breathing that she had finally fallen asleep. He held her tenderly in his arms.

"No one will ever hurt you or Matt again, Faith." Kieran whispered the promise.

Chapter 14

Faith awoke feeling comfortably cozy and unusually rested, not to mention hungry. It was only when she attempted to stretch that she realized she was not on her bed at all, but sprawled across an expanse of warm male flesh. Kieran lay beneath her, his arms protectively at her waist, sound asleep.

She took the rare opportunity to study him closely. There was a dark shadow of stubble gracing his cheeks and the underside of his jaw; his hair was splayed like wild black silk over the arm of the sofa. In sleep, his youthful face looked even more so, so peaceful and angelic.

So impossibly *good.*

As if he sensed her watching him, he opened his eyes without giving any other indication that he was awake. Faith sucked in a breath. She didn't know if she'd ever get used to the power in those eyes.

"Comfortable?" she asked with a little smirk.

Kieran's fingers flexed at her waist. "Very."

She propped herself up on his chest. "You're still here."

* * *

Fighting to withhold his sigh, he studied her face. How could she not see it? She was such a beautiful, intelligent, caring woman, yet she seemed either unwilling or incapable of believing that he wanted nothing more than to be with her. Damn those that ever made her view herself as anything less than the gift she was.

"Is there a reason I shouldn't be?"

Her eyes clouded. "I thought once you knew, you might feel differently."

Kieran pulled her up and over his body until she was nose to nose with him. "Well, you're right about that," he breathed. His hand cupped the back of her head, bringing her to him for a searing kiss. He was beyond trying to explain it to her with words alone. He would just have to show her.

"I'm sick," she protested weakly when he allowed her a short break to breathe.

"I don't care," he mumbled, nibbling her lower lip.

"I'll get you sick, too."

There was no hesitation. "Then you can take care of me."

Her eyes softened, and her body melted into his. "I can do that."

"I'm in love with you, Faith O'Connell," he said. He hadn't meant to just blurt it out like that, but apparently parts of his brain had had more than enough of his 'be-a-good-friend-until-she-realizes-what-she-is-to-me plan'. They decided to conspire against him and get on with it already. His cock, feeling impossibly thick and hard beneath all her soft female heat, was totally on board with that. His heart and lungs froze, no doubt waiting to see what would happen next.

Faith's eyes widened and she sat up, straddling his midsection. He couldn't stop his abs from rippling and contracting beneath her inner thighs and other, far more sensitive places. Her hands flattened against his chest, the one currently exposed to her short nails. Kieran closed his eyes lest she see the stark, raw hunger she was inciting with such actions.

"You love me?" she blinked in disbelief.

There was no sense denying it now. He could try to minimalize it, but more parts were ganging up on him. They wanted her. Now.

"Yes," he confirmed, his voice lower and huskier than usual. The Eeyore pajama bottoms were worn thin enough that he could feel her feminine heat resting just above what was fast becoming one of his hardest erections ever, and he swore if she continued to paw his chest with her little tiny claws he could not be held responsible for his actions.

At least she wasn't running. If anything, she seemed genuinely surprised by his blurted admission. Stunned, even.

“Since when?” she asked.

Kieran’s hands flexed around her hips in an attempt to keep her still. Every breath caused the subtlest of motions where their bodies met, but it was enough to have him worried. He’d gone so long without relief that the anticipation alone might unman him.

“I think from the first time I saw you,” he said honestly. “But I knew for sure that day when you held my hand at the Open House.”

Her eyes widened and she shifted her weight. “And you’re just telling me this now?”

He closed his eyes and tried to fight the compulsion to roll her over and claim her as his body demanded. She was sick. Her body needed to heal, and she needed time to adjust to the bombshell he’d just dropped on her. His mind parroted the same phrases back to him over and over again as he struggled to regain some semblance of control.

“You weren’t ready to hear it before. Now you are.” It sounded good. He wasn’t about to admit that he’d simply been too afraid to tell her for fear of scaring her away.

Faith stared deeply into his eyes, searching. Her fingers curled again, though she didn’t seem to be aware of it; he was fairly certain she didn’t realize her inner thighs were contracting on either side of his hips, either.

He was, though. He liked it. Too much. Didn’t she know that every minute of every day she owned another piece of him? God, he couldn't wait until he felt those nails scoring his back, those legs wrapped around him in blind, mindless passion.

"You sound very sure of that," she said.

She didn't believe him; doubt clouded her soft gray eyes.

"I am. Because now I know you feel the same way." His voice, growing huskier with each passing moment beneath her, was almost a growl.

She stilled above him. Fear and disbelief etched her features, and he knew with absolute certainty that he had been right. Faith knew there was something special between them. What he didn't know was why she was so afraid to admit it.

"And how do you know that?" she asked, her voice a frightened whisper.

"Because," he said gently, needing her to understand this if nothing else, "you never would have trusted me with the truth if you didn't. If you didn't want more, there would have been no reason to tell me any of that."

She remained perfectly still as she processed that. The feel of her beneath his hands was distracting. With much difficulty he pried his fingers from her hips and propped his hands beneath the back of his head, daring her to disagree. It was a risk letting go of her like that, but he wanted her to know, and to accept, that the next move was hers.

He watched in awe as several emotions flitted across those expressive gray eyes even as her facial expression remained relatively neutral. Fear, followed by surprise, then acceptance. He would always know what she was thinking by her eyes.

After several moments, those little claws flexed again and he saw a sparkle in her eye that hadn't been there before. The knowledge that he had been the one to put it there turned half of his mouth into a decidedly masculine smirk.

"You're very arrogant," she said with a twist of her lips. "I haven't seen this side of you before."

His smirk became a full-fledged grin. "I can be very arrogant when it comes to you, Faith. Simply knowing you love me makes me feel invincible."

* * *

Faith couldn't quite wrap her mind around that. Surely she was dreaming, an erotic, romantic fantasy brought on by her recent fever. It must have returned with a vengeance while she was napping.

He certainly *felt* real enough, all warm and hard beneath her.

Some unseen barrier between them had been breached, and there was no going back. She needed time to process it. Faith couldn't fully accept Kieran's declaration any more than she could accept what was in her own heart, but she couldn't bring herself to openly offer resistance to his presence or the things he tried to do for her, not after he'd said *those* words.

So she said nothing. To his credit, neither did he. He seemed to understand. He didn't pressure her for the same words, or even validation, and she was grateful for that.

They snuggled on the couch and watched some DVDs together. She caught Kieran snooping through her sketchbook when she went to take a bath, but was secretly pleased when she saw him smiling as he turned the pages.

He made a couple of business-related phone calls, too. Faith tried in vain to suggest that he should go take care of whatever he needed to, that she'd be fine, but he refused to leave her, saying he could take care of everything he needed to over the phone.

He waited on her hand and foot, ensuring she drank enough fluids and rested, even making her soup and tea throughout the day. She couldn't remember ever feeling quite so pampered. As unfamiliar as it was, it was also very nice.

After several hours of resisting Kieran – something that proved to be impossible under such an onslaught of tender care – she finally gave in and just tried to enjoy it. For more than two months, Kieran had been a constant presence in her life - always helping, listening, making her laugh. In the past two days, Kieran had shown Faith more gentle care than anyone ever had.

And he'd told her he loved her.

Maybe that's why Faith invited him to share

her bed that night. It had been a big decision on her part, but it was the natural progression of things. Not that Kieran seemed to be expecting anything. Other than that earth-moving kiss he'd given her earlier, he'd done nothing to pressure her into anything further than snuggling beneath a blanket. He wanted to, at least physically; there was no mistaking the blatant evidence of his arousal. And as she had such strong feelings for him, it seemed like the right thing to do.

He agreed easily enough, sliding in behind her fully-clothed, but made no move to do anything further. His arm came around her waist and pulled her body against his. She waited, holding her breath, expecting his hand to caress a few inches above or below where it splayed across her abdomen; to feel light kisses along the sensitive skin of her neck or the grind of his hardened length against her backside. Yet he did none of that, settling her in to fit all of his hard planes and dips and nothing more.

"Kieran," she asked in the darkness. "Don't you want to…?" She let her question hang in the air; she couldn't bring herself to say the words. The invitation had been her not-so-subtle hint. Perhaps he had misunderstood?

"More than you can possibly imagine," Kieran breathed, his breath a sensual caress behind her ear. He pulled her closer, pressing his hips against her so there would be no doubt. "But you're not ready for me yet, Faith."

Her body didn't agree, screaming protests in the form of a radiating ache deep in her center, but her inner self – the one who guarded the securely locked chamber of her deepest thoughts and feelings - was nodding emphatically.

"You seem very certain of me," she said.

"I am," he said simply, without a trace of arrogance. "You are my *croie*, Faith, and I am yours. I will always be able to sense what you are feeling, even if I don't know your exact thoughts. You will be able to do the same for me, but first you must truly accept this connection we have between us. And when you do, it will be nothing less than magical. Until then, I will just hold you and try to convince you what you are to me."

His croie? Her? Earlier he had said he loved her, and that had been a revelation. But for him to say that she was his soul mate? That shook her to the very roots of her foundation. Love was fleeting, but soul mates implied a much deeper, unbreakable type of bond; one that, once forged, could never be broken.

She didn't know what to say to that. It seemed… unbelievable. Too much for her to even contemplate. And he was right. There was no way she could simply accept that and believe it. Not when he just blurted it out like that. Not when she was tucked in his arms, pressed against that fabulous physique that would scatter her thoughts on a good day.

And definitely not while her mind ran rampant with naughty fantasies arising from that especially large, rigid part of him currently nestled against her behind.

Yet he wouldn't take advantage of her, even though he could, easily. It was unnerving, in a way, that Kieran seemed to know more about what she needed than she did sometimes. And he was right. Though he claimed that he knew she loved him, she had not yet uttered the words herself. Hadn't confirmed them in any way, in fact, unless he saw her lack of resistance to his care as an unspoken affirmation of sorts.

The fact that it was true was completely irrelevant. She did love him. She'd come to that same, inescapable conclusion herself. So the question then became, why was she unable to say what she knew in her heart to be true? When she knew that is what he wanted to hear?

The answer was simple: she was afraid. Afraid of being wrong. Of opening herself up to love and hope and being devastated again. She had thought she loved Nathan Longstreet, but she had been wrong about that. It had been nothing more than an adolescent crush based on a handsome face and lies; the attention given to a naïve young girl by a privileged high-school star who saw her as a temporary, disposable fling. Stupidly, she had thought Nathan cared for her, too.

She had also believed that her family loved her enough to forgive her transgressions, to help and support her. Believed it right up until the time she came home from school to find a raggedy old cloth-covered suitcase packed with a few meager belongings waiting for her near the door and those words she would hear in her mind forever: *Get out. You are no longer welcome here, whore.*

Every time she had believed in love, she had been wrong.

Faith closed her eyes, but not before a single tear managed to escape. Nathan, she understood. After all, she had been the one to see things that weren't there. But her family? Your parents were supposed to love you no matter what. Weren't they?

She certainly loved her son, more than anything. There was nothing he could do, nothing he could ever say, that would change that. She would always be there for him, no matter what. Even if she had the chance to go back and change things, she wouldn't, because if she did, she wouldn't have Matt.

And, despite the circumstances, she had loved her baby from the very moment she realized she was pregnant. It had been a source of great contention between her and her father. When she refused to consider giving up her baby, he had reminded her of one of his favorite Biblical passages – where God commanded Abraham to offer his only son as a sacrifice. It was the right thing to do, he insisted. Penance for her sins. Proof of her devotion.

She'd said no then, and she'd say it again today. She offered a quick prayer of apology to God. She knew that if she was ever given the choice between helping her son and obeying the rules of the church, unlike her parents, she would pick her son every time. Somehow, she believed God understood that and loved her anyway, sins and all. How could she do any less for her child?

But what about Kieran? Did she love him?

Yes, of course she did. What she had felt – or thought she had felt – for Nathan all those years ago was nothing compared to what she felt for Kieran now, although the thought of Nathan still brought a lance of pain to her chest. Time and maturity had dulled it, but enough remained to haunt her and make her wonder if she would ever truly get past the hurt and humiliation of Nathan's rejection and outright denial that the baby she'd carried was his.

Did she believe that Kieran loved her? If she was truthful, yes. It made no sense to her why he would, but she believed that he did.

So what was the problem? Why wasn't her heart singing in joy instead of cautiously peering around the corner, scared of what might happen next?

You know why, that little voice said inside her. *Because eventually he's going to figure out that you're not good enough for him.* Nathan's rejection had been difficult. Her family's casting out, even more so. But if she gave her heart fully to Kieran and he decided one day that he no longer wanted it, it would destroy her.

Even now, the very thought of it manifested as a sharp physical ache deep in her chest. She needed something – anything – to distract her from it.

"Kieran," she whispered quietly, even though she sensed he was every bit as awake as she was. She'd replayed the entire day over in her mind, not wanting to forget a single moment of it. It was then that she realized that while Kieran had spoken of his brothers, his father, his sisters-in-law, cousins, nieces, and nephews, he had never once mentioned his mother. Somehow, she sensed it was a significant omission.

"Hmmmm?"

"Tell me about your mother."

Right away she knew she had been right; this was a sensitive topic for him. His arm flexed, holding her tighter, squeezing as if she was a life-sized teddy bear. Faith didn't mind; it made her feel cherished. If holding her comforted him, all the better.

"She's been gone a long time," Kieran said quietly.

"She passed?"

Faith tried to turn around to see his face, but Kieran kept her where she was, resting his chin on her head. She settled against him and stroked his arm. If it was easier for him this way, so be it. The idea of taking care of this man, of doing anything for him, really, was appealing on a level that scared her.

"I don't remember much. More feelings than actual memories, if that makes any sense."

It did. Images faded, but the memories of how someone made you *feel* never did. They were so much more powerful than fleeting, tactile impressions, encompassing more than a single sense or two. A perfect example of that was that no matter what happened, Faith would never forget how she felt at that very moment, safe and warm in Kieran's arms.

"How old were you?"

"Almost six." Deep in her chest, her heart ached for him as an image of Kieran as a little boy rose in her mind. A sweet, caring child who lost his mother.

"What happened?"

"Pneumonia," he said so softly she could barely hear him, despite the fact that he was so close she could feel his breath caressing her cheek. "It was a bad winter. Everyone was sick – my dad, all my brothers, me. She took care of all of us. None of us realized that she was sick, too. Not until it was too late."

"I'm so sorry, Kieran." Faith suddenly had a greater understanding of why Kieran had been so adamant about staying around and helping her, hovering over her like a mother hen when she just had a case of the flu.

"Thank you." He squeezed her a little tighter. "I see how you are with Matt, and it reminds me of how she used to make me feel. Loved. Safe. Adored."

He couldn't have spoken sweeter words to her. She sensed the pain and grief he still held deep inside, as well as something else, too: fear.

"Is that why you're here with me now, Kieran? Because you're afraid the same thing might happen to Matt that happened to you?"

He was quiet for so long she didn't think he'd answer. "When I saw you on the floor, pale and sick…" Kieran let the sentence hang, unwilling to give voice to the memories that haunted him. His arms tightened around her. "I won't let anything bad happen to you, Faith." His words, as softly spoken as they were, held all the weight of a steel promise.

Was he thinking of Matt? Or of himself? Maybe, she thought, if she was truly blessed, a little of both.

She tried again to turn in his arms. This time he allowed it. She cupped his face with her hands. She heard him draw in a breath, waiting for her to say it. *I love you, Kieran.* The words were there, on the tip of her tongue, but she couldn't speak them. She knew if she did, it would make him happy.

If she did, he would make love to her and ease that horrible ache that was beginning to extend far beyond the physical. If he took her now, he would want to claim not just her body, but also her heart and soul.

But no matter how much she might want to give them to him, she just couldn't. Not yet.

Several moments ticked by in awkward silence before his barely audible sigh. "Go to sleep, Faith," he commanded softly, kissing her forehead before he tucked her beneath his chin.

"Pleasant dreams, Kieran."

She felt, rather than saw him smile. "Pleasant dreams, Faith."

Chapter 15

Matt arrived home the next day, and things returned to normal. Well, almost. Kieran was a greater presence in their lives, spending as much free time with them as Faith would allow. Faith didn't resist him quite as much when he tried to do things for them, although she was still quite adamant about paying for things herself. That irritated Kieran to no end, but she was immovable on that point. He was hesitant to do anything that might negate some of the progress they'd made, especially since she was including Kieran in just about everything they did, from nightly dinners to weekend chore runs. It was all very comfortable and domestic.

Like they were a real family.

"Are you and my mom, uh, …?" Matt finally blurted out one night. Kieran looked across the table to find the normally friendly face looking pinched and uneasy. Faith had run a quick errand, leaving the two of them in the house alone.

Matt squirmed uncomfortably under Kieran's steady gaze, but to his credit, didn't look away. Normally Kieran wouldn't even think of discussing his and Faith's physical relationship (or lack thereof) with Matt, but he understood the kid's need to know where things stood. More importantly, Kieran wanted him to know what his intentions were, because they would affect Matt greatly.

"No," Kieran said finally. Truthfully. "But I am very much in love with her."

The relief in Matt's features was obvious, though his eyes did widen at Kieran's open confession. Then a frown creased his youthful brow. "Does she know?"

Kieran's lips thinned a little. "I've made my feelings clear to her, yes."

"And?"

"And what?" Kieran grumbled almost irritably, sitting back and running his hand through his hair. The truth was, he was trying to figure that out himself. Several weeks had passed since his confession, and while Faith was no longer actively pushing him away, they hadn't made significant progress forward, either.

She had yet to say the words he longed to hear, even though he *knew* she loved him. It was hidden in her softly spoken words, in her eyes when she looked at him, and in the quiet way she included him in their daily lives.

He wouldn't trade any of that. But he wanted more. Each day his physical need to join with her grew. Over the past several years, he'd watched his brothers go through similar periods. He understood that it was all part of the natural progression of things. Although, he thought wryly, they all seemed to have better success of getting their *croies* into their beds.

Maybe that was what they needed to get past this plateau. Maybe once she felt the magic he knew they would create together it would chase the last of doubts from her mind. He'd been extremely patient. Maybe too patient. Perhaps she needed a little nudge. A little romance…wine, dinner, flowers, a private room at the Goddess…

"What did she say?" Matt asked, interrupting Kieran's train of thought. Kieran's blue eyes flashed, and Matt seemed to understand. He exhaled, as if he, too, was frustrated by his mother's lack of action. "Yeah, she's like that. Are you going to ask her to marry you?"

Yes. Without question. Once she accepts who and what she is to me. Yet he didn't feel like getting into a discussion about *croies* with young Matt just yet. The boy was just beginning to fully enter the realm of female awareness, he couldn't be expected to grasp that concept. Hell, Kieran was twenty-eight and the very idea of being inexorably linked to another soul left *him* dizzy.

Instead, Kieran posed a question of his own. "How would you feel about it if I did?"

Matt sat back in his chair and seemed to give it serious consideration for several long minutes.

"I think I'd like it," he said finally. "I mean,

you're cool. And I'm pretty sure she's in love with you, too."

Yeah, Kieran thought so, too. Faith seemed to be the only one not readily accepting of that fact.

"Plus," Matt continued logically, "you make her happy."

"Do I?" Kieran wondered, though he hadn't meant to say so out loud.

Matt rolled his eyes. "Duh."

Kieran sighed. Hearing Matt say so (sort of) made him feel slightly better, but then what was holding her back? The truth was, things were more complicated than that. Loving her and making her happy obviously wasn't enough.

"You make it sound so simple."

"Well, it is, isn't it?" Matt asked. "At least it should be, anyway. You've got to make her see that, Kieran. I don't think anyone else could." Matt's voice grew quieter. "She doesn't think I know, but I do. All the shit she puts up with, just so we have food on the table and a place to sleep. How she pretends to eat, but doesn't so there's more for me. It hasn't been easy, but she made it work. She's sacrificed too much. And she's too smart to spend the rest of her life cleaning up after other people. She needs a chance, Kieran. She needs *you*. You are the only one I've ever seen her listen to."

Kieran was floored by Matt's insight, and by the depth of his feelings on the matter. Weren't teenagers supposed to be too self-absorbed to notice things like that? Then again, Matt was no normal teen. He had Faith for a mother. Kieran felt a surge of pride for the boy.

"When did you get so smart, anyway?"

Matt smirked, and the cocky teenager was back. "Adults," he said, shaking his head, making Kieran chuckle.

* * *

The knock at the door surprised her. Very few people came to visit. Matt was at *BodyWorks* with Kieran working on his next belt, and she had the place to herself for a few hours.

"Hi, George," Faith said when she saw the older man on her porch. Looking quite sharp in the navy blue knee-length shorts and light blue cotton shirt that comprised the standard warm-weather uniform of the US Postal Service, he smiled warmly. His eyes matched the color of his shirt, and his short-trimmed hair was snowy white beneath his cap.

Faith didn't get to see him often. He usually left the mail in the box up along the roadside, but if Faith was working outside when he came by, he'd stop and chat for a few moments. She suspected it had something to do with the iced tea or lemonade and cookies she always offered him, but she didn't mind. George was one of those people who knew how to be friendly without being intrusive.

"I've got a certified letter here for you, Faith. I'll need you to sign for it."

Faith looked at the envelope, a plain white 8.5 by 11 number, her blood chilling when she saw the name of the law firm and the return address: *Longstreet & Son, Athens, Georgia.*

"Thanks, George," she said, signing the electronic receipt with the stylus he held out for her, glad to see that her hands weren't shaking too much for the task. Remembering her manners, she asked, "Would you like some sweet tea? I have a batch of sugar cookies I just took out of the oven, too."

"Thanks, but not today, Faith. I'm running a little behind; my knee's acting up again. But if it's not too much trouble, I'll take a couple of those cookies for my wife. She loves them. Which reminds me – I'm supposed to ask you for the recipe."

"I'll write it up and leave it in the box tomorrow," she said automatically as she slid a dozen or so cookies into a plastic container, then put a couple into his hand.

"That would be great, Faith, thanks."

Faith remained frozen to the spot for several minutes after George left. The envelope felt like a hundred pound weight in her hand. She held it away from her by the tips of her fingers as if it might suddenly grow teeth and snap at her. What in the world would Nathan's family law firm be sending to her?

She laid the letter on the table, her mind racing. It couldn't be good, whatever it was. Anything to do with lawyers usually wasn't, and anything that had to do with Nathan *definitely* wasn't. All the times his father had gotten in touch with her, he'd done so discreetly. Ethan Longstreet would never contact her through his business.

She tossed it onto the table and went about making some hot tea to give her hands something to do and chase away the sudden chill that seemed to settle in her bones despite the unseasonably warm weather. Maybe she shouldn't have accepted it. Maybe she should have refused to sign for it. What would have happened then? What if she simply refused to open it? Would they send another?

She was still staring at the envelope two hours later when Kieran and Matt came through the door. Their laughter sounded loud and foreign after sitting in the silence for so long.

"Mom, what's wrong?" Matt asked the moment he saw her face. What could she tell him? *Oh, it's nothing, dear. Just that I received a certified letter from the father you've never known and has never tried to contact you.*

She opted for cautious honesty. "I'm not sure, really. This came in the mail today."

Matt looked at the envelope. "Longstreet & Son Legal?" The name held no meaning for him, but he knew enough to sense that anything with

"Legal" in the name probably wasn't good. "What is it?"

"I don't know. I haven't opened it yet." Faith felt Kieran's eyes on her. Knew that he recognized the name even if Matt didn't.

"You have to open it, Mom."

"I know."

"Do it now, while me and Kieran are here." Even though she was a wreck, Matt's words made her heart swell. Protecting her, comforting her, even though she was the parent. And including Kieran, as if he understood how much he had come to mean to her.

She nodded, her fingers shaking so much as she tried to peel apart the sealed lip that she gave herself a paper cut. Before the blood could soak through the expensive vellum stationary, she handed it to Kieran. "Would you mind?" she asked, reaching for a tissue to wrap around her finger.

Kieran extracted two items – a long, rectangular, legal-size envelope also bearing the name of the firm, and a smaller note-sized one, hand-written and addressed to Faith. Faith regarded both as if they might bite her.

"Start with the official-looking one," she said. Kieran nodded and opened the legal letter. His expression gave nothing away as he scanned the paper. Faith didn't even realize she was holding her breath until he folded it back into thirds and slipped it into the envelope.

"It's a notification that you and Matt have been named as beneficiaries in a will."

"Who's will?"

Kieran met her eyes meaningfully. "Ethan Longstreet." Faith's face softened. "Oh, no. Not Ethan."

"Old Ethan?" Matt asked, a frown on his face. "The guy that used to take me fishing?"

Faith nodded. "What did he leave stuff to us for?" Matt asked.

Because he's your grandfather. "I think he wanted you to remember him. You two always seemed to have a good time together."

"Yeah, we did," Matt agreed. He looked at Kieran. "Does it say how much?"

"Matt!" Faith scolded. "It doesn't matter! What matters is that he remembered you. Have a little respect."

Looking properly abashed, Matt apologized. "I'm sorry, Mom. You're right."

"Actually, Faith," Kieran said, his face unreadable. "I think it might matter in this case."

"Why?" she asked, though the sinking feeling in her stomach already presented her with a possibility.

"Because he left you one million dollars and his son is contesting it."

"Holy shit," Matt breathed. Faith couldn't even bring herself to admonish him for it, not when the same words were sounding in her own mind.

"One *million* dollars?" Faith whispered.

Kieran nodded. *Oh, Ethan*, she thought. *What have you done?*

Kieran handed her the small, sealed envelope with her name written across the front. "This is addressed to you. It looks personal."

Faith looked at it, recognizing Ethan's scrawling script. At least it wasn't from Nathan.

Dearest Faith,

Yesterday I was told by a snot-nosed doctor barely old enough to shave that I have a particularly aggressive form of cancer, and that I should start getting my affairs in order as soon as possible. I told him that I am pretty aggressive, too, but he doesn't seem to think I have much of a chance.

If you are reading this, it means that he was right and I was wrong. I hate being wrong.

I didn't want to tell you, not when you and Matt are so excited about starting a new life. I wish I could have been a part of it. I'm sorry I wasn't there more for the two of you. You are raising a fine boy, Faith. I'm grateful for the time you allowed me to spend with him. You are a good woman. I would have been proud to call you my daughter.

Nathan will no doubt pitch a fit, but these are my final wishes. He doesn't know about the cancer yet, but it's inevitable that he will soon.

It is my hope that I can do for you in death that which I did not have the courage to do in life. I know that you and my grandson will make good use of it.

Ethan Longstreet

Tears were rolling down her face by the time she finished. She didn't even think of protesting when Kieran pulled her into his arms.

"Mom? What does it say?"

When Faith didn't answer, Matt carefully took the letter and read it for himself. Faith didn't stop him. He was old enough to know.

"He was my grandfather?" he asked quietly. There was none of the anger or hurt in his voice that she would have expected.

"Yes," she answered, her voice thick.

Matt nodded. "I kind of figured," he said, surprising her. "And this guy he mentions – Nathan. He's my dad, isn't he?"

"Yes."

"Will you tell me?" Matt asked, pinning Faith with soft gray eyes so like her own. It was a reasonable request, and one long overdue.

She looked at him, at her beautiful son, with his dark coppery hair and velvety gray eyes. Those he had gotten from her, but in everything else, he took after his father. Matt was a big kid, taller and broader than most kids his age. Spending the last couple of months with Kieran only developed him further. The varsity coaches were already chomping at the bit, trying to coax him onto every sports team they had. He was so much like Nathan that way.

"Yes," she answered.

And so she told him the tale of how a naïve young girl became involved with an older boy, star-struck and blinded by romantic notions and misinterpretations. She didn't go into excruciating detail, but she didn't sugar coat it, either.

As hard as it was to confess her sins in front of her son, it was even harder to try to explain how his father wanted no part of them. Matt listened quietly, his normally expressive face showing interest but not giving away any of his inner feelings. He asked a few questions, which Faith answered honestly and to the best of her ability.

When she had finished, a heavy silence fell over the room. She glanced at Matt, trying to get a read on his feelings, but it was hard to glean anything from his neutral expression. He seemed neither angry nor hurt as she might have expected, but thoughtful, as if he was sorting through it all.

"I need to think about this. I'm going up to my room," Matt announced suddenly, grabbing his backpack and starting up the stairs.

"Matt - " Faith called after him, but Kieran gave her hand a gentle squeeze. "Let him go, Faith," he said quietly. "He needs some time to assimilate this. It's a lot to take in."

Faith nodded, knowing it was true, but longing for the time when Matt would have sought comfort in her arms. He was growing up, and it was hard to accept that a hug and a cookie wasn't enough to ease him anymore. Hadn't been for a long time, she realized.

Faith sank into the chair and put her head in her hands. "Have you eaten?" Kieran asked softly.

She shook her head. The sun had long since set. The crock pot filled with chicken and vegetables still simmered on low, the tray of fluffy biscuits still waiting for its turn in the oven. Kieran kissed the top of her head and rose. He slid the tray into the oven, then filled the old-fashioned tea kettle with water and set it on the stove.

Before long the kettle whistled and Kieran fixed a cup of tea for her, using the special blend Maggie had prepared and gifted her with weeks earlier. He knew it was her favorite.

She offered him a grateful smile as he placed the mug in front of her. When he sat down and tugged her onto his lap, she didn't even think of resisting.

Faith leaned back upon this man who had become such an integral part of her life. He believed she was his soul mate. Warmth curled through her, and for the first time, she realized that he was hers as well. She could no longer imagine her life without him in it, nor did she want to.

But no matter how far or fast she ran, she would never escape her past. It would always be there, looming over her like a great shadow. For a little while, she'd managed to fool herself into thinking that she might be able to outrun it by moving away from all that she knew, and, more importantly, from everyone that knew her. By making a fresh start with a new job in a new place with a new home and new friends. Hoping against hope that she could bury her mistakes and let them rest in peace.

As if anything could really be that easy.

She felt the strong, steady beat of Kieran's heart against her side. God help her, she was so in love with him. But while she might be able to finally admit that to herself, she could never admit it to him. Ever since he told her how he felt about her, her life had become an emotional thrill ride. High one minute from the thought that someone as wonderful as Kieran could care for her as more than a friend, low the next when she remembered that they were from two different worlds.

Did she love him? Yes, she thought, without question. Would she ever find anyone better? No, not a chance. Those questions were easy. But if asked from his point of view, the answers were a lot different.

Did he love her? He said he did. Kieran didn't have a deceptive bone in his body, so he probably believed it, too. But how much of that was because he wanted what his brothers had? She'd learned enough over the past few months to know that all of the brothers had found their wives during some unexpected circumstance, most of which involved the sudden appearance of someone new into their lives.

Maybe that's what Kieran had been looking for – someone new. Maybe it wasn't so much her as the fact that she fit the profile of circumstance – a young woman who happened to appear out of nowhere and face some kind of life challenge. Ever the knight, Kieran might see that as a sign. And he wanted to find his *croie* so badly that maybe the situation blinded him to the grim possibility that she wasn't it.

The second question was even more difficult. Would he ever find anyone better? The answer was unequivocally yes, and that was a bitter pill to swallow. She could offer him her love and fidelity, but that was about all.

It was a fact she was reminded of every time she took a good hard look around her. There were so many women who would be a better choice for him. Women who had more than their GED.

Women who had better than blue collar jobs, who made more than minimum wage cleaning up after the wealthy. Women who weren't forced to sometimes choose between eating and making the mortgage payment. Women who didn't have teenage sons to raise as their first priority.

As difficult as they'd been, the last few months had also been some of her happiest. But now she had to face facts, and the biggest one was that Kieran deserved so much better.

And she would never survive the day he woke up and finally realized the same thing.

As if on cue, the oven timer went off. Faith reluctantly slid from his lap, aware of the proof of his arousal as she did so. Another reason she had to end this. He wanted a whole lot more than she could give him.

It wasn't that she didn't want to. Lord knew, the man had a way of making every feminine part of her sit up straight and put their hands in the air shamelessly vying for his attention. But despite her feelings for him, despite the powerful feelings of desire he awoke in her, the thought of being intimate with him scared her senseless. The one and only time she'd been with a man had been, at best, uncomfortable, not to mention downright painful and humiliating. While she was fairly certain things would be much different with Kieran, she couldn't take that chance.

Not to mention that inviting him to her bed was

probably not the best way to push away.

Then again, it had worked with Nathan.

Which led inevitably to the next thought: what if she got pregnant again?

Unaware of the inner battles waging between her heart and her head, Kieran was by her side, pulling out shallow bowls, grabbing some silverware and a tub of butter from the fridge. Faith tipped the biscuits into a bowl and covered them with a heavy linen napkin, then ladled them each a bowl, putting significantly more into Kieran's than hers.

"What do you want to do about that?" Kieran asked, inclining his head toward the envelope. She said a silent prayer of thanks that he hadn't guessed her thoughts. So many times it seemed like he knew what she was thinking before she could puzzle it out.

Her shoulders sagged. Thinking all of those depressing thoughts about putting distance between her and Kieran had temporarily blocked Nathan's legal notice from her mind.

"What are my choices?"

"Well," Kieran said thoughtfully, "I think we should have Shane take a look at the papers."

Faith nodded. It made sense. Shane was a lawyer, and a damn good one for all that she'd heard. His advice would be welcome, and as much as she hated to ask, there was no way she could afford a legal consultation with someone else.

Kieran made a quick phone call while Faith took a tray up to Matt. Within an hour, Shane and Lacie were in her living room, with Shane pouring over the documents.

"Well?" Kieran finally asked when Shane neatly refolded the papers and put everything back into the larger envelope.

Shane leaned forward, his forearms on his knees. Lacie placed her hand on his shoulder in a silent show of support. "Basically, Faith has two options. She can sign a release refusing the bequeathal, or she can try to claim it."

"Why would she refuse it?" Kieran asked immediately.

Shane exhaled. "Nathan Longstreet claims that his father was intentionally misled into believing that Matt was his grandson, and that the terms of his will were predicated on a falsehood and therefore not valid. Faith can sign the waiver, which in effect says that Matt is not a direct blood descendent of Ethan Longstreet, and thus has no legal claim on any of his holdings."

Some of the color drained from Faith's face. Did Nathan really believe that she would be capable of doing such a thing? That she would deliberately deceive an old man into thinking he had a grandson simply to get her hands on some of his money? The very thought that anyone could think that of her made her feel slightly ill.

"That's bullshit," Kieran said firmly, rallying

on her behalf. "Faith would never lie about something like that."

Shane nodded as if he agreed. "If Faith refuses to sign the waiver, then Nathan demands proof of her claim before releasing the holds he's placed on Ethan's personal assets."

"Proof?"

Shane's lips thinned. "Matt will be required to undergo a paternity test to prove that Nathan is the father."

"So?" Kieran asked. "Mick can do that." But Shane was shaking his head.

"It's more complicated than that, Kier. Nathan's motion specifically states that the test must be performed by a certified, non-biased agent, and offers three acceptable choices, all located in Georgia."

Faith, who had been quiet up to this point, cleared her throat. "Then he's already won," she said, her voice too calm. "He must know I can't afford to travel back to Georgia to have the tests done."

"Don't worry about that," Kieran said. "We'll get you there if that's where you need to be."

Faith was about to argue, but Shane spoke again. "You might not want to."

"Why not?" Kieran demanded. "It's about time the bastard did right by his son."

"Therein lies the problem. If Faith proves that Matt is indeed Nathan's son, then he might be able to claim some parental rights himself. Visitation, custody, - ”

“NO!” Faith said vehemently, shooting to her feet. “Give me the waiver. I’ll sign it right now.”

“But Faith - ”

“No!” she repeated, searching frantically for a pen. “One million dollars is nothing compared to losing my son. We’ve made it just fine without him or his money. He can keep it, and shove it right up his arrogant - ”

“Mom.”

Faith looked up in horror to discover Matt sitting at the base of the stairs.

“Matt! How long have you been sitting there?”

“Long enough.” He stood, looking much older than he had only a few hours ago. “Don’t sign anything yet, Mom.”

“Why not? I have no intention of putting you through that, Matt. No amount of money in the world is worth that.”

“I don’t care about the money, Mom,” Matt said carefully. “I’ve thought about it and… I want to meet him.”

“What?!” Blood turned to ice in her veins at the very thought. She would *not* lose her boy.

“I want to meet him,” Matt repeated evenly, watching her with guarded eyes. “I want to see him for myself.”

“Absolutely not. I forbid it.”

He smiled, and Faith wondered exactly when

her son had acquired Kieran's smirk. "He can't hurt me, Mom. And he could never take me away from you." He looked at Shane. "He couldn't, could he?"

Shane looked thoughtful. "By law, he could claim certain rights as your biological father. As a lawyer, he would know this."

"But we live in Pennsylvania now."

"True, but he could petition for joint custody or at the very least, regular visitation." Shane hesitated. "There are ways, of course, to delay things, drag them out over the course of several years until you turn eighteen and it becomes a non-issue."

"Absolutely not," Faith said again adamantly.

"But… to do so would also mean that Nathan has been shirking his responsibilities for a long time. I imagine the interest alone on fourteen years' worth of child support is staggering. It might make him a little reluctant to pursue something too aggressively. He's probably counting on the fact that Faith wouldn't know that, though."

"You can do that?"

Shane shrugged modestly. "There is some precedent for it."

Faith was shaking her head. "No. I don't want anything from him. Give me the paper."

"Mom, please." Matt's voice was so much more composed than hers. "I won't do the blood test if you don't want me to. And I'm okay with you signing the paper. All I'm asking is that you wait a couple of days."

"Why? What's going to change in a few days?"

Matt shifted his feet. "I want to meet him first."

All of the fight drained out of Faith; she felt numb. "Why, Matt?" she asked.

He shrugged. "I don't know. I just know it's something I have to do. You can understand that, can't you, Mom?"

Faith looked at her son. When had she lost her little boy and gained such a strong young man? She might not be accepted by her family anymore, but at least she knew who they were. She knew them enough to understand why they had made the decisions they had, even if she didn't agree with them. Didn't Matt deserve the same thing?

She sighed heavily. She had to do this. No matter how much she wanted to protect him, she had to face the fact that he was growing up and old enough to understand the situation. And damn it, he had a right to meet his father.

Matt was right. She wouldn't lose him by allowing him to meet Nathan. But if she forbid it, it might drive a wedge between them. At least this way, she could ensure she was right there with him.

"I suppose I can." What she didn't know was how she was going to make it happen. She'd have to take time off work; he'd miss school. Their car might not survive another trip down to Georgia and back; it was about a thousand miles each way, give or take, and she was already at the point where she offered up a silent prayer of thanks when it brought her safely home from work every day.

Lost in those thoughts, it was a while before she realized the Callaghans had it all figured out.

"Sean says he can fly you guys down Friday night," Shane said, tucking his mobile back into his pocket, "and have you back by Sunday night."

"What?" *Sean could fly a plane? He had a plane?*

"It's only a two hour flight," Kieran explained. "We'll have all day Saturday and most of the day Sunday."

"What?" *Kieran was going, too?*

Kieran offered her a patient smile and turned to Shane. "Want to come along?"

"I've always wanted to go down South," Lacie said with her usual gentle optimism. "See the big plantation mansions, maybe get some fresh peaches and Vidalia onions."

"Looks like that's a yes," Shane grinned, kissing Lacie's cheek. "Besides, if it's alright with Faith, I could act as her legal counsel." He looked expectantly at Faith; she barely heard him over the loud buzzing in her ears.

"Faith?"

She blinked, and Kieran laced his fingers with hers. "Of course it is. Right, Faith?" She looked at him blankly. "You'll let Shane handle the legal stuff, right?"

She blinked. He took that as a yes.

"Awesome. We'll meet you at the private airport Friday?"

"Yeah. Sean said to be there around six."

"Done."

"NO!" someone yelled, and Faith realized it was her. Everyone's eyes turned to her, surprised.

Kieran's face was a mask of concern. "Faith, what - "

"No," she said, shaking her head and taking a step backward. "No to all of it."

"But Faith - "

"No. No more hand-outs. No more charity." She looked at Kieran, trying to summon the courage to say what she had to say. "No more *anything*."

The silence was deafening as the meaning of Faith's words sunk in. "What are you saying, Faith?" Kieran asked.

"You know what I'm saying," she said, forcing the words out, praying she could hold back the bile in her throat at what she was doing. "We can't be your little cause anymore, Kieran."

The words tasted like acid in her mouth; the hurt in his eyes nearly had her on her knees. But this was for the best. She had to do it. For him as much as for her.

"You don't mean that." He whispered the words. "You can't mean that."

"I'm not who you think I am, Kieran. I can't be what you need. Stop wasting your time and find the one who can."

Matt stepped forward, his face just as stricken as everyone else's. "Mom, no. Don't do this… "

"Go to your room, Matt."

"But Mom - "

"I said go to your room! I am still your mother, and you will do as I say!"

Matt's eyes widened for a moment before he turned around and ran up the steps two at a time. Faith's hand came up over her mouth. She'd never once yelled at him like that before. A slight movement reminded her that she was not alone. Kieran was moving toward her slowly, as if she was a frightened animal. She put her hand up to stop him.

"Please. Just go."

She couldn't look at him anymore. Couldn't bear to see the look in his eyes and know that she had been the one to put it there. Sometimes doing the right thing was painful. That's how you knew it was the right thing. The wrong things, the bad things, they were always easy.

She walked past all of them into the kitchen, closing the door behind her. She heard the murmur of soft voices – Kieran's and Shane's and Lacie's. Then it was quiet again until she heard the sound of gravel as two vehicles made their way out of her driveway.

Chapter 16

Matt didn't speak to her for several days. That was okay. She didn't know what to say to him anyway. Her heart felt as if it had been shredded; but that was nothing new. There was enough precedent for her to know that she would survive it, no matter how much it felt otherwise.

Disappointment and heartache were part of life, and no amount of pretty words or good intentions could change that.

It was a hard lesson to learn, but Matt was strong. He'd make it. Even if he didn't understand it now, someday he would, and hopefully he'd be able to look back and know that she had done what was best. Someday he'd understand what it meant to love someone so much that you would sacrifice nearly everything for them.

She'd loved Matt that way from the moment she found out she was pregnant. He was a precious Gift, and everything else was second to that. She suspected she loved Kieran that way, too. It was exactly why she couldn't allow herself to be selfish. To constantly take and never be able to give back.

A few phone calls confirmed her initial thought

that she could not afford air fare to Georgia and back.

She cursed softly as she drove through Pine Ridge in search of a garage, alternately coaxing the wipers and the defroster in turns, since running both at the same time played havoc with the electrical system. The earlier warm front had long since moved on, plunging the temperatures back to where they should be.

Faith released a sigh of relief when she finally pulled into the brightly lit station. It was a testament to how distracted she was that she didn't realize who owned it until a large, muscular man with jet black hair and all-too-familiar blue eyes came out to speak to her. He looked exactly like Shane – if Shane had suddenly developed a badass attitude since the last time she'd seen him.

Sean Callaghan wiped the grease from his hands and walked into the customer waiting area, looking like a doctor forced to give bad news. Faith's eyes looked up when he entered, but the little bit of hope she had died quickly.

"Faith, right?"

She nodded. "Did it pass inspection?"

She knew it was a silly question, but she asked anyway. The look on his face said it all. His eyes darkened, and his jaw clenched as if holding back what he really wanted to say. But she had to hear the words.

"No, I'm sorry," he said.

And there they were.

Her hope faded, but she wasn't all that surprised, not really. She took a deep breath, straightened her shoulders and looked him right in the eye. "What will it take to make it passable?"

"A miracle," he said honestly. He started to explain when she held up her hand and stopped him. "I'm not a mechanic," she said. "In English, please."

He took a deep breath. Faith almost felt a pang of sympathy for him; he was clearly trying to soften the blow. She appreciated that, but in her opinion, it was better to just say it and get it over with.

"The only thing that's good for is the junk yard."

It wasn't the first time she'd heard that. The middle-aged fry cook she'd bought it from had said the same thing when his conscience nagged him at the last minute. So had every other mechanic she'd dealt with since. Despite their words of doom, they'd always been able to find a way to make it last a little longer. They didn't have all the shiny, fancy equipment Sean Callaghan did, so they'd had to get creative. But surely, with all this high-tech gadgetry he could do *something*.

"You can't fix it?"

He scratched the back of his head and exhaled. "I can, but it would be a hell of a lot cheaper to buy a new one. The truth is, I would have sold it for parts years ago."

"How much?" she persisted.

Sean named a figure that had her eyes widening. She swallowed hard. Blinked once. It would be cheaper to fly first-class to Georgia and back.

"Well, thank you, Mr. Callaghan," she said quietly, her face pale. "I appreciate your honesty."

She held her hand out for the keys. "Sorry, Faith," he said, sounding like he really was. "I can't let you drive that home."

"Excuse me?"

"It's not safe, Faith."

"But it's all I have," she sputtered before she could think better of it. "How will I get home? How will I get to work? How will I pick up Matt?"

"I have a loaner I could give you till you find something."

The words hit her like a slap across the face. It was charity. More charity. Just like all the home improvement materials. The labor. The MMA classes. Offers of flights to Georgia and free legal counsel.

And she was *so* done taking charity from these people. The trembling stopped, and she stood taller again. "No, thanks. How much do I owe you?"

Sean waved her off. "Nothing. I feel awful about - "

"*How much do I owe you?*"

"*Nothing.*" Sean stood up to his full height and crossed his arms over his chest. He towered over her, fixing her with a laser-like stare that told her he was used to being obeyed. Faith bit her lip, then reached into her purse for her wallet anyway.

* * *

Sean snorted, though he had to respect her spirit. There was no way he was taking money for telling Kieran's *croie* that her car was a piece of shit and confiscating the keys to the damn menace. He was going to have a word with his younger brother, though, for letting Faith and her son drive around in the screaming metal death trap in the first place. Oh, he'd seen where some minor repairs had been made – Kieran's doing, no doubt – but the truth was, the car was finished.

Had it been anyone else, Sean would have laughed. He could hardly believe the thing even made it down the mountain. If she had been a man, Sean would have ripped him a new one for being stupid enough to allow that deathtrap on the road.

He turned and went back into the bays, reasoning that she couldn't pay him if he wasn't there to take it. He'd call Kieran - he knew her best – and let him handle it.

* * *

Faith stared at his back as he walked away from her, stunned. At least until the anger began to overshadow everything else. She stomped right into Sean's office and looked at the posted rate charges. She figured he'd spent a good hour on the car. By emptying her wallet, her coat pockets, and every last purse compartment she scraped together enough for one hour of labor and left it on his desk, then turned and walked out.

No wonder pride was considered a deadly sin, she thought sometime later as she walked the five miles in the cold October rain back to her cottage. Hers just might kill her.

"Where the hell have you been?!" Matt shouted when Faith finally walked through the door.

"Can we talk about this a little later?" she said, struggling to speak through her chattering teeth. "I'd really like to get into something dry first." She ignored the urge to chastise him for his disrespect and language choice when she saw the stark fear in his eyes.

It took him a minute to realize that she was soaking wet and shivering. "Jesus, Mom," he said, following behind her as she headed straight for the stairs. "What happened? Are you alright?"

"Car trouble. And I'm fine. Just a little cold and wet at the moment." If she'd been thinking clearly, she might have realized that fall rain in Pennsylvania was a lot colder than fall rain in Georgia *before* she'd decided to walk home.

"Why didn't you call?"

In answer, Faith reached her hand into her

pocket (which wasn't easy because her fingers were numb) and extracted a thoroughly soaked cell phone, thrusting it into Matt's hands. Then she left him standing there as she closed the door to the bathroom and cranked up the hot water.

The cold had seeped so far into her bones that she didn't think she'd ever feel warm again, but a full tank of hot water later, she was feeling much better. Tugging on thick sweats, a t-shirt, a hoodie, and two pairs of Matt's sweat socks, she made her way back downstairs for some hot soup.

Faith found a steaming bowl waiting for her, as well as a cup of tea. Matt was just sliding his cell phone back into his pocket and spooning out some soup for himself. Judging by the way he attacked the rolls she'd made the night before, he hadn't eaten either.

She thanked him for getting supper on the table and sat down, physically and mentally exhausted. "I'm sorry you were worried," she said.

"What happened, Mom?"

Faith sighed. She'd never lied to Matt and she wasn't about to start now. "I took the car into town hoping to get it tweaked enough to make the trip to Georgia," she said with a hesitant smile when Matt's head jerked up. "But it turns out the old gal's on her last legs, and the mechanic said it wasn't safe to drive anymore."

"Sean said that?"

Of course Matt would know Sean Callaghan.

He knew all of the brothers. She nodded.

"So we don't have a car."

"No. I'm sorry, Matt." She looked at the soup, her appetite suddenly gone.

Matt was quiet for a long time. "We've been without a car before," he finally said. "But how will you get to work?"

She shrugged, having giving that a lot of thought on the long walk home. The Goddess was cut into the side of a mountain, and unless she suddenly developed leg muscles like the Callaghan men, she wouldn't be riding a bike there.

"I'll have to bum a ride from someone until I figure something out." It would kill her, but she'd find some way to pay them back. "But Matt, this means I won't be able to pick you up in town anymore."

"Kieran can bring me home."

"Matt, you can't take advantage of him like that," she said quietly.

A familiar fire lit his eyes, his chin lifted defensively. "He doesn't mind. And just because you don't want him around anymore doesn't mean that I don't."

"Matt… " She didn't finish what she was going to say. Matt was right. There was no reason for her to forbid Matt from seeing Kieran, especially as long as he continued to pay for his own classes. She sighed, forcing another spoonful into her mouth and trying to swallow past the lump in her throat.

"Alright. But just until I get us some new wheels." Which, judging by the way things were going, might happen around the same time Matt left for college.

Matt's phone vibrated again, the third time since they'd sat down. "No texting while we're eating," Faith said, reaching for the phone, but Matt was faster. "Who is that anyway?" she demanded, her eyes narrowing.

"Kieran," Matt said, scrolling down the message. "He wants to talk to you."

"Maybe later," she hedged. She had been avoiding him since the night she'd asked him to leave. She'd have to face him eventually, but not now. She was exhausted; she didn't have the strength to stand up against the force of nature that was Kieran, not when all it took was a look from those blue eyes to melt her defenses.

There was a knock at the door, and Faith sighed. She didn't have the strength for company, either.

"Get that, will you please, Matt?" Faith said, her voice weary. "Tell whoever it is to come back another time." She felt a slight pang of guilt at the uncharacteristic rudeness, but she knew her limits, and right now smiling and being neighborly was beyond her capabilities.

She heard Matt open the door and speak softly, then exhaled when she heard the door close again.

She rose to empty the remainder of her soup back in the pot for another time when she might be able to stomach it.

"Faith." Kieran's low voice rumbled through her as he stepped into the kitchen. "Are you alright?"

"Obviously," she snapped. He shouldn't be here. She hated that some part of her really liked the fact that he was. It was the same part that ached to run into his arms and tell him how much she missed him, how much she wanted to stop fighting these feelings she had for him and let him take care of everything.

But she couldn't. She'd lain awake every night going over and over it in her head. And by the time dawn rolled around, the conclusion was always the same: they were from completely different worlds. Her life had been a series of lessons, proving that it would never work.

"How did you get home?" he asked, unfazed.

"She walked," Matt said, exchanging a glance with Kieran as he resumed his seat at the table. He seemed to have gotten his second wind, tucking into another roll.

Faith didn't have to turn around to know that Kieran's eyes had narrowed and were now focused on her back. Apparently laser-vision was a genetic trait among the Callaghans.

"She did what?" Kieran's voice was whisper soft. Faith shivered; she didn't think she'd ever heard anything quite so menacing. Even Matt stopped chewing, his wide eyes looking from one to the other.

“What were you thinking, Faith?” Kieran asked, his voice still too soft, too even to be anything good.

“I was thinking that your brother wouldn’t let me drive my car home,” she hissed, turning around so quickly she felt lightheaded for a moment. As if it was Sean’s fault her car wasn’t even worth the price to tow it to the junkyard.

It wasn’t fair; she knew that, but in that moment all she cared about was releasing the ball of frustration and misery and heartache that had lodged in her chest and threatened to suffocate her if she didn’t do something. It had been building ever since that damn letter came.

“He offered you a loaner,” he said, confirming her suspicions that Sean probably called Kieran right after she left, no doubt to tell him how pathetic and stubborn she was. Maybe even to offer kudos to Kieran for getting out before it was too late.

“I don’t want your charity!” she practically yelled.

Kieran blinked, nonplussed. “Then why not at least call a cab or something? It would have only cost a couple of bucks.”

Her spine stiffened, proving to her once again that they came from completely different worlds. A couple of bucks might as well have been a hundred when she left every last dime she had on his brother's desk.

He ran his hand through his hair and blinked again as he read the answer in her eyes. "Jesus Christ, Faith. You could have called *me*."

"No, she couldn't," Matt interrupted, tossing Kieran the ruined cell. He looked at it as if he'd never seen such a thing before. A few more drops of water leaked from its innards, landing right on the tips of his size fourteen shoes.

"You were out wandering in the dark, in the rain, by yourself, without even a working phone?" If she thought his voice was dark before, it was doubly so now. The fact that he spoke through clenched teeth didn't help. It pissed her off.

"News flash, *Mr.* Callaghan," she said, feeling the heat rising within her. "Not all of us have Droids and a garage filled with Porsches and Jaguars and H2s. Not all of us own our own businesses and can come and go as we please. Not all of us can afford to be financially philanthropic. And those of us who can't do any of those things sometimes do whatever we have to *just to survive*."

Kieran snapped back like she had slapped him. Out of everything she'd hurled at him, one thing stood out. "Is that what you think? You think I'm here because I'm philanthropic?"

"No, not entirely," she said, her voice softer as the last of the wind left her sails. "I think you are an incredibly kind, generous man who wants something so desperately that he's willing to see it, even when it's not really there."

He stared at her, long and hard, as the seconds ticked into minutes, the muscles working in his jaw.

"Maybe you're right," he said finally. "Because if you were what I thought you were, you could never have said those words to me."

Without another word, Kieran turned around and walked out of the kitchen, taking the last remaining piece of Faith's heart with him.

Chapter 17

The weather turned cold faster than she had expected. At least she had a car with a working heater. She bought the old Buick from Mrs. Campbell, who said that it had been sitting in the garage since her late husband died. Thankfully, Mrs. Campbell had been willing to sell Faith the car on a "payment plan". To each installment, Faith added on a free housecleaning every two weeks.

It turned out to be a good thing. Mrs. Campbell raved about Faith's cleaning skills and soon Faith found herself turning away potential clients when nearly every night and every weekend was booked.

The downside was that between her job at the Goddess and cleaning houses, she had very little quality time to spend at home with her son. The upside was that she was so busy she barely had time to recognize her broken heart.

She hadn't seen or heard from Kieran since the night she'd walked home in the rain. She'd picked up a new Go phone, but she had the number changed to a local one. Not that she expected him to call. Why would he? Given the look in his eyes that last night, she didn't think she'd ever hear from him again.

Lacie stopped by a few times, but Faith couldn't bring herself to ask about Kieran, and Lacie didn't mention him.

By the end of November, Faith had saved enough to purchase two coach tickets to Georgia. The holidays made people generous. Between the tips she'd received from her personal clients as well as the rich and famous vacationing at the Goddess, she had more petty cash than she'd ever had at one time. It was enough to cover mid-week airfare for two, plus a night or two in a budget motel. Her hopes of getting Matt something nice for Christmas were dashed, but she was going to give him something he really wanted instead – a chance to meet his father.

When Matt came home, she was packing a small travel bag for each of them.

"No MMA tonight?" she asked, surprised to see him home so early.

"No," he said simply, but his steely tone immediately caught her attention.

"Why not?"

He shrugged, asking a question of his own. "What's with the bags?"

"I got us a red-eye into Atlanta tonight. We need to be at the airport by nine, and it's about a two hour drive from here, so we should leave about seven. Why no class tonight?"

"Atlanta? What about school?"

"I've already cleared it with your teachers. The rates are cheaper mid-week." She stood up and blew a lock of hair from her forehead. "Matt, what's going on with you and Kieran? Did he tell you that you can't take class anymore?" She didn't really believe Kieran would do such a thing, but she also knew Matt loved the classes.

"No," Matt said. "I just don't want to do it anymore, okay?"

"No, it's not okay. I thought you loved it."

"Things change."

"Matt."

"Leave it, Mom. Are we going to eat before we leave? I'm starving."

Faith looked up at her son. So tall, so proud. And stubborn enough that she would get no more from him until he was ready to share.

"I made a lot in tips last week," she said, dropping the subject for now. She'd have the next couple of days with him; hopefully he'd open up. "Maybe we could stop and grab something on the way."

He nodded, looking relieved when she didn't question him again. "Cool."

* * *

"You look like shit, Kier," Ian said as he stacked a few more mugs in the behind-the-bar freezer to frost up.

Kieran saw no reason to argue. Ian was right. That's what happened when you felt like your heart was ripped right out of your chest. It tended to affect things like eating and sleeping and working out. As it was, he could barely stand to make it through the day until he could get back to the Pub and try to numb the pain a little. He didn't have to worry about drinking and driving; all he had to do was manage the stairs to his room on the second floor when he'd had enough. He simply nodded and accepted the longneck Ian handed him.

"Still no word from Faith, huh?"

Even her name was a sharp dagger to his chest. How could he have been so wrong? "Nope."

ESPN played on the flat screens hung on each wall. Kieran glanced up occasionally, but he couldn't follow the game. He didn't care. None of it mattered.

"How's Matt handling all this?" Ian prodded.

Kieran took a long swig. "Don't know."

"What the hell?" Ian said, his voice low enough that the other customers didn't hear him. "You see the kid every day, don't you?"

"Not anymore. He quit."

"Why?"

"How the fuck should I know?" Kieran said, slamming his beer down hard enough to earn a few curious glances from the other patrons.

"You have to do something, Kier."

"Yeah, you're right." Kieran lifted the bottle to

his lips and drained it. "Give me another, will you?"

"No." It was Lexi's voice denying him, not Ian's. Kieran looked up and saw not the eyes of his brother's wife, but those of the scrawny little girl he'd befriended and taken under his protective wing so many years ago.

"Let it be, Lex," he warned.

"I don't think so." She stubbornly pulled herself up on the stool next to him. "White," she said, pointing at herself. "Rice," she said, poking him in the chest. "That's how I'm on you, Kier. At least until you talk to me and say something that makes sense."

Kieran looked pleadingly at Ian, who just put both hands up in the air and found something else to do at the other end of the bar.

"You're not going to go away, are you?" he said with a martyred look.

"Nope. So start talking."

Kieran remembered how he used to bully her into telling him what was bothering her. He liked it a lot better when he was the one pushing for info.

"You're a bully, anyone ever tell you that?" He couldn't completely stop the quirk at the corner of his lips.

"Ian tells me that all the time," she said, waving her hand and completely unrepentant. "And quit stalling. Why aren't you with your *croie*?"

Kieran clenched his teeth so hard he thought he

might have cracked a few molars. "I was wrong about that."

He was met with stunned silence. It was a few moments before Lexi could speak. "Are you saying that Faith is not your *croie*?"

"Yes." It was a hiss, not a word.

Lexi exchanged a concerned glance with Ian. He shook his head slightly. A Callaghan man was never wrong about his *croie*.

"So… Faith is not your *croie*," she said slowly.

His jaw flexed. "No."

"And you aren't missing her at all."

His knuckles whitened as he tightened his grip around the bottle. "No."

"And it doesn't bother you in the slightest that she's leaving for Georgia tonight?"

"N- *what?!?*"

"Lacie said she and Matt are headed down to Georgia."

"What the fuck for?"

She smirked. "Thought you didn't care."

"I … don't."

"Well, that's probably good then," she said, patting his forearm. "Because Lacie also said she's planning on meeting Matt's father tomorrow morning, and if you did care, it would probably be driving you batshit crazy right about now."

Kieran let a vile curse fly from his lips, and the next second he was on his feet.

"You are an evil woman," Ian growled into her

ear a moment before he nipped it. “You make me so fucking hard.”

Lexi laughed as they watched Kieran’s fast-retreating form disappear toward the stairs that led to their private living area.

Kieran fired up one of the computers in Ian’s “office”, his fingers working magic across the keyboard as he logged into the secure FAA site. Ian might be the acclaimed digital genius, but Kieran had a few tricks of his own. Within minutes he’d located Faith and Matt booked on a red-eye to Atlanta on one of the economy airlines.

He sat back and stared at the manifest as the strangest feeling came over him. It began somewhere in the middle of his chest and rippled outward from there, an icy, tingling fire that was uncomfortable as hell. Kieran shifted and rubbed at the spot right over his heart.

What the hell was she thinking, going down there like that? If Lacie was right about the flight, then she was probably right about Faith meeting Nathan Longstreet as well.

The sensation flared from uncomfortable to downright painful.

Did Matt still want to meet his father? Is that why she was doing this? He could understand that. Faith would do anything for her son, and if the kid really needed the closure, then hell, he was onboard with that plan. Except he should be there, too. Protecting Faith and being there when Matt learned what a piece of shit his father was.

No matter what Faith said.

Oh, yeah, Kieran had done his research. He knew exactly the kind of man Nathan Longstreet was. High school superstar with a rich daddy, lauded college athlete until he graduated and came back for an instant and unearned partnership in Daddy's law firm.

But his privileged youth wasn't what bothered Kieran. It was the fact that Nathan Longstreet was still every bit the smarmy bastard he used to be. Despite the fact that he was married, he had a long trail of mistresses. No more illegitimate kids, though. At least Nathan seemed to have learned the benefits of using a condom.

Did Faith still have feelings for Longstreet, Kieran wondered? She'd obviously cared for him once. She'd said as much. Faith was no liar, nor was she the kind of woman that would give herself freely. He was willing to bet that Nathan Longstreet was the only one she'd ever given that particular gift to, and that alone was enough for Kieran to want to kill him.

At least until him. Faith had offered herself to him, too, that night when he'd slid beside her in bed and held her in his arms. And he'd turned her down, thinking he was doing something honorable. He should have listened to his heart and accepted her gift. He should have spent the entire night making love to her, showing her exactly what she was to him and what he was to her, erasing every doubt, every fear she had.

If he'd done that, the ring he'd purchased specifically for her would be comfortably ensconced on her finger instead of making time in his nightstand drawer. Hell, maybe they'd even be married by now, and he'd be spending every night wrapping his body around her, inside her. And – the pain reached a fever pitch at this point – a little brother or sister for Matt might already be growing inside her.

Faith was his *croie*. He could try to deny it, bury it beneath layers of self-pity, but that didn't change the truth.

The sound that ripped out of him was of one of such power and torment that the desk lamp actually shook.

Two floors below, heads tilted toward the ceiling. "Sounds like he's finally ready," Ian sighed. "Didn't take him nearly as long to figure it out as it took me."

Lexi smiled.

Fifteen minutes later Kieran was racing down the steps with an overnight pack slung over his shoulder. His hair was still wet from his shower, his face once again shaven boy-smooth.

"Hey, Ian, I'm heading over to Sean's to see if he can - "

He stopped, pulling up short when Sean stood up. He grabbed the bag from Kieran and gave him a hard shove toward the door. "About fucking time. Move it, man. Our flight plan says we leave in thirty, and I *hate* refiling flight plans."

Chapter 18

It was surreal; that was the thought that struck her as they were lifting into the air. Her knuckles turned white as she gripped Matt's hand tightly. This was the first time either of them had been on a plane, but Matt was apparently handling it better than she was. Faith said a silent prayer for having the foresight to pass on the greasy burgers at the fast food place they'd stopped at on the way to the airport.

"This is so cool," she heard Matt remark from beside her. Inside, she felt the same way, but apparently she had a fear of flying that she'd never known about.

Or maybe it wasn't the flying at all. Maybe it was the thought of where they were going and why that had her stomach feeling like it was filled with little squirmy creatures.

A small smile graced her lips as she heard Kieran's voice in her head, as clearly as if he was sitting beside her. "Breathe, Faith," he would command softly, not realizing that whenever he spoke to her like that it would take the rest of her breath away. Then he would lace those long, sexy fingers through hers, giving her an anchor and a whole head full of nothing but Kieran Callaghan and fantasies of what it would be like to have the rest of their bodies as intertwined as their hands…

She missed him so much, more than she thought possible. Missed seeing his boyish face and that cockeyed grin that never failed to make her weak in the knees. Hearing his deep, rumbling laughter when she invariably did something that amused him. Feeling the heat of his hard body when he was nearby. Smelling that delicious scent that was uniquely his.

It had been hard to keep her distance from him in Pine Ridge, but at least she had always known he was close, even if he wasn't right there with her. Now she was acutely aware of each mile between them as their flight headed into the unknown, making her feel increasingly alone and vulnerable and downright twitchy.

The plane leveled out and Faith relaxed a little, allowing her to take in her surroundings. The seating was comfortable enough for her, but she felt bad for Matt when she saw how his long legs were scrunched up. She tried to imagine Kieran or one of his brothers on a plane like this, and couldn't. Maybe that's why they had one of their own.

And just how much money did you have to have to own your own plane, she wondered?

She shook her head, stopping herself before she

went down that road. *Again.* The bottom line was that Faith O'Connell and Kieran Callaghan came from completely different worlds.

So? her subconscious piped up. She told it, in no uncertain terms, to shut the hell up, thank you very much. She'd been over this same argument so many times even she was bored by it. Kieran deserved more than she could give him. Period. End of story.

* * *

"What the hell is she thinking?" Kieran muttered to himself, sitting in the copilot's seat next to Sean. "She shouldn't be doing this alone. The guy's a complete poser, *and* he's a lawyer. That makes him doubly untrustworthy."

"Don't let Shane hear you say that," Sean chuckled.

"You know what I mean," Kieran said, shooting a disgusted look at Sean. Sure, it was easy for him. He had his *croie*. He'd already been through his trial of fire.

Kieran sighed. That's what this was, he realized. The test he and every other Callaghan man had to pass before they could claim their true life mates. It was a complete pain in the ass and scary as hell, but the rewards were phenomenal.

"Yeah, I do. And I know a fuck of a lot more than that, too."

Kieran's lips thinned as he braced himself. With six older brothers, he knew the signs of a lecture coming on and braced himself for the torrent soon coming his way.

"Don't fuck this up."

Kieran sat quietly, waiting for more. It didn't come. He felt strangely cheated.

"That's it? That's all you got?"

Sean smirked. "Do I look like Dr. Phil to you? That's all you've got to know. She's your *croie*. Your life is shit without her. *Don't fuck this up.*"

Well, duh.

One of the many benefits to having your own plane and standing privileges at every U. S. military base was that you didn't have to go through all the bullshit associated with a commercial flight. It also meant that they arrived well before Faith and Matt did.

"You cool?" Sean asked, stepping out only long enough to talk to a couple of the guys and refuel.

"Yeah." There was no need to say thanks. It was understood.

"I'll be back for you in two days. And I'd better be picking up three, feel me? 'Cause if you think I'm coming all the way back down here just for your sorry ass, you'll find yourself keeping a couple of gators fat and happy in the swamp." Sean punctuated that statement with an unnecessarily heavy hand to the shoulder.

Ah. The joy of big brothers knew no bounds.

* * *

After two layovers, they arrived in Atlanta just before dawn. With only their carry-ons, they were able to bypass the baggage claim and head out into the hustle and bustle of the busy area. A wall of warm, humid air filled with the fumes of the city hit them hard the moment they did. Faith choked back a cough, thinking longingly of the cool, clean air of Pine Ridge. And just when had she managed to become such a Yank, she wondered?

Faith checked the bus schedule posted outside the terminal and did a few mental calculations as she worked out the best way to get to where they needed to be. It was an hour or so later when she finally worked up the courage to pull out her Go phone and make the call that just might change their lives forever.

With slightly trembling fingers, Faith punched in the number from the legal letterhead. It took several attempts for her to press the buttons in the proper sequence and remain on the line while it rang. A woman answered, her voice crisp and very business-like.

"Longstreet and Son. This is Pamela. How may I assist you?"

For several long moments, Faith forgot to breathe. This was it. She could still hang up right now and pretend they had just used up all of her savings and flown to Georgia for some other reason.

"Hello?" the woman said, efficiency now laced with annoyance.

Faith looked at Matt and summoned her courage. "Uh, hello. I would, um, like to speak with Nathan Longstreet, please."

"Do you have an appointment?" The question, crisp and efficient, came before Faith had even finished speaking.

"Uh, no, but - "

"Then I would be happy to make one for you," the woman said, cutting her off, sounding not very happy at all. There was a brief pause with only the clicking sound of long nails on a keyboard audible over the connection. "His first opening is a week from next Wednesday. If you would give me the reason for your call, please."

"That is not acceptable," Faith heard herself saying, wondering where in the hell the confidence in her voice was coming from. "My name is Faith O'Connell. I am in town for one day only – today. And as for what it regards? Tell Mr. Longstreet that it concerns his *son*."

Silence.

Faith's entire body was shaking now. Matt looked at her, pride etched across his beautiful, youthful face, and he gave her a two-thumbs up – a well-timed reminder that this was not about her.

"Hello." Faith recognized Nathan's voice

immediately. Even that single word held the command of a quarterback calling out a play to his team mates, the smooth Southern drawl so familiar. "Hello? If this is some kind of prank - "

"Nathan," she finally managed. She heard him pause on the other end. "Who is this?" he asked, his voice a little less authoritative.

Faith took a deep breath for strength. "Nathan, it's Faith. I – I got your letter."

The silence on the other end of the line stretched for so long Faith thought he might have hung up, at least until she heard him sigh. She looked at Matt, who gave her a smile of encouragement. When she spoke again, her voice sounded more confident.

"I thought maybe you and I could talk for a few minutes."

Another long stretch of silence. "Alright. Come to my office and - "

"No, Nathan," Faith said before she lost her nerve. "Neutral ground."

"Neutral ground?" Nathan asked, sounding surprised. "Are we at war?"

Faith ignored that. Nathan Longstreet might have been able to charm her once before, but no longer. She wasn't a scared, naïve fourteen year old anymore.

"How about Pappy's Diner, ten a.m.?" Pappy's was a twenty-four hour place right off the interstate. A very busy, very public location that would hopefully keep the drama to a minimum.

"I'd prefer to do this in a more private setting."

This was not about what Nathan preferred. Faith didn't give a damn about that. "That's a no, then?"

Again, she sensed his surprise. He wasn't used to her having a spine, she realized.

"You aren't going to be reasonable about this, are you?"

"I am trying to be reasonable, Nathan," she said, just a hint of annoyance staining her otherwise even tone. "But if you prefer to handle this in court - "

It was a bluff, of course. Faith had already decided she would not have Matt submit to a paternity test. One million dollars was a hell of a lot of money to someone who'd been eking out a living day to day, but things were finally starting to look up. She and Matt were happy (broken heart notwithstanding). She had a decent job, and Matt was doing phenomenally well in school, making lots of friends. They had their own home. It might not be much in most people's eyes, but it was theirs. She liked her new life. And she wouldn't give it up for anything.

Another sigh, but this one was definitely forced. "Alright, Faith. I'll meet you at Pappy's. But if you think for one minute that I am going to - "

"I don't," she said, cutting him off. "Ten a.m.,

then. Goodbye, Nathan."

Her hands were still shaking even after she flipped the mobile closed. "Well?" Matt asked.

"We're meeting him at a diner just outside of town. I was thinking we could stop by Ethan's grave on the way, pay our respects."

Matt nodded soberly. "I'd like that. And Mom? Thanks."

* * *

Kieran sat in the rented sedan, waiting impatiently. His heart nearly leaped out of his chest when he saw her. Well, to be truthful, he saw Matt first - the kid literally towered over his mother – but had he not, Kieran would have had difficulty picking her out of the constant ebb and flow around the airport.

He stepped out of the car, ready to pull an intercept. He wasn't exactly sure what he was going to say. "What the hell were you thinking?" probably wasn't the best opener. Neither was, "You belong to me," or "Get in the fucking car, we're going home." It seemed all of the things in the forefront of his mind weren't suitable. After much thought, he decided to wing it based on her reaction to seeing him.

By the time he got to the cab waiting area, they were gone. He knew she didn't have a rental lined up; the reservation would have appeared in the searches he'd done. And there hadn't been time to grab one once their flight landed.

He very nearly smacked his palm on his forehead. Of course she wouldn't get a rental! Just like she wouldn't get a cab. Maybe he was every bit as insensitive to her situation as she'd accused him of being. Even as the thoughts found purchase, he spotted the bus pulling away. He quickly pulled out his phone and dialed Ian with the number of the bus as he sprinted back toward his rental.

"Lost her already, did you?" Ian chuckled into the phone. Kieran let loose with a few colorful expletives. He was *so* not in the mood for Ian's shit.

"Relax, little bro. Just activate the GPS in your phone. I chipped Matt's cell. As long as it's on, you'll be able to find him."

"You couldn't have told me this earlier?" Kieran grumbled into the phone.

Ian's laughter was rich. "And miss the groveling? Not a chance in hell."

Sometimes being the youngest sucked.

* * *

It wasn't hard to find Ethan Longstreet's final resting place. The aboveground vault bearing the Longstreet name was noticeably larger than anything else around it, and there were still plenty of greens and flowers placed around the exterior.

Faith kneeled just before the structure, placing the small bouquet they'd purchased in front. She murmured a few soft words, a prayer maybe, as she and Matt held hands and bowed their heads together.

Pappy's was just close enough to the interstate to be filled with tourists and travelers, but not a lot of locals. It was for primarily that reason that Faith had chosen it. She had been gone a long time, but Faith didn't want to take the chance of being recognized. An added benefit was that Nathan wouldn't be on his home turf. Faith would take any advantage, no matter how slight.

After some consideration, Faith thought it might be better for her to speak with Nathan alone first before introducing Matt. That way she could feel him out and decide whether or not to move forward. As much as she wanted to fulfill Matt's wish to meet his father, she wouldn't hesitate to leave if Nathan was acting particularly nasty.

She explained this to Matt. He agreed, reluctantly, but only on the condition that he remain close enough to intervene if necessary. Faith didn't think it would come to that, and tried to convince him otherwise. If this meeting went anything like the last time she saw Nathan, he might have some less than kind things to say, and she didn't want Matt to hear those kinds of things about his mother.

But Matt was adamant (a trait he seemed to develop after spending several months around a certain willful Irishman) and assured her that he knew the truth, no matter what he would hear. Sighing, Faith agreed to the compromise. Sometimes it was hard for her to remember that her little boy was growing up, and that he had one heck of a protective streak in him.

With that in mind, Matt took a seat at the counter, while Faith slid into a nearby booth. Faith ordered a cup of coffee and a muffin, though she doubted she could eat anything. She was so nervous her stomach churned. She alternated her glances between the front door and where Matt sat. Matt's face was shadowed by the brim of the ball cap he wore, but he was close enough to hear every word.

Promptly at ten, a familiar looking figure came into the diner. Familiar, though the passage of time had definitely left its mark. He still had his blonde hair, but there was significantly less of it than there once was. His form, while athletic, had softened somewhat over the years. He was handsome enough to turn a lot of feminine heads, in any event, and the expensive cut of his suit didn't hurt, either.

As he looked around the diner, Faith held her breath, waiting to feel…. Something. Anything. Some spark, some interest, some residual tenderness, but found … nothing.

When Nathan's eyes finally settled on her, they widened perceptibly.

"Faith," he said, his voice every bit as rich as

she remembered, though it had deepened slightly. "You look positively – *stunning*. Christ. You still look like a teenager."

The color rose in her cheeks a little bit. Nathan had never called her stunning, had never complimented her on her appearance at all, actually, she realized. Of course, then she'd been fourteen, only on the cusp of womanhood. Motherhood and time had changed things significantly. Though she remained on the slim side, she had more than her share of womanly curves, thanks in large part to her pregnancy early in life.

But then Nathan wouldn't know that, because he'd never believed her, and she'd been long gone before she'd shown a baby bump.

She smiled, just a little one, and inclined her head at the compliment as Nathan slid in across from her with athletic grace, bringing with him the scent of expensive cologne. It was a struggle not to wrinkle up her nose. Kieran always smelled so fresh, so naturally masculine; she had become so accustomed to it that she found this offensive. She wondered idly if Kieran even wore cologne at all, then decided he probably didn't. He was just naturally delicious.

"Thank you," she said quietly, wrenching herself back to the situation at hand.

He continued to stare at her, not taking his eyes off of her even while he gave his order to the waitress. Faith fought the urge to squirm, as well as the even stronger urge to look at Matt. She could feel his eyes on them. Protective. Watching. Waiting.

She felt his presence as keenly as if he'd been sitting beside her, giving her the strength she needed. *Her* son. Practically a man. And though Nathan might be Matt's biological father, he had absolutely no claim whatsoever on the young man eyeing them warily.

And it made her realize something else, too: Nathan Longstreet couldn't hurt her anymore. Whatever hold he once had over her was long gone. She no longer felt the anger, the betrayal, the hurt that she once did. If anything, she felt a kind of detached gratitude. If not for Nathan, she would have never had Matt. If not for Nathan, so many things would have been different. What happened made her stronger, and, she hoped, a better person because of it.

"I just can't get over how young you look, Faith. So young and sexy and *beautiful*."

She didn't bother thanking him again. The waitress brought more coffee and a plate of biscuits covered in sausage gravy, placing the plate in front of Nathan. Automatically, Faith tried to picture Kieran eating that and couldn't. Kieran took great care of his body, keeping to naturally low-fat and organic foods. She bit back a smile, recalling how much he had raved about her cooking, how he liked that so many of her dishes were filled with fresh vegetables from the farmer's market and those she'd canned from her own garden. Of course, it probably never occurred to him that she did so because meat was so expensive…

Faith shifted uneasily. It seemed that everything reminded her of Kieran. No matter where she looked, there was something that made her think of him, or something he said, or the way he looked or smelled or laughed.

Nathan continued to stare at her across the table, and that only served to increase her discomfort. Only Kieran had the privilege of looking at her like that - like he wanted to taste her. She liked when *he* did it, but Nathan's ill-concealed appreciation was unwelcome.

Damn it, she cursed inwardly. She'd just gone and done it *again*. Couldn't she go five seconds without thinking of Kieran Callaghan?

"I'm sorry about your father, Nathan," she said finally, because someone had to say something. "He was a good man."

Nathan nodded, but his expression hardened as he no doubt remembered the circumstances that had precipitated this meeting. "He was. But he was also a soft-hearted old fool," he said. Faith wondered how his eyes could go so quickly from blatant admiration to suspicious accusation and still remain condescending the entire time.

He watched her carefully for a reaction. She offered him none. Ethan Longstreet had been kind and generous to her and Matt, both with his time and his money. Faith always refused more than the bare minimum she needed at the time, and always paid it back with interest when she could.

"Are you married?" he asked suddenly, shooting a glance toward her left hand.

"No," she answered simply. She supposed it would have been polite to inquire in kind, but the truth was that she didn't really care, especially when it had absolutely no bearing on the reason she was here. All it took was a brief glance downward to note the gold circlet around his left ring finger anyway. She wondered idly if he had married Carla Martin; her daddy had a lot of strong political connections.

The interest in his eyes increased. "Why not?"

She could tell him it was because she'd never met the right one, but that wasn't true. She had. It just so happened that something between them wasn't possible, especially since she had pushed him away. Kieran hadn't tried to contact her in several weeks. Some part of her believed that if what he had said were really true – if they really were soul mates – then nothing would have kept him away, not even her panicked decree. Faith took absolutely no pleasure in being right.

And how ironic was it that each passing day had her missing him more, and him getting on with his life? She was now convinced that Kieran *had* been the right one – her true soul mate – just as

Kieran was discovering that she wasn't his.

Regardless, she hadn't the slightest wish to discuss any of it, and certainly not with Nathan. It was irrelevant.

"Nathan, the reason I wanted to speak with you was because - "

He held up his hand, halting her. "I know why, Faith."

"You do?" Faith couldn't help but steal a glance over at Matt. His body was still angled away, though she could tell by the way he held himself he was listening intently. The baseball cap he wore did a good job of covering his dark coppery locks, but it was probably unnecessary. Nathan hadn't looked his way even once.

"Yes." He offered her an indulgent smile and placed his hand over hers. "We shared something once, a very long time ago."

Nathan's hand felt heavy and foreign; she reclaimed hers almost immediately and gripped her coffee mug. She opened her mouth to speak, but he continued on. "You were there for me once, and I do appreciate that. But I'm afraid that I cannot allow sentimentality to hold sway in this situation. One million dollars is a lot of money, Faith, no matter what happened between us."

It took her a moment to process his words. "You think I'm here to use our previous, uh, relationship, to persuade you to drop your motion?"

"Aren't you?" he asked, spreading his arms

open, once again the consummate lawyer. In the back of her mind, Faith pictured Shane. He'd made her a little nervous at first, but he was nothing like this. None of the Callaghans fit the standard stereotypes, come to think of it. Sean cared more about her and Matt's safety than he did about making money. Shane wanted to be her legal counsel, pro bono. And the others – Ian, Jake, Michael, and even the big scary guy, Kane, had been very good to Matt.

"…for someone like you." Nathan was saying. "Not that I blame you."

Faith sat up a little straighter, her hand gripping the coffee mug so tightly her knuckles started to whiten. Certainly she hadn't heard what she thought she had. "I beg your pardon?"

"Come now, Faith. We both know your family didn't have a decent pot to piss in. That kind of money is enough to make anyone think twice about stretching the truth a little, eh?"

Faith stiffened. She'd never realized what a snob Nathan was before. Yes, his family had lived in a big house on the wealthier side of town, and her family hadn't. Because her father was a minister, they lived in whatever the parish church provided them, which often didn't amount to much. But they always had food on the table and clothes on their backs, and they thanked God for whatever other blessings they could list at any given time, some days leaner than others.

Pushing the hurtful slight aside – he didn't even seem to realize he'd said anything offensive, she tried to remember that she was here for Matt's sake. And somehow, she had to explain that to Nathan.

"Although," he said, dropping his voice into what he no doubt believed was a sensual tone, "perhaps we can make some arrangement." He reached over for her hand again as his leg found hers beneath the table. "I can set you up," he said softly. "A nice place on the outskirts of town for you and your boy." He lifted her fingers to his lips and pressed a kiss to them. "And we can… renew our acquaintance."

She heard the coffee cup slam down onto the counter much harder than it should have, and reigned in her own growing revulsion before Nathan said even one more thing. "I don't want your money, Nathan," she said as she tugged her hand out of his grasp and wiped her knuckles on her leg. She was proud of how even and calm her voice sounded when all she really wanted to do was up-end that plate of sausage and biscuits over his receding hairline. The contents of that steaming carafe of coffee would look pretty good in his lap, too.

He blinked. "Of course you do. Why else would you be here?"

"Matthew," she said very clearly. On cue, Matt stood slowly, then turned around and started walking toward her.

"Matt, this is Nathan Longstreet. Nathan, I want you to meet my son, Matthew O'Connell."

Nathan looked at the young man standing beside their booth. The boy had her dark coppery hair and gray eyes, but there was little else in the way of similarity. He was big, towering over Faith, with broad shoulders. *His* build. *His* features.

Matt nodded tersely, and slid in next to his mother. The expression on his face looked like he was just barely containing himself from giving the older man a good beat down.

"Mr. Longstreet," he said with forced politeness.

"Jesus, Faith." Nathan, stunned, looked at Faith, then back to Matt. There was no denying the boy was his. Just by looking across the table, he knew what the results of a paternity test would be. For several moments, Faith indulged in enjoying his very obvious discomfort. She ignored the little pang of guilt at taking such a pleasure.

"What do you want?" he asked softly.

"Me? I want nothing," Faith said quietly. "But Matt wanted to meet you."

Nathan paled. "How old are you?" he asked, but he already knew.

"Fourteen, as of September second," Matt replied evenly, his gray eyes analyzing Nathan's every feature. Faith knew he was comparing it to the face he saw in the mirror each morning.

"Fourteen," Nathan whispered. He looked

back to Faith, the shock on his face almost as hurtful as his denial all those years ago. "I didn't believe you," he said. "I thought you were trying to get back at me because Carla and I…"

He shook his head, and for the first time, Faith saw a hint of regret in Nathan's eyes. "And then you left. All these years I let myself believe… I heard rumors, of course…" His eyes widened. "Jesus Christ, Faith. Your family really kicked you out, didn't they?"

She didn't have to answer. The look on her face said it all.

"Mom?" Matt asked, and now she felt her son's eyes on her, too. She had never told Matt the full truth of it, of exactly what her decision to keep him had cost her.

"Yes," she said, drawing courage from somewhere way deep inside.

"*Jesus*."

For some unfathomable reason, Faith actually felt sorry for Nathan in that moment. It hadn't always been easy, but she had her son. "It wasn't all bad. Your dad helped us find a place to live. He'd come and visit sometimes, spend some time with Matt, but never told him who he was."

"I'm sorry, Faith. Forgive me."

Faith inclined her head. "Thank you." She looked into Nathan's eyes, saw real torment there. "And I forgave you a long time ago, Nathan." She didn't realize the truth of those words until they came out of her mouth. All these years she'd blamed him, but it was herself she'd needed to forgive, not Nathan.

She slipped her purse over her shoulder and turned to her son. "Okay?" Faith asked Matt.

"Yeah," he said, exhaling. "I've heard enough. Thanks, Mom."

"Wait!" Nathan said. "You're not leaving are you? You just got here. And I don't know anything about you."

Matt turned calm, thoughtful eyes to him. "No," he said. "You don't." There was not a trace of the hurt or anger she had feared this meeting would bring, just acceptance and a sense of closure.

"Can you stay? Just for a little while? Please?"

Matt looked to Faith. "It's up to you," she said, so proud of him in that moment.

"Nah," Matt said finally. "I'm good." He stood and offered his hand to Nathan. "It was nice meeting you."

Stunned, Nathan took his hand. "You've got a good, strong grip," he murmured.

One side of Matt's mouth curved upward in a grin, so like Kieran's that Faith stilled for a moment as yet another realization hit: Matt was as attached to Kieran as she was.

"Thanks, Nathan," she said, grabbing her check, leaving Nathan's. "We won't bother you again."

"Oh," she said, reaching into her bag and extracting a familiar looking envelope. "Here. Your papers. Burn them, shred them, do whatever you want with them. We've gotten what we came for." Matt draped an arm around his mother's shoulders as they walked away from the table, leaving Nathan Longstreet in a mild case of shock.

Chapter 19

"You okay, Mom?" Matt asked once they had walked out of view.

No, she thought inwardly. She was not alright. Her head was throbbing with the potential for a full-blown migraine, probably brought on by the stress of the last few hours and Nathan's heavy cologne. And her stomach felt like there were a bunch of miniature leprechauns doing a jig in there.

But that was nothing compared to the ache in her heart.

The events of the last hour or so had made a lot of things crystal clear. Not the least of which was that she was hopelessly, desperately in love with one big, blue-eyed Irishman. Sitting there across from a man she thought she had once loved, Faith couldn't help but compare everything about him to Kieran, and there just was no comparison. Kieran was everything she'd ever wanted in a man and more.

And it had absolutely nothing to do with his money or his family or his success.

Despite being worlds apart on the socio-economic scale, he had always treated her as an equal. With kindness. Generosity. Respect. Love. She'd been the only one to allow things like wealth and status to cloud her judgment.

And in a few short months Kieran had been more of a father to Matt than his real father – or anyone else for that matter – ever had.

God, she was such an idiot.

"Yeah," she finally answered, blowing out a breath. No sense laying any more burdens at her son's feet. He'd had enough drama to last him a while. "How about you?"

He grinned. "Yeah. Wouldn't have picked him for my dad, though. The guy's a complete tool."

After a brief moment of surprise, Faith couldn't help but laugh. She wound her way through Matt's arm; thankfully he was not the type to be overly embarrassed by the show of affection. "That he is," she agreed.

"What did you ever see in him?"

Wasn't that the million-dollar question, literally? "He was very good-looking," Faith said, smiling when Matt rolled his eyes. "He was smart, athletic, and popular. But I think what really did it was that he was nice to me."

"Other guys weren't?" Matt asked, as if the very thought was inconceivable.

"Not like him. The ones who came from good families. Who had nice clothes and expensive cars." Like Kieran. Kieran was all those things, and he had been nice to her. And he never once asked her for anything more than to share her life with him.

As if she was the one who had everything *he* wanted.

"Your family didn't?"

Faith was done carefully constructing answers out of partial truths to make things sound rosier than they were. If he wanted the truth, she would give it to him. He'd already proven he could handle it.

"No. We were church-mouse poor. My dad was a preacher, so we lived in whatever house, shack, or trailer the parish provided. It was one of the benefits of the job," she explained when Matt gave her a questioning look. "And the members of the congregation gave us stuff – food, secondhand clothing, an old beat-up station wagon."

Faith swallowed a pang of regret. Her whole childhood, everything she had had been based on the charity of others. Maybe that's why she was so vehemently against accepting it now.

They walked in silence while Matt processed that. "You never told me they kicked you out." Matt's voice was soft, slightly reproachful.

"No," she agreed. And she didn't want to talk about it now, either, but this trip was turning out to be all about facing demons, wasn't it? What were a few more? Matt wasn't a baby anymore. If he asked, she would tell him, no matter how painful the truth was. He deserved that much.

"Because of me," he frowned.

"No," Faith said firmly. "Because of *me*, Matt." She still remembered the look of tremendous relief on her mother's face the day she picked up that suitcase and walked out the door without causing a scene. No teary goodbyes. No I love yous. Just profound relief.

It still hurt.

Faith never understood why her father seemed to hate her so much. She'd tried to be good, she really did. But she was never good enough. And her father never looked at her the way he did his other children. Her mother hadn't been much better, but then Faith assumed she was afraid of bringing John O'Connell's wrath down on her, too.

She hadn't realized she'd voiced a few of those thoughts out loud until Matt squeezed her hand.

"You grew up around here, right?" Matt's voice brought her back from her musings. Faith nodded, surprised to find that her feet had unknowingly carried them in that direction. "Yeah, just a couple of miles, actually."

"Will you show me?"

"Why?"

Matt shrugged. "We're here till tomorrow, right? Seems like as good a thing to do as any."

There was more to it than that, Faith guessed. Matt wanted to know where he came from.

"Okay," she agreed after only a moment's hesitation. Maybe she needed this, too. Maybe it would help her come to grips with a few things, provide some closure. Just like saying their final goodbyes to Ethan, and letting go of all the emotional baggage she'd carried around over Nathan. It seemed like this trip was about laying the past to rest so they could begin to move forward again.

The parish-provided house didn't look like she remembered it. It was much smaller. Older looking. More rundown. Judging by the state of disrepair, the congregation wasn't as diligent in providing free labor and supplies as they used to be, but Faith supposed things were tough all over. It had never been a wealthy parish at the best of times.

"This is where you grew up?" Matt asked in disbelief. The place made their tiny cottage look like the Taj Mahal.

The house was behind the big church hall, out of sight of the main road, but close enough for the preacher to be at the church in a matter of minutes.

"Excuse me. Can I help you?"

Faith stiffened. The last fifteen years melted away in that moment at the sound of that voice. Matt turned around first. The woman had graying hair, was on the thin side. A well-worn pale blue dress, faded from too many washings, hung on her thin, bony frame.

When Faith faced the voice, the woman's eyes widened, and she dropped the basket of fruit she held in her hands. "*Faith?*" Both hands came up to cover her mouth.

"Mama."

The woman looked as if she had seen a ghost. She broke her gaze away from Faith and looked up at Matt.

Faith attempted a smile. "This is Matthew, Mama. Your grandson."

The woman shook off her shock and anger contorted her expression into something so ugly Faith instinctively placed herself in front of Matt and took half a step back.

"He is no grandson of mine!" the woman spit with vehemence. She spun on her heel and began to stomp toward the house. An inexplicable rage built inside of Faith. It was one thing for her mother to treat her this way. But her son?

Before she realized what she was doing, she ran after the woman, then reached out and grabbed the other woman's arm, beyond caring about propriety and manners. "He is your *grandson*, Mama. Matt is my son."

"He's not my blood," the old woman said bitterly, her face as white as a ghost's. "Because you aren't."

Her words froze Faith in shock. "What?"

"You didn't come from my womb," the woman hissed. "And you turned out to be every bit the slut your mother was." The woman wrenched her arm away and practically ran toward the little house. This time Faith didn't try to stop her.

It felt as though a wrecking ball had just hit her in the very center of her chest. Faith was vaguely aware of Matt saying something, something he shouldn't be saying. Some innate parenting sense had her mouthing an admonishment, but her words were lost in the inexplicable fog. It was as if her brain was shutting down in self-defense.

None of it made any sense. The woman's words echoed in her head over and over again, drowning out everything else. Matt was talking, but she was incapable of hearing anything over the constant buzz in her ears. He led her away from the church, but she didn't even realize they were walking until Matt pushed at her shoulders and guided her onto a park bench.

* * *

"Mom. *Mom*. Look at me. *Jesus*." The words left his lips right before a string of curses that would have earned a raised eyebrow or two from the Callaghans. Matt pulled out his cell, realized it wasn't turned on, and cursed again. It took less than a minute, but it felt like an eternity. The moment the start-up message faded, he hit a preprogrammed number.

It was picked up before the first ring fully sounded; Matt silently thanked God and prayed Kieran wasn't too angry with him, and would still talk to him. Matt simply didn't know who else to call.

"Kieran. Yeah, I'm sorry to bother you, but it's Mom…"

"What's wrong?"

"We're in Georgia, and we just ran into Mom's mother, except it's not really her mother. She said some hateful things and Mom's in shock or something… I don't know what to do…"

"Are you someplace safe?"

Matt looked around. "Yeah. A park or something. Nobody else is around."

"Good. Don't let her out of your sight. Stay there and keep your phone turned on. I'll be there in a few."

"But we're in - "

Matt didn't get a chance to finish before the connection ended. Obviously Kieran missed the "we're in Georgia" part. He sank down next to Faith on the bench and tried to think. What should he do? Was it better to sit here a few minutes and hope his mother snapped out of it? Or should he try to walk her around a bit? They hadn't checked into a motel or anything yet, so he didn't even have a place to take her.

"Matt."

Kieran's voice roused him. Matt's head snapped up, wondering just how long he'd been sitting there. It hadn't seemed like five minutes had passed, but Kieran was in Pine Ridge…

Kieran kneeled in front of Faith. "Faith," he

said, his voice soft but commanding. "Look at me, sweetheart. Look at me."

She blinked once, but there was no recognition in her eyes. "Shit," Kieran muttered under his breath as he took in her pale complexion, the coldness of her skin. "She's in shock."

"When is the last time she ate?" he asked, shooting the question over his shoulder as Matt jogged behind them with their carry-ons.

Matt tried to think. The muffin she'd ordered at the diner this morning was untouched when they'd left. She hadn't had anything the night before when they'd stopped at a restaurant on the way to the airport, saying she'd eaten earlier and didn't want too much on her stomach for her first flight. Come to think of it, he couldn't remember the last time he'd actually seen her eat anything.

Kieran cursed again. He led them to a sleek black rental sedan, instructing Matt to get in the back. Then he carefully handed Faith to him and climbed into the driver's seat.

* * *

Kieran drove them back to his hotel, glancing frequently in the rearview mirror. The flood of relief he'd felt when the GPS on his phone came to life was now replaced with concern. He'd driven around the bus route for several hours, blindly hoping to catch sight of them when the GPS failed to pick anything up. The moment the app lit up, he'd hung a quick U-turn and sped back toward the blip which, thankfully, had been only a few miles away.

Thank God he'd been there. Matt was close to freaking out, and Faith was as pale as he'd ever seen her. When he'd scooped her up into his arms, he'd been shocked by how light she was. She'd lost weight since he'd last seen her.

How did you get here so fast?" Matt finally asked. He sat in the three-room suite at the Marriott, staring at Kieran as he hung up the receiver after ordering nearly everything on the room service menu.

"I followed you down here last night," Kieran admitted, his eyes shooting back to the bedroom where he had placed Faith. She still had yet to say a word, but she seemed to be resting comfortably, at least. Kieran left the door open so he could keep an eye on her.

Matt blinked, surprised. "You knew?"

Kieran nodded soberly. "Lex told me, but you guys had already left. I'm sorry, Matt. Sean flew me down last night. I was waiting at the airport, but somehow I missed you."

"I'm glad you're here," Matt said. "I've never seen her like this. Is she going to be okay?"

Yes, she would, Kieran thought, because he would make sure of it. Even if it meant he had to raze the whole goddamn town on her behalf.

To Matt, he said, "How about telling me what happened? Start at the beginning and don't leave anything out. You can begin by telling me why you quit the mixed martial arts class."

Matt nodded. He told Kieran that it just got to be too hard to pretend that nothing was wrong when it was obvious both Kieran and his mother were miserable. Without going into too much detail, he managed to paint a clear picture of what life had become for them. Faith spent all day working at the Celtic Goddess, then came home, made sure there was something for Matt to eat, then worked cleaning houses around the neighborhood to earn some extra cash. Weekends weren't much better.

"I didn't get to see her hardly at all, and the times I did, it was like she was in another world or something." He looked accusingly at Kieran. "And you weren't doing anything about it, even though you were every bit as miserable as she was."

The muscles in Kieran's jaw clenched, but he said nothing. The kid was right.

Matt went on to tell him that he'd come home from school and Faith had surprised him with tickets to Georgia. "I would have told you," Matt assured him, "even though I wasn't sure you even cared anymore."

Kieran stoically took that hit, too, though he suspected Matt did know better. The fact that Matt was so angry with him was a good thing. It meant he cared a hell of a lot.

Matt spoke in great detail about their meeting with Nathan. Kieran couldn't help but smile at the way they'd handled themselves, and was relieved that neither Faith nor Matt had any interest in cultivating any further relationship with Nathan Longstreet.

It was when Matt started talking about their walk to Faith's childhood home that the true unease began to settle in Kieran's gut. Matt told him everything, tears in his eyes when he ended with his frantic call to Kieran.

"It's my fault," Matt said. "I made her go there."

Kieran placed his hand on Matt's shoulder, commanding his attention. "Listen to me, Matt. It's not your fault. There was no way you could have known what would happen. Even your mom didn't know. She never would have taken you there if she did."

The food arrived, and Kieran suggested they take a break and eat. He left Matt wide-eyed in front of the huge cart of food and went to check on Faith. She was right where he'd left her, though she'd turned onto her side, curling up with a pillow in her arms for comfort.

"I'm so sorry, baby," Kieran said, stroking her hair. "I'm here now. Me and Matt, we're going to take care of everything, so just rest." He wasn't sure if she heard him or not. He hoped she did. He wasn't going to give up until he was sure she understood that he would never, ever leave her again.

It was well past midnight when Kieran finally shut down his laptop and rubbed his eyes. With Ian's help, he'd managed to gather a lot of information about the pious pastor, John O'Connell and his wife, Mary. Most of it, he had no intention of ever sharing with Faith unless she asked for it outright, and possibly not even then. It was true what they say – those that protest the most vehemently are often the greatest offenders, and John O'Connell had a very loud voice indeed.

Matt was sound asleep in the second bedroom, having made a significant dent in the room service that had been delivered. Kieran had already given him a heads-up that he would be sharing a room with Faith. He wasn't sure how the kid was going to take it, but Matt seemed relieved. He told Kieran that he'd sleep a lot better knowing that his mom was safe.

Kieran changed into some loose sweats and a T-shirt, then climbed into bed with Faith. She sighed softly and rolled right into his arms. He could only hope she'd be as willing when she was awake.

* * *

It was as if someone flipped a switch. One minute she was completely oblivious to everything around her, the next all of her neurons were firing and her senses were back online. She opened her eyes to find herself tucked neatly into Kieran's strong arms, her face buried in his neck.

Memories drifted back to her. The plane. The diner. Her mother…. *Oh, God.*

"Kieran! How did you - "

"Ssshhhh," Kieran said, his low words rumbling through his chest and into hers. "It's okay, baby. I've got you."

"Matt?"

"He's good. Well-fed and sound asleep in the next room."

Faith felt an instant and profound sense of relief. If Kieran said Matt was safe, then he was.

And she was being given a second chance. "Kieran, I - "

"Sssshhh," he repeated. "It's been a hell of a day. Just let me hold you, Faith. Please."

There was something in Kieran's voice. A quiet, heartfelt plea that was impossible to ignore. He'd made a simple request, but Faith could sense him holding his breath, as if what she chose to do or say next was monumentally important.

Kieran was in Georgia. At least she thought they were still in Georgia. They could be anywhere, really, and she wouldn't be the wiser. She had no memory of what happened after those few horrible moments with her mother… or the woman she had believed was her mother.

Faith felt herself tensing up again and shut her eyes tight against those images, concentrating instead on the warmth of Kieran's skin, the unique male scent of him, the feel of his body wrapped protectively against hers. The things she never thought she'd get to experience again. It felt like she was finally home.

It was then that she knew. *Really* knew. Finally understood what Kieran had been trying to tell her all along.

He would always be there for her, no matter what. No matter what she said, or what she did. No matter how many times she tried to fool herself into thinking otherwise, this was the real truth of it.

Things like where they came from, what kind of education they had, the jobs they held – they meant absolutely nothing. They were simply circumstances. Circumstances, she realized, that had conspired over time to bring them to this exact moment. Right here, right now.

Every muscle in her body relaxed as a soothing warmth spread through her and her mind grew calm.

Everything really was going to be okay.

* * *

Kieran held his breath and closed his eyes,

offering silent prayers without even realizing he was doing so. Faith had been entrusted to him. To love. To cherish. To protect. He would do all those things and pay for the privilege, but it sure would be easier if she understood and accepted it.

Several tense moments passed, then he felt her relax. As if magically commanded, every soft curve of her body conformed perfectly to his much harder planes. He felt a delicate whoosh of warm, moist air against his collarbone as Faith released the breath she'd been holding, too. And her arm wound its way around his waist, settling on his back, holding him to her as if he might be the one to decide to move away.

Kieran knew then that at least for now, his prayers had been answered.

Chapter 20

Faith tried to extract herself from Kieran's locked embrace (he was a full-body contact sleeper), earning herself a low, rumbling growl of denial.

"Kieran," she said quietly. "It's been nearly eighteen hours since I've… well, I really have to use the bathroom."

One eye popped open, a luminous blue surrounded by thick black lashes, reminding Faith once again how incredibly gorgeous he was. She offered him what she hoped was a sincere, yet desperate, smile.

"You're not leaving," he rumbled. It was not a question, but a statement.

"No," she said, fighting the oddest urge to grin at his grumpy command, instinctively adding, "I promise."

Kieran gave a grunt, a sound so masculine it couldn't possibly have been generated by anything with double-X chromosomes, and released the steel trap of his arms. "You've got five minutes."

"Ten," she countered, scooting away quickly in

case he decided to change his mind. "Maybe fifteen."

He growled louder, his muscles coiling as if he might literally spring from the bed and pounce on her. His hair was mussed from sleep; the shadow of a beard graced his jaw. It was so hot. The thought of seeing him in the same position – but completely naked – had her squeezing her legs together and swallowing a whimper or two. How could she have even thought about running away from something like that? Talk about self-delusional.

"I need a quick shower and to brush my teeth, too."

Dear Lord, was he actually baring his teeth?

Faith forced herself into the bathroom and took a deep breath. Now that she'd made her peace with it, it all seemed quite simple really. They belonged together. Period.

The suite rivaled the Goddess for space and comfort. Two bedrooms, both with queen-sized beds. Real dark wood furniture – not the cheap laminate-over-flake-board stuff. A spacious living area, complete with a sofa, two swiveling reclining chairs, and a sizable flat screen with stereo surround sound. There was even a small kitchenette with a sink, fridge, stove, microwave, and, thank God – a coffee maker.

Faith made a beeline for that. Opening one of

the prepackaged filter-sugar-creamer bags, she set about making a pot. Kieran would forgive her for not heading straight back to bed, especially if she brought a cup of coffee for him, too.

"Hey Mom," Matt said tentatively. He emerged from the other bedroom, his gray eyes filled with concern.

"Hey," she answered softly. "You okay?"

"Yeah. You?"

She smiled and wrapped her arms around him. "Yeah. I really am." Matt returned his mother's hug; judging by the almost-desperate feel of it, he'd needed it every bit as much as she had.

* * *

Kieran watched the scene from the doorway. He'd been ready to bark at Faith for not keeping her word, but he changed his mind when he saw them together. As much as he wanted Faith back in his bed, in his arms, they needed this. And he was fairly certain Faith wasn't going anywhere. If she was, he would find her.

He slipped back into the room quietly, opting for a shower and shave instead.

When he returned, he found Matt in one of the La-Z-Boys and Faith on the sofa. Both had cups of coffee in their hands, and looked as though they were in the midst of a deep, serious discussion. Two sets of unique gray eyes turned to him in unison, and Kieran felt a possessive tug deep in his chest. They were his. Both of them.

"Here," Faith said, patting the seat beside her. "Matt was filling me in on everything I, uh, missed, yesterday. I made you some coffee."

Kieran gladly accepted the cup with thanks, but he didn't sit down. There were some things they had to get straight, and the sooner that was taken care of, the better off they would all be.

He drained his cup, briefly taking note of the fact that Faith had made his exactly the way he liked it (of course she did, she was his *croie*, she would do everything perfectly for him), and faced the two of them.

He gave a meaningful glance to Matt, who nodded soberly. The kid knew what was coming. Kieran had a long heart-to-heart with him the day before, and Matt had given his full and whole-hearted support.

"Know this, Faith," he began, keeping his voice carefully modulated – soft, yet firm. "You are my *croie* – my heart and my soul. I'm sorry if you can't accept that just yet, but you will, and I won't give up until you do. If you run, I'll be two steps behind you. If you hide, I will find you. Because there is no other option."

Faith gazed up at him, her eyes widening slightly. "Okay."

He stood there, immense and immovable, ready for a battle. He was through with stepping lightly.

Faith was his, that's all there was to it. And now that he'd started, he had no intention of stopping until she'd heard him through till the end.

"And I'll tell you something else, too," he said, refusing to be sidelined by her willful pride. "I couldn't care more for Matt than if he was my own flesh and blood. I don't know much about being a father, but I can promise I'll do my damnedest to do right by him, and I'll always be there for him, whatever he needs."

"Alright."

She was not going to wear him down with her illogical arguments, he decided stubbornly. "You can just forget all that bullshit about having to carry every burden on your own shoulders, because mine are a lot broader than yours, sweetheart. And while we're on that subject, you *will* drive a safe and decent car and you *will* have a workable phone so I am not batshit crazy with worry over whether you're broken down or laying bloody in a ditch somewhere."

He paused as he blew out a breath and crossed his arms over his chest, setting his face in what he hoped was a stern look that let her know he meant business. She stared up at him with those big, soft gray eyes, her face much more relaxed than he'd expected.

"Anything else?"

Kieran blinked, the fury he'd prepared for not yet forthcoming. She meant to lull him into a sense of complacency first, obviously. A clever trap, but one he would not be falling for today.

"Yes, actually. I want you to be happy. If you want to work? Great. Go to school? Awesome. Stay at home? Fine by me. I am totally cool with whatever you want to do, but you *will* allow me to provide for my family, which, in case I wasn't clear enough, now includes you and Matt."

The corners of her mouth twitched. "Are you done?"

"Almost." This was going much easier than he'd expected. It made him suspicious, scared the hell out of him, really, but Callaghan men were renowned for their courage and fortitude in the face of danger. He fumbled around in his pocket for a moment, then went down on bended knee.

"I want you to marry me, Faith. Be my wife, and let me take care of you for the rest of our lives."

* * *

She stared at him for a full minute while she tried to control the irregular pounding of her heart against the walls of her chest, as well as how to breathe. Finally, when she was capable of speech again, she opened her mouth.

"No," she said softly.

A flash of pain appeared momentarily in his eyes, replaced almost immediately by grim determination. Before he could say another word, however, Faith was before him, sitting on the edge of the couch. With him down on his knee, it put them at eye level. Her hands gently cupped his face, forcing his eyes to hers.

"I have a couple of demands of my own," she said. "First, *you* will not take care of *me*. *We* will take care of *each other*. Secondly, I want to pick out my own car and my own phone. You can have a say in it, and you can have Sean check it out, but ultimately, it's my choice. Third, I will continue to work, but I am willing to cut down my hours so we can have more family time together."

She smirked at the look of total shock on his face. "How does that work for you?"

Kieran didn't move for several long moments. He remained on the floor, with one knee down and the other bent at a ninety degree angle. His blue eyes darkened, then lightened to their perfect celestial blue again. And the corners of his mouth began to quirk.

"That's a yes, then?"

Faith rolled her eyes, but she was smiling, too. "A bit slow this morning, are we?"

The quirk became a full-fledged grin. "Apparently." He looked at Matt, whose face was twisted in that smug, cocky look only a teenager was capable of. "You heard her, too, right? She said she'd marry me."

"She did."

"She can't back out now."

"Nope."

Kieran slipped the exquisitely cut diamond onto Faith's waiting finger and captured her mouth in a possessive kiss.

"Ugh. If you guys keep that up I might just change my mind," Matt grumbled.

Faith looked at her son over Kieran's shoulder. "You were in on this?"

"Well, *duh*."

"I need to see my father."

Faith blurted out the words in between bites of the buttery croissant. Her mother's – or at least the woman she had believed was her mother all this time – words kept repeating in her head. As much as they shocked her, Faith sensed an underlying truth in them. It was as if some dark monster was hiding in the depths of her awareness, trying to avoid being dragged out into the light.

Kieran looked up from his plates of eggs, pancakes, home fries, ham, and, since they were in the South, grits. Matt had already polished his off and was taking his turn in the shower.

Kieran finished chewing and swallowed, wiping a napkin carefully across his mouth. "You sure?"

She drew in a breath. "Yes. I need to know." She exhaled. "I want to put all this behind me so I can start enjoying my new life," she said, touching

Kieran's hand. "I need closure."

Kieran nodded, his concern evident in the darkening of his blue eyes, the serious set to his boyish features. He wasn't happy about it, but he understood.

"You don't have to come with me if you don't want to."

His full, male lips thinned slightly; his eyes darkened further, a luminous midnight glow. He gave her a look of such possession that it made her heart stutter slightly, but then softened it with a smile.

"Have you already forgotten?" he chastised gently. "You will never have to face anything alone again."

Faith beat down the feeble protest that tried to rise up out of habit, and allowed the wave of intense relief to carry it away. It would take a while for her to learn how to share her doubts and worries, and it wouldn't always be easy, but for this man, she would do her best.

"Thank you," she said sincerely. With Kieran by her side, Faith felt like she could face – and conquer – anything. "I don't think Matt should go, though."

"Agreed. Think he'll be okay hanging out here?"

Faith took a look at the bank of digital electronics and chuckled. "Yeah, I think he'll be okay roughing it for a few hours."

* * *

Matt wasn't entirely happy about being left behind, but it was a sure sign of his ever increasing maturity that he said he understood when Faith explained where they were going and why. Kieran knew he had no desire to meet his maternal grandparents, not after the scene he'd already witnessed. As part of their heart to heart the night before, Matt had confessed that if that was what his heritage was, he didn't want to know any more.

Maybe that would change someday. If it did, Kieran would be there to help him through it.

At this point, though, it was probably for the best. Kieran wasn't sure he would be able to completely suppress the urge to lay the man out for everything he'd made Faith suffer.

Kieran and Faith slipped quietly into the back of the church, taking their seats on the far end of the pew before the service began. The idea was to avoid as much interest as possible. Avoiding it completely wasn't realistic; they were outsiders, after all, and a man like Kieran definitely stood out anywhere he went.

They remained quiet and still, Faith's head bowed in what looked like respectful prayer while Kieran kept his eye on everything and everyone and made no secret of the fact that he did. Only a few of the curious were brave enough to hold his intense blue gaze for more than a second or two before looking quickly away. No doubt many felt the weight of that laser-like stare on the backs of their heads, too, preventing them from turning around and gawking.

He heard Faith's breath hitch when the pastor finally stepped up to the pulpit. He squeezed her hand reassuringly, reminding her that she was not alone.

John O'Connell was barely fifty years old, but every one of those years showed in the lines in his face. He kept his dark gray hair shorn close, emphasizing his dark, piercing eyes. Kieran studied his sharp, angular features, but there was absolutely no sign of his beautiful *croie* anywhere in them. Faith must have taken after her mother, he realized. That simple fact alone probably doomed her to their scorn.

Finding that the longer he looked at the preacher the more his dislike for the man grew, Kieran turned his attention elsewhere. When they'd first arrived, Kieran automatically made note of every possible entry and exit point. Out of habit, he checked again to make sure they were all clear.

As John segued into his sermon (ironically enough centered upon the sacrifice of Abraham's son and the need to put God above family), Kieran took the opportunity to study the surroundings. It was definitely an old church, built around the turn of the century if he had to guess. The exterior was the traditional white, a narrow building with a steeple and a bell tower on top. Inside, the wooden benches showed their age, worn smooth over the years. A few stained glass windows remained, though most had been replaced with less-expensive plexi-glass. The carpet up the center aisle was threadbare.

The seats were a little more than half-full. Most of the parishioners looked as worn as the church. The older ones dressed up to attend services - the men in suits and ties, the women in dresses, accessorized with hats and hairpins. From the look of things, their finery was from an age long past, but Kieran thought that God would appreciate the effort nonetheless.

The younger ones sported jeans – though Kieran was sure they were their "nice" jeans, and clean shirts and shoes. But there was no mistaking this parish for anything but what it was – a very poor community where the people struggled to survive and held on to their faith regardless.

It angered Kieran that a man like John O'Connell would take advantage of that. He didn't realize he'd let his control slip until he felt Faith squeezing his hand, giving him the same quiet reassurance he had given her. He smiled, and her earlier words came back to him: *We will take care of each other.*

* * *

After the service, they waited quietly in the shadows while the pastor spoke to the departing parishioners.

"I thought you might come," John said, closing the church doors as the last of his flock walked away with a wary backward glance. "Mary told me she saw you yesterday."

Faith looked at the man that had once cast her so easily from his home and inhaled deeply. "Are you my father?" she asked suddenly.

A lifetime of pain crossed his features, and he suddenly looked very, very old. "Yes."

"Is Mary my mother?"

Seconds ticked by in the silence that followed, but it felt like an eternity. Faith was sure her heart had stopped beating in the time it took for him to answer.

"No."

"You *hypocrite*." Several phrases flowed through her mind at that moment. That was the most Christian-friendly word she could think of.

John's features hardened, but he nodded. He walked toward the front of the church and sat down heavily in the first pew. After a few moments, Faith followed with Kieran's hand on her lower back. Faith slid into the pew behind her father, shifting to the side so she could see his face.

John turned and looked not at her, but at Kieran. "You're married?"

"Will be soon."

"And the boy?"

"My son in every way that matters."

John nodded, but his eyes remained cold and impassive. "Our sins always come back to haunt us, don't they?" he said, his voice rough. "We fool ourselves, thinking that if we pray fervently enough, go to church, say and do all the right things, that we're worthy, but we're not. It's futile. God knows this."

"Is that what I am?" Faith asked, her voice as small as a child's. "A sin?"

"Yes," he said without hesitation. "You, Faith, are the physical manifestation of my weakness. My *Scarlet Letter*, if you remember your classics. God's reminder that no matter what I think I am, I am still only a man. A sinner at heart."

That sounded like a load of bullshit to her, nothing but a convenient excuse, but she heard herself saying, "Tell me."

For a long while she thought he wouldn't. The silence was deafening in the empty church, as if even God was listening. Kieran ran small circles over her hand with the pad of his thumb, keeping her anchored, confirming his words in deed. It didn't make it easy, but having him there made it easi*er*.

"I didn't know your mother was pregnant," he said finally.

"Did you love her?" Faith asked.

John didn't answer that question. "I couldn't marry her. She came from a bad family. Her father was a drunk and a criminal, her mother the town whore. Not exactly ideal for a pastor's wife." He smiled weakly. "But she was beautiful. And smart. And funny." His eyes raked over Faith as if seeing someone else. "You look just like her."

Two different worlds, Faith mused, but maybe not so different. "Where is she now?"

John's face clouded. "She's dead. She died in a house fire shortly after you were born when her father passed out in bed with a lit cigarette. I didn't even know about you," he said quietly, "until the police chief came around with you in his arms. He said I was the next of kin, that I was listed as your father on the birth certificate."

For several moments, his nearly black eyes glittered with the regret and pain of loss. Faith was very familiar with both. "And?"

"Mary, oh, Mary was livid. Hasn't let me forget it a single day of my life. But I had to take you in, didn't I? It was the Christian thing to do, and I was the pastor. God was using me as an example."

It was all becoming clear; the pieces were finally following into place. Why Faith had gray eyes but her parents and all of her siblings had brown ones. Why the woman she thought was her mother and her father resented her so much. Faith felt like part of her was slowly leaking away; had it not been for Kieran, she might have slid down the pew.

"When you came home pregnant, Mary couldn't handle it. She said you had to go, that you were just like your mother. I had no choice, Faith. She stood by me all those years, kept my secrets. Gave me five more children - legitimate children not born in sin."

Whatever self-pity Faith was feeling faded, replaced slowly with anger. "I am your daughter."

He stiffened, the lines on his face hardening. "I took you in. Put food in your belly and clothes on your back until you went and got yourself pregnant. I did right by you."

"If that's what you think parenting is, you're even more pathetic than I thought. Leaving was the best thing I ever did."

John didn't deny it. "I prayed for you."

Faith laughed, a cold, empty sound that surprised them all. It echoed in the empty church. "Well, then. I guess that makes everything okay. Goodbye, *Dad*."

Faith rose and began to walk down the aisle, Kieran protectively at her back. She was nearly at the doors when John stood up. "Faith, wait."

Faith paused and turned slowly. "You've obviously done well for yourself," John began, and for a moment Faith thought he might be about to tell her that he was proud of her. But those hopes were shot to hell with his next words. "We've fallen on hard times here. You have an obligation to your family."

Nothing could have prepared her for that. She gaped at him, open-mouthed, for several seconds before she finally found her voice. "Don't worry, Dad," she said, turning away again. "I'll *pray* for you."

"You okay?" Kieran asked, once they were in the comfortable rental and headed back to the hotel.

"Yeah," she said, blowing out a breath. It was the first full breath she'd taken all morning. The fresh air, combined with the scent of the man she loved, filled her lungs and burned away some of the residual angst. "I really am."

"Good," he said simply, lacing his fingers through hers.

"Yeah."

"So. What do you think about a New Year's Eve wedding?"

Chapter 21

They went out to dinner that night to celebrate - Kieran, Faith, and Matt. They had shared a meal so many times together that it felt quite natural. But there was something new there that wasn't there before. The invisible bond that tied them together was now a tangible thing. It felt right, as if the last pieces of the puzzle had finally clicked into place.

When they got back to the hotel, Matt surreptitiously excused himself and went to his room to watch some of the premium movie channels (each bedroom had a small television). Faith was about to warn him against trying to watch some of the unrated shows, but Kieran nudged her.

"He's giving us some time alone," Kieran breathed into her ear. "I'd say that deserves a little good faith on our part, wouldn't you?"

Faith blushed and Kieran chuckled when they heard the television in Matt's room come on loud enough for them to hear what he was watching, but guessed that the excessive volume was more to keep Matt from hearing anything that might be going on *outside* of his bedroom.

Kieran picked up the ice bucket with the bottle

of champagne and two flutes and walked into the bedroom. Faith followed feeling a bit nervous. Was he planning on staying with her again tonight, even though she was no longer ill?

"You bet I am," Kieran said, leaving Faith to wonder if she'd voiced her thoughts out loud. "Now that I've finally got you, there's not a chance in hell I'm letting you slip away again."

He chuckled softly when Faith said she really needed to take a shower, granting her a generous hour to do whatever she needed to do, but warned her that he would come in and get her if she wasn't out by then. Faith wasn't sure if the thrilling shiver that ran through her body was a result of anticipation or nerves.

She used every minute of her allotted time. She scrubbed, shaved, plucked, exfoliated, flossed, and brushed until she was hairless, smooth, and glowing from the neck down. With five minutes to spare, she spritzed a soft musk along her pulse points. Spotting Kieran's shirt hanging from the hook on the back of the door, she decided to slip it on.

She swore Kieran's eyes glowed when she stepped somewhat shyly out of the bathroom. He was propped up on the bed, shirtless and barefoot, remote in hand. He stilled when he saw her. Only his eyes moved; she felt them on her as keenly as a caress. With every step she drew closer, the sheer hunger on his face intensified.

"I need a shower, too," he said, his voice somewhat strangled. Kieran leaped out of the far side of the bed just as she approached the other and sprinted into the bathroom, leaving Faith looking uncertainly at the back of the door.

She heard the water come on. The muted sounds of a zippered bag opening and closing. A few muttered curses (the reason became clear shortly afterwards).

In less than five minutes, Kieran emerged from the bathroom, his hair towel dried, a few nicks along his jawline (she guessed he had shaved a bit hurriedly), and a towel slung low on his hips. It really had been an eight-pack she'd glimpsed that one day so very long ago. An eight-pack that was nestled into the most perfect "V" of muscle and dark hair she'd ever seen.

"Lord have mercy," she whispered.

Kieran slid into the bed beside her, dropping the towel on the floor as he did so. He sat next to Faith, his left leg rubbing up against her right. It was all she could do not to stare at the very prominent erection he sported, but what she glimpsed in her peripherals was enough to have her core burning and preparing itself for him.

They sat in silence for several minutes. Faith felt like a pubescent teen, jumping slightly when Kieran made the first move by placing his hand lightly on her thigh.

"Matt's in the next room," she breathed, her

heart fluttering like a hummingbird's.

Kieran exhaled slowly before turning toward her. "I guess we'll have to be extra quiet then." His hand reached up under the shirt she wore – his shirt – and skimmed across her flesh. "No matter what happens," he said softly, his voice a sensual caress in itself, "*don't* scream."

* * *

Faith whimpered. Kieran moaned softly when his fingertips soon discovered she had neglected to put on panties. His lips met hers, capturing her outcry when his fingers found her slick wet center.

He was going to do everything he could to bind her to him. He'd already openly laid claim upon her heart, now it was time to imprint himself on her soul.

"How I've dreamed of touching you like this," Kieran breathed as he kissed his way down her jawline, her throat, stopping only to place his fingers upon his tongue. "Like the sweetest honey," he murmured.

He made quick work of the two or three buttons she'd fastened, opening the sides slowly and with anticipation, as if he was unwrapping a present. "So beautiful…" he praised, the only words he managed before drawing one hardened tip into his mouth. At the same time, his hand found its way back down to her molten core. Faith hissed loudly, arching beneath him, her hands tangling in his thick, silky hair.

"Sssshhh," he scolded, nipping the underside of her breast and then licking away the sting.

He made sure to treat her neglected breast with the same attentiveness, while his fingers continued to strum along her center. Without warning, he began to ease a finger inside her. Reflexively, she tensed all over and clenched hard on his fingers.

"Damn, baby," he choked around her breast. "You're going to unman me before I even make it inside you."

Faith was too highly strung to even consider penetration any time soon, he realized, which did very little to ease the horrible ache that had taken root deep in his groin. His cock was thick and heavy with need, the tip already wet and slick. If he tried to take her now, as his body was screaming for him to do, he would hurt her. He needed her softer, more pliant before he could even consider claiming her.

With that in mind, he called upon his inner control. As if he had all the time in the world, he licked, teased, and suckled her breasts, leaving not a spot untouched, as he continued to thumb her now-swollen nub and coax another finger inside.

"Don't fight it, baby. Let it take you." He nearly sobbed with relief when he felt her inner muscles tightening. He stroked faster, sucked harder, and scissored and curled his fingers with consummate skill. Faith released the death grip she had on his hair and grabbed a pillow, slamming it over her face to cover the sounds of the wail she could not completely contain.

Kieran chuckled against her skin, pleased with her response. "Oh, Faith, sweetheart, I can't wait for the day I have you alone and you don't have to be quiet." He lightened the pressure on her sex, bringing her down gently. His fingers were coated in her creamy heat, her sex swollen and hot in his hand. His cock pulsed in agony.

"I'm sorry, baby," he breathed as he drew himself over her. "I wanted to make our first time last all night, but I can't wait any longer. I need you, Faith. I need to be inside you more than I've ever needed anything in my entire life."

Faith moved the pillow aside and opened herself to him, allowing him to settle in the cradle of her thighs. She felt the thick head of his erection nudging against her entrance, her ultra-sensitive nerves more than ready to welcome him.

"Then come inside me," she whispered huskily. "Come inside me and make me yours."

Kieran didn't need to be told twice. He kissed Faith, a passionate, soul-searing kiss, and rocked his hips forward. She was so well-lubricated that it eased his penetration, but it was still a very tight fit. He felt her stretching to capacity all around him.

Faith held her breath, as did he, caught somewhere between awe and ecstasy at the feel of entering her for the first time. "Breathe, baby," he commanded with the last of his ability to speak. She did, and when she took that first big inhale, he slid in up to the hilt in one smooth, final thrust.

He stayed like that, suspended and still, as he let the wonder of finally being joined with his *croie* overtake him.

* * *

It gave Faith the opportunity to adjust to his girth. If she'd had any doubts about being too stretched down there from giving birth, they were quickly laid to rest. She tried to imagine what it would have been like to accommodate someone of Kieran's size without having the benefit of natural childbirth first. Granted, it was a long time ago, and she'd been very young, but she still believed it had to have helped somewhat. He was as big there as he was everywhere else.

Despite his size, there was none of the pain she'd expected, none of the discomfort she'd felt the one and only time she'd ever had sex. On the contrary, this was the most wonderful thing she'd ever felt. Kieran's big, hot body held over hers, the feel of all that hard muscle and silk beneath her fingertips. His thickness lodged snugly in the very core of her, filling her, heating her, joining them, making them one. It went far beyond the physical. As she stared into his eyes, she understood what he had been trying to tell her all along. It was not only their bodies that were now connected, it was their very essences.

Faith and Kieran. Kieran and Faith. No longer two separate entities, but *One*.

* * *

Even though he wasn't moving, she was. Her internal muscles were working his cock, flexing and rippling against his intrusion. After a few minutes, he realized that she could make him come by that alone. Maybe he'd test that theory one day, but today he wanted his first climax inside Faith to include hers as well.

With that specific goal in mind, he began moving inside her. Extracting himself, then pushing forward, penetrating her again and again. What started as slow, thorough strokes soon became faster, shallower, as they both did nothing to fight the apex coming fast and hard. Kieran buried his face in her neck and pistoned his hips, heeding her breathy but near silent moans for more. Some part of him worried that he would hurt her if he let himself go, but then another part reminded him that she was his *croie*, and that she had been fashioned for him, just as he had been for her.

He felt her sheath clenching his cock even as his balls tightened and the seed rose in his shaft. She was almost there, and he was going to come so fucking hard…

He thrust once, twice, three more times until Faith opened her mouth in a silent scream. Kieran was right there with her, his body tense and stiff as he began to fill her. He pushed harder, settling himself deeper, shooting right into the entrance of her womb.

She held him close to her, milking his body with hers, demanding everything. He reveled in the feel of his liquid heat scorching her insides with every powerful pulse. He was powerless to do anything but give it to her.

An eternity later, he rolled to the side, taking Faith with him. Still joined, they passed out in each other's arms.

It was the first of several times they would do so that night.

* * *

It was hard to drag themselves out of bed the next morning, but the sound of Matt very deliberately banging around the living area and the smell of coffee proved to be adequate motivators. Faith had trouble looking her son in the eye at first, but Kieran had no such compunction.

Sean was beaming from ear to ear when they met him at the private airport. He spotted the ring on Faith's hand right away and hugged her, saying he was glad to be the first to officially welcome them into the clan.

The plane ride home was more pleasant than the ride down. Sean let Matt sit up front in the cockpit with him, which, according to Matt, was "beyond sick." Faith felt none of the unease she had on the commercial flight, but she wasn't sure if it was because of Sean's mad skills or because nearly all of her attention was focused on the impossibly perfect man she now found herself engaged to marry.

Kieran started moving some of his things into Faith's cottage as soon as they got back. One night, he said, had only made him realize he never wanted to sleep alone again. Matt, surprisingly, was accepting, though he did manage to let Kieran know it was only because they were getting married right away.

Less than a month was not a lot of time to plan a wedding, but the Callaghans rose to the challenge. Apparently Taryn, Lexi, Maggie, Nicki, Rebecca, and Lacie had been mentally planning the event since mid-summer (after the infamous county fair incident), and already had most of the details worked out. It had been relatively easy, they said, since both Faith and Kieran were very much alike in preferring the simpler things, neither one being prone to lavish or extravagant tastes.

Christmas was a blur. A near foot of powder painted everything in glistening white. The Callaghan men – much less concerned with the myriad of details involved in pulling together a last-minute wedding, made sure that Matt got the full benefit of experiencing his first NEPA winter wonderland. They took him skiing and snowboarding and snowmobiling over the mountains. Sean even let Matt ride along in the big plow truck, much to Matt's great delight.

Faith was shielded from much of the details, a fact she was secretly happy for but felt slightly guilty about. It became clear very early on that it would take time for Faith to adjust to the skills and resources of their clan, and accepting so much help was proving a hard thing for her to do.

Kieran did his part by attempting to distract her at every opportunity, but letting others do for her after so many years of doing for herself took a lot of effort on her part. After nearly hyperventilating when she caught sight of the pricelist for various wedding items, they decided it was better for everyone involved to just tell her where to be and when. That worked for her.

They broke up into teams. Maggie and Lacie took Faith for her gown (a classic and simple candlelight white with a fitted bodice, modestly full skirt and train, and off-the-shoulder long sleeves) and all the necessary accessories (shoes, purse, veil, and bustle). They handled the flower arrangements, too, selecting colors that best complimented the bride, but tried to stick to a wintry theme with deep cranberries, forest greens, and pale, shimmery silvers.

Lexi and Aidan naturally assumed control of the reception arrangements. They reserved a private ballroom at the Goddess – one with an entire wall boasting a spectacular view of the valley in its snowy splendor. They planned the custom menu and had their professional decorators make sure everything was picture-perfect.

Taryn, Nicki, and Rebecca threw together one hell of a bachelorette party, and were ultimately in charge of the extra-special tradition among the Callaghan women that had Kieran shackled to a bed in his room at the Pub and Faith arriving in nothing but sheer veils via a dumbwaiter. It was the special gift offered from one *croie* (or several *croies*, as the case was) to another: a night of total sexual domination over her alpha male. It was a tradition and gift Faith embraced heartily.

The wedding was a simple but breathtaking candlelight ceremony, held in the church in Pine Ridge. Kieran and Faith exchanged vows before the entire Callaghan and Connelly clans. Matt gave his mother away, then proudly took his seat next to the stunning blonde in the first pew.

Epilogue

Faith sank into the chair, rubbing her feet discreetly beneath the table, feeling deliriously happy, but exhausted. She couldn't remember the last time she had felt this worn out. Granted, the last few weeks had been a whirlwind of activity, and her nights with Kieran left her a bit sleep deprived. And last night's stint as a Domme – the one night when she might have been able to sleep soundly for more than a few hours – had her running on fumes. It was only adrenaline keeping her going now, and she feared even that wasn't going to last much longer.

Thank goodness Rebecca's gift to her had been a pair of cloud-soft satin slippers that matched her gown. She never would have made it through the last few hours without them; tradition required that the bride dance with each and every one of the Callaghan and Connelly males. It was a rite of passage that every new bride was expected to take, though it had the obvious benefit of annoying the groom as well.

Poor Kieran had been trying to get to her for the last hour, but was foiled by several well-executed defensive maneuvers. When Faith expressed concern, Ian laughed and told her that she should not feel sorry for him, given that he had gladly partaken in the tradition when it was everyone else's bride involved.

"Congratulations, Faith."

She looked up into the slightly exotic golden eyes of Aidan Harrison. He was every bit as imposing close up as he was from a distance, and Faith could not help but feel a little nervous. Even as she had tried to embrace and become accustomed to her new lifestyle – which included the financial security of the Callaghan family - she was unused to being in direct contact with someone as wealthy and important as the CEO of the Celtic Goddess.

Technically, she was rather well-off herself now, too. Nathan dropped his challenge of Ethan's bequeathal after their visit to Georgia, but her mind was still having trouble adjusting to that. All she knew was that Shane was handling the legal aspects and Kane was already creating a financial portfolio.

She forgot about all of that in the presence of the powerful man next to her. Her falling adrenaline levels made a valiant rally to at least appear relatively coherent.

"Thank you," she said, feeling the words woefully inadequate. She still hadn't been able to wrap her mind around the fact that all of this had been done for her wedding. "Everything is beyond perfect."

He grinned easily, pleased, as if he was a regular guy and not the wealthiest man she'd ever met. "Mind if I sit for a moment?"

"Of course not. You do own the place, don't you?" Faith immediately lifted her hand up to her mouth, mortified that she had allowed the words in her head to be spoken aloud. She had a sneaking suspicion that the last drink someone had placed in her hand was made by Brian McCain, the devil.

Aidan's eyes glittered with amusement. "So I do."

Faith sipped her drink and sighed. Yep. If she hadn't been so distracted she would have recognized the signature taste of a Brian McCain special, a.k.a, the potent Virgin Slayer. She glanced over toward the bar, and Brian gave her a big smile and a friendly salute. It was impossible to be annoyed with him, but she really wanted to be.

"You also work for me, I believe," Aidan was saying, snapping her attention back to him. Faith immediately sobered, wondering where this was heading.

"Yes, sir. I do."

"Call me Aidan. Environmental, right?" She nodded warily, wondering where this was going.

"Well, I think we need to talk about that."

"Sir?" Was he firing her?

"Aidan," he corrected patiently. He extracted a familiar-looking tablet and placed it on the table between them. Faith froze as she realized she was looking at one of her sketchbooks. "These are yours?"

Faith nodded, feeling the numbness seeping through her limbs.

"You have talent, Faith. May I call you Faith? 'Mrs. Callaghan' applies to more than half the women in this room."

She nodded again, dumbstruck. *She was on a first name basis with Aidan Harrison.* Add that to the fact that she was in the middle of a fairy tale wedding and now married to her soul mate, and she felt downright stupefied.

She took another sip of the Virgin Slayer and fought the urge to giggle at the improbability of it all. If she saw a dancing unicorn, she was soooo going to go lay down in the ladies room. Actually, she might just do that anyway. Just five minutes, maybe ten, to recharge and she'd be good as new.

"Well, Faith, I love your ideas. I'd like to hire you to re-design the interiors of the latest set of luxury suites."

She gawked at him. Not quite a dancing unicorn. But close.

"It'll be a bit different than what you're used to. You'll have an office on the same floor with Lex and me, well, more of a design studio, really. You'd design exclusively for the Goddess. You'll be expected to attend meetings and travel to the Corporate headquarters in Georgia with us from time to time. I think once they see your ideas we'll be renovating all of the Goddesses, and perhaps some of our other chains as well."

Faith was glad she was sitting down, because otherwise she was certain she'd be slumped on the floor. That feeling only intensified when Aidan started throwing out mind-numbing possible starting salaries and signing bonuses and stock options.

"Aidan, you're not talking business at our wedding are you?" Kieran chastised, joining them at the table. He leaned down and kissed his bride. She gripped his hand. Hard.

"Just wanted to put my bid in before you left on your honeymoon," he said, offering Faith a wink. "I see Johnny over there chomping at the bit. Think about it, okay?"

She nodded numbly.

"Baby? You okay?" His eyes grew concerned when he saw her weak smile. Out of the corner of her left eye, she saw him signaling for someone.

Somehow she managed to relate what Aidan had told her, though she thought she might have messed up a few of the words along the way between her mind and her mouth. She was just so tired. And maybe just a bit in the grips of shock.

"Faith?" Michael's soothing voice registered about the same time she realized his long, warm fingers were discreetly checking her pulse. "How are you holding up, sweetheart?"

"I'm tired," she breathed. "Really, really

tired."

Michael exchanged a glance with Kieran, who had lifted up Faith's barely-touched drink and sniffed it suspiciously before shooting Brian a scathing glance.

"Would you like to lay down for a little bit?"

"Oh, yes, please," she said, her voice growing dreamy. To Kieran, she offered a smile. "Your brother's really nice."

"Yeah, he's a prince. Come on, baby. Put your arm around me. There you go." Kieran lifted his bride into his arms.

"Hey, is she okay?" Maggie asked, joining them.

"I'm just tired," Faith said sleepily. "I'm sorry."

"Let's get her up to Lex's office," Michael said quietly. "I'll grab my bag and meet you there in five."

* * *

"Well?"

"She's fine," Michael said confidently.

"Are you sure?" Kieran asked, looking worriedly to where Faith was sleeping soundly on the sofa in Lexi's office, covered with Michael's tux jacket.

"Yes," Michael said, his eyes twinkling. "Quite sure."

Kieran narrowed his eyes at his older brother. "Mick…"

Michael put his hand on Kieran's shoulder. "Relax, Kier. It's perfectly natural for Faith to experience fatigue at this stage. It should only last a couple of weeks, then she'll get her second wind. In the meantime, plenty of sleep and some good prenatal vitamins should help."

Kieran blinked. One minute he was standing next to Michael, the next he was on his knees, looking up at him. All of the breath left his lungs in a single whoosh. "Faith's pregnant?"

Michael laughed. "I'd bet my license on it. Where the hell have you been the last seven years or so? Congratulations, little brother. You're going to be a father."

"I can't believe I fell asleep at my own wedding," Faith moaned later. Kieran fluffed the designer accent pillows behind her back and held the glass of orange juice to her lips.

"I can't believe you didn't tell me."

"Tell you what?" she asked innocently.

Kieran might have thought she was joking, but there was nothing but confusion in her soft gray eyes. "I guess it just finally caught up to me," she said. "Working all day, running around in the evenings, making love half the night," she said, her face coloring a lovely pink. "Your family must think I'm a complete ingrate."

She didn't know. "Faith," he said slowly. "No

one thinks any such thing."

"Yeah, right. I bet none of them fell asleep at their receptions, did they?"

"No," he admitted, wondering how he was going to tell her. If anyone but Michael had told him, he might have his doubts, but Mick was never wrong about that sort of thing (his own firstborn notwithstanding). Faith groaned and leaned back onto the pillows.

"Faith, have you been overly tired lately?"

"Yeah," she sighed. "But you know how busy things have been."

He nodded. "How about your appetite? You don't seem to be eating much."

"Nerves. My stomach's been full of butterflies lately, but I guess that'll ease now that the wedding's over. Oh, boy. I need to apologize to everyone before we leave tonight."

"Trust me, they understand."

"How could they possibly understand?"

Kieran took a deep breath. "Because they've all been through it."

Faith looked at him doubtfully. "But you just said - "

"Faith. You're pregnant."

She froze. Blinked once. Twice. "I'm pregnant?"

He nodded.

"But I can't be pregnant. I'd certainly know, wouldn't I? I mean, with Matt I was tired all the time, nauseous for the first three months, wildly emotional, …" She stopped, mid-sentence, clamping her mouth shut as the truth dawned. Her eyes widened and filled with tears and she looked at Kieran, terrified. He didn't need their special connection to figure out what she was thinking. It was all right there on her face. She was terrified of his reaction.

"Faith," he said, sliding onto the sofa with her and pulling her into his arms. He sensed her fear keenly and wanted to reassure her as quickly as possible. "You are my *croie*. I've known from our first time together that this was a possibility. And I couldn't be happier."

She sniffed against his chest. "Really?"

"Really." He kissed the top of her head, and chuckled. "Surely after having met my family you realized we tend to be a prolific bunch. You didn't doubt my virility, did you?"

"No," she smiled weakly, sniffling. "Maybe that's one of the reasons I fought you so hard. I was afraid of what might happen. That history would repeat itself, and that you'd leave me, too."

"Faith," he crooned, holding her to him. "My Faith. Don't you know that a child will only strengthen the bond between us? I'm afraid you're stuck with me, woman, and if I have to keep getting you pregnant to prove that, I will."

Her lips twitched. "Well," she said, her little claws petting his chest, "you just might. I'm kind of a cynic, you know."

"Are you now?" His hand rubbed possessively over her still flat stomach as he leaned in for another kiss. "Because that sounds like a challenge..."

IT'S NOT OVER!

I hope you enjoyed reading KieraFaith's story – thank you!

Writing the Callaghan Brothers seis been an amazing experience. The cha have become very real to me, and from you are telling me in your emails, posts, and re – you, too!

Before you worry that this is the don't. There is still more to come.

Aidan might not technically be a Can, but he is close enough to the family to be ered an honorary brother. Book 8 in the serBottom Line – is available now.

THANK YOU SO MUCH for corong on this crazy, wonderful ride with me. It'ver yet ☺

Abbie

nks for reading Kieran and Faith's story

u liked this book, then please consider posreview online! It's really easy, only takes a fnutes, and makes a huge difference to indent authors who don't have the mega-bud the big-time publishers behind them.

n to Amazon (or Goodreads) and just tell othat you thought, even if it's just a line or two's it! A good review is one of the nicest thin can do for any author.

ways, I welcome feedback. Email me at abbersromance@gmail.com. Or sign up for my iling list on my website at httpv.abbiezandersromance.com for up to datnd advance notices on new releases, Like my page (AbbieZandersRomance), and/or foll on Twitter (@AbbieZanders).

s again, and may all of your ever-afters be nes!

Also by Abbie Zanders

Contemporary Romance

- Five Minute Man (Covendale Series #1)
- All Night Woman (Covendale Series #2)
- The Realist
- Dangerous Secrets (Callaghan Brothers #1)
- First and Only (Callaghan Brothers #2)
- House Calls (Callaghan Brothers #3)
- Seeking Vengeance (Callaghan Brothers #4)
- Guardian Angel (Callaghan Brothers #5)
- Beyond Affection (Callaghan Brothers #6)
- Bottom Line (Callaghan Brothers #8)

Time Travel Romance

- Lost in Time I
- Lost in Time II

Paranormal

- Vampire, Unaware
- Black Wolfe's Mate (writing as Avelyn McCrae)

About the Author

Abbie Zanders loves to read and write romance in all forms; she is quite obsessive, really. Her ultimate fantasy is to spend all of her free time doing both, preferably in a secluded mountain cabin overlooking a pristine lake, though a private beach on a lush tropical island works, too. Sharing her work with others of similar mind is a dream come true. She promises her readers two things: no cliffhangers, and there will always be a happy ending. Beyond that, you never know…